WILL TANNER
U.S. DEPUTY MARSHAL

William W. Johnstone
with J. A. Johnstone

PINNACLE BOOKS
Kensington Publishing Corp.
www.kensingtonbooks.com

PINNACLE BOOKS are published by

Kensington Publishing Corp.
119 West 40th Street
New York, NY 10018

PUBLISHER'S NOTE
Following the death of William W. Johnstone, the Johnstone family is working with a carefully selected writer to organize and complete Mr. Johnstone's outlines and many unfinished manuscripts to create additional novels in all of his series like The Last Gunfighter, Mountain Man, and Eagles, among others. This novel was inspired by Mr. Johnstone's superb storytelling.

All Kensington titles, imprints, and distributed lines are available at special quantity discounts for bulk purchases for sales promotions, premiums, fund-raising, educational, or institutional use. Special book excerpts or customized printings can also be created to fit specific needs. For details, write or phone the office of the Kensington sales manager: Kensington Publishing Corp., 119 West 40th Street, New York, NY 10018, attn: Sales Department; phone 1-800-221-2647.

PINNACLE BOOKS, the Pinnacle logo, and the WWJ steer head logo are Reg. U.S. Pat. & TM Off.

ISBN-13: 978-0-7860-3799-5
ISBN-10: 0-7860-3799-7

First printing: June 2016

10 9 8 7 6 5 4 3 2 1

Printed in the United States of America

First electronic edition: June 2016

ISBN-13: 978-0-7860-3800-8
ISBN-10: 0-7860-3800-4

CHAPTER 1

"You're just lookin' for trouble, Boss," Shorty Watts cautioned as Jim Hightower put his boot in the stirrup. "You better let Will take the starch outta that one."

"You just hold on to his ears till I get in the saddle," Hightower replied confidently. He knew Shorty might be right. He was getting too old to try to break the really rank ones, and this horse must have been gelded much too late because there was still a helluva lot of stallion in him. He was a handsome devil, though, a blue roan, about fifteen hands high, and Jim couldn't help admiring him. But so far, no one had been able to saddle-break him, and Jim thought it would be the perfect way to cap off his farewell to the cattle business. He decided he could use one more good ride on a bucking horse before he retired to the rocking chair.

Walking out of the barn, Will Tanner called out, "Hey, Boss, why don't you let me ride that one? Shorty's right, he's got a mean streak in him." The horse did have a mean streak, and it had been at least a couple of years since Hightower had decided his bones were getting too brittle to dust his britches on the hard ground of the corral. Will was usually the man to break the ill-tempered horses, but he hadn't gotten around to this one.

"Too late," Hightower said as he settled his weight in the saddle. "I'm already on him. Let him go, Shorty." Shorty shook his head, concerned, but he released the roan and backed away. The horse remained motionless, surprising all three of them. "Well, I'll be . . ." Hightower started. "I believe he's just a big bluff."

"Watch him, Boss," Will warned when the roan's ears pricked up and he raised his tail, even though there was no other indication that he was going to move away from the rail. The words had no sooner left his lips when the horse exploded. Bucking stiff-legged, it slammed Hightower against the corral rails repeatedly before rearing back so violently that it seemed about to fall on its back. His leg already shattered by the corral rails, Hightower tried to hold on to the saddle horn, but the horse bucked so violently he was thrown to the ground, landing hard on his back. Still bucking insanely, the horse reared up over the stricken man and came down fiercely with his front hooves on Hightower's chest, crushing the life out of him.

Will was quick to climb over the rails, but it was too late to help his boss. It had happened so suddenly, and the horse almost seemed intent on killing the man. Shorty managed to back the horse away to the other side of the corral, where it stood calmly with no sign of violence other than the wild look in its eye and the flared nostrils. Will knelt beside the broken body of the man he had known as a father figure since he was a boy. Looking at him lying there in the dust of the corral, his eyes flickering like a candle about to go out, and blood trickling from the corner of his mouth, Will wanted to cry out in anguish. Devastated by his inability to help, as he witnessed the last feeble gasps of breath leaving the dying man, he said his silent farewell to a man he loved and respected.

Jim Hightower had taken in a fatherless boy, the son of a drunken whore, and taught him how to work with cattle and horses. He seemed to delight in the boy's natural ability to ride and rope. And when Will developed into the kind of man a father could be proud of, Jim made him his foreman. This was in spite of the fact that he was younger than most of the men who worked for him. The decision proved to be a wise one, for there was never any doubt among the men concerning Will's qualifications. He was just as proficient in handling an unruly cowhand as he was a bad-tempered horse. But now, on this tragic day, he was as gentle as if working with a newborn foal when he carefully lifted Jim's body up in his arms.

"Go on up to the house and tell Miss Jean," Will said to Shorty. "Tell her that I'm bringin' Boss."

"Is he dead?" Shorty asked anxiously as he hustled to open the corral gate. Will nodded solemnly. "My Lord . . ." Shorty declared, at a loss for words. "I swear . . ." He stood there and held the gate for Will.

Then he closed it again and hurried up ahead of him to the house to alert Jim's wife.

Jean Hightower, affectionately known to the men of the J-Bar-J as Miss Jean, was not the typical pioneering woman often found standing shoulder to shoulder with her trailblazing husband. In fact, Miss Jean was a rather fragile woman, the daughter of a Presbyterian minister in a little town east of Fort Smith, Arkansas. As Will expected, she almost collapsed when told of her husband's tragic death. She was fortunate to have the support of her long-time cook and housekeeper, Sally Evening Star, an Osage woman. Sally helped her clean Jim's body and lay him out in the bedroom in his one suit coat. Miss Jean would sit with her husband's body all night, saying her farewells before he was buried in the morning.

Will was grieving privately for the loss of the man who had given him a life, but he was angry, too. He found it difficult to understand how Jim Hightower's life could be snuffed out so suddenly, and at a time like this, when the man was retiring. Jim was planning to take Jean back close to her people in Arkansas. Most of the cattle had been sold. There was only a skeleton crew left to take care of the ranch—Shorty, Cal, Slim, and himself. There were no buyers for the small ranch there in northeast Texas, so Boss had planned to leave it to Will. And now Will wasn't sure he wanted it. He didn't even know if he wanted to stay in the cattle business or just sign on with another rancher. He had lost his desire for it. And he was angry, damned angry, because he had been really happy that Boss could retire while he was still young enough to enjoy it. *He had to try to ride that one devil horse*, he thought.

After Will and Shorty did all they could for their grieving mistress, they returned to the barn. "Whaddaya want me to do about that horse?" Shorty asked as they approached the corral. The roan was still standing where Shorty had tied it. "Want me to pull the saddle off?"

Will took a long, hard look at the horse before answering. "No, you go find Cal and Slim and a couple of shovels. Miss Jean said she wants Boss buried over near the creek, close to those willows where that bench is. I'll take care of the horse."

When Shorty went inside the barn, Will went to the corral gate. He stood looking at the big blue roan for a long moment, then he opened the gate and went into the corral. He walked purposefully toward the horse, looking it in the eye as he untied the reins from the rail. The roan did not resist when Will led him away from the side of the corral. "Now, you evil son of a bitch, I wanna see if you're really a killer," he said, and stepped up in the stirrup. Just as before, the roan made no move when Will settled down in the saddle. Then, also as before, the horse exploded suddenly, but this time the rider was not taken by surprise. Around and around the corral they went, the roan bucking and rearing as if to fall over on its back, then landing stiff-legged to buck again. Time and again, it tried to pin Will against the side rails of the corral, only to have Will pull his foot from the stirrup and raise his leg, further frustrating the belligerent beast.

Hearing the pounding hooves and the horse's squeals, Shorty ran to the barn door to observe the contest between man and horse. "My Lord," he muttered as he watched the battle of wills on display, neither man nor horse willing to yield. He was certain that he was witness to a ride like he had never seen before, or was likely to see in the future. Will drove the horse relentlessly on until it began to take pauses between its violent attempts to throw the demon on its back. But Will would not let him rest. Shorty stood spellbound, holding a shovel in each hand, for a solid three-quarters of an hour before the final surrender, when the roan stood defeated, its head and tail drooping. Will kicked his heels into the roan's sides, forcing it to a slow trot around the corral. Then he reined the horse to a stop and dismounted. He was not satisfied that the horse was really broken, however, sensing an evil streak that was inborn.

"I'll get a pick and help you dig that grave," Will said as he walked past Shorty. "We'll let that devil horse rest for a spell, then one of you take him for a little ride to make sure he's fully broke."

By the time the three men had dug Jim's grave, the blue roan had had plenty of time to become rested, so Slim volunteered to try him out. Will's instincts had been right about the horse, however, and when Slim got on him, the horse repeated his attempts to maim his rider. Slim escaped the fate that had befallen Jim simply because, like Will had, he managed to get his leg out of the way before it was shattered. He could not prevent being thrown, however, and barely escaped being trampled by the belligerent horse's hooves. Rolling over and over, he scrambled to his feet and went over the side of the corral just before being bitten.

"That damn horse is a man-killer," Slim gasped breathlessly. "He's out to do you in, and that's a fact."

"I'm afraid you're right," Will said. He thought about it for a long moment before deciding what needed to be done in regard to the wrathful beast. It was a hard decision, but he finally went inside the corral and approached the leery horse. It backed away, rearing up on its hind legs, its front hooves pawing the air as if daring the man. When it dropped its hooves to the ground again, Will grabbed the reins. Holding the bridle, he forced the roan's head down, so he could look him in the eye. "Go back to hell where you came from," he said. "You killed a good man today." Then he drew the .44 he wore and put a bullet in the horse's brain. Stepping back to keep the horse from falling on him, he turned and walked back to the gate.

Slim was still standing, speechless, when Will came out of the corral. In over four years riding for the J-Bar-J, he had always known the young foreman to be kindhearted when it came to horses. Fair and even-tempered as a rule, Will Tanner could be riled over some things after all—if they were important to him. Slim learned that today.

"You or Cal hitch up a team and drag that damn carcass outta the corral. I'm gonna ride in to Sulphur Springs and see if I can get the preacher to come out and give Boss a proper funeral in the morning."

* * *

Jim Hightower was buried before noon the next day. Thanks to Will's diligent efforts the night before, Sam Harvey, barber and undertaker, drove a wagon carrying a pine box and the Reverend Edward Garrett out to the J-Bar-J. With Will's help, Harvey placed Jim's body in the simple coffin. Before he nailed the lid on, Miss Jean came in and said one final good-bye to the man she had been married to for thirty-one years. She placed a scented linen handkerchief in Jim's cold hand. "So that something of me will always be with him," she said tearfully. Acting as pallbearers, Will, Slim, Cal, and Shorty carried the coffin out to the willows by the creek, and Reverend Garrett delivered a fine eulogy, considering the deceased had never set foot in his church. Will compensated Sam Harvey for the pine box, but Sam said there was no charge for the four-mile trip from town to deliver it. Reverend Garrett graciously accepted a donation to his church. When it was all done, Will had spent fourteen dollars of the money he had saved up over the last few years. He didn't begrudge the expense and felt good about spending the money.

After the eulogy that turned into a sermon, Jim was lowered to his eternal rest on two lengths of ropes held by the pallbearers. Miss Jean expressed her appreciation to the reverend and Sam Harvey for making the eight-mile round-trip, and to all the cowhands involved. After the funeral party was fed one of Sally Evening Star's beef stew dinners, and the wagon departed for town, Miss Jean pulled Will aside. She wanted to thank him for his thoughtfulness in arranging a real funeral for her husband. "I know Jim appreciates it," she said. "You know you've always been someone very special to Jim and me, and I'm just sorry that we didn't have something to leave you besides this ranch. I do have a little bit saved back, though, and I want to give you money for what you've spent for the funeral. I know it cost you a lot to get them to come out here, all the way from town."

"No, ma'am," he insisted. "It didn't cost nothin' at all. The preacher don't charge, and that coffin was one Sam had already made. They were glad to do it for Boss 'cause he was such a fine, upstandin' man, they said."

She smiled gently, obviously pleased by the sentiment. "Will," she said, "you're a man any father would be proud to call his son—and such a splendid liar."

The next couple of days were sad and worrisome days for Miss Jean as she went through the process of closing out her life on the J-Bar-J. In preparation to leave for Arkansas, Jim had already closed out their bank account and settled up with anyone he owed in Sulphur Springs. So she was left with the question of how best to go to her family's home, now that her husband was no longer there to take her. It was possible to go by train, but it would require a long, roundabout journey to make railroad connections. And it would also mean she could not take most of the possessions she had planned to carry by wagon. She was spared the sorrow of leaving her precious keepsakes when Will told her that he would take her to Arkansas. It was what she had counted on, but she still questioned his decision. "Won't you be needed here at the ranch?" she asked.

"No, ma'am, not really," he said. "Shorty and the others can handle everything here. There aren't but a handful of cattle left to worry about, and the horses. They don't need me."

So it was settled, then. The wagon was packed with the sentimental keepsakes Miss Jean was fond of, as well as the cooking supplies needed for a trip that Will figured to take close to three weeks. Planning to keep one of the team of horses to use as a packhorse on his return trip, he put a pack saddle rig in the back of the wagon. When all was ready, the party prepared to depart early one June morning. Will had planned to drive the wagon, but Sally Evening Star insisted that she knew how to drive a team of horses. That was good news to Will, because he preferred to ride his buckskin gelding instead of sitting on a wagon seat for three weeks. It also meant a little more room in the wagon. The three remaining cowhands stood by to wish the travelers a safe journey, each one stepping forward to shake Miss Jean's hand. "We'll make sure Boss's grave don't grow up in weeds," Cal assured her.

"I know you will," she said. "Jim was always talking about how pleased he was to have you boys working for him."

"What about you?" Shorty asked Will after he helped Miss Jean up on the wagon. "The ranch belongs to you now. Anythin' you want done while you're gone?"

"You know what needs to be done," Will said. "Just

take care of things like you usually do. The ranch is yours till I get back. Run it like I ain't comin' back." It was not an idle suggestion, because he had given the possibility serious thought. "In fact," he said, the idea suddenly striking him, "I'm making you my partner, if you want it. Half owner, whaddaya say?"

Totally flabbergasted, Shorty blurted, "Hell, yes, I want it!" He immediately offered his hand to shake on it. "What about Cal and Slim?"

"I'll tell 'em," Will said. The two hands were good men, but Shorty had been working the J-Bar-J since Will was a boy, and he was the most capable to run the ranch. Will led his horse over to Slim and Cal and told them that they were working for Shorty now. They had already assumed as much. That done, he stepped up into the saddle. "Let's go to Arkansas, ladies," he sang out, and started out to the northeast, toward the Red River.

The journey that Will had figured to take three weeks stretched into a month, because of a spell of bad weather that delayed them and forced a detour miles out of their way to find a ferry crossing. The two weary women gratefully rolled into Fort Smith on the Fourth of July amid that city's celebration of the holiday. Miss Jean had planned to stay one night in a hotel to give herself the opportunity to recover from the grueling trek through Oklahoma Indian Territory. Because of the celebrations, however, she was unable to find accommodations in the better hotels. So she decided to push on to camp overnight east of town. They found a camping spot by a creek where she could bathe and freshen up before meeting her brother and sister-in-law at the family farm near a little junction called Ward's Corner, named for her father, Henry C. Ward.

Not one of the three travelers was happier to see Miss Jean's old home place than Will Tanner. He felt satisfied knowing that Miss Jean and Sally had been safely delivered, with all the contents of the wagon intact. But he was weary himself after the wagon's slow pace of travel. It had given him many hours to reflect on his life to this point, however, and to decide if he was content to return to the little ranch near Sulphur Springs. In spite of this, he had still come to no decision, primarily because he didn't know what else he wanted to do. So he put it aside to deal with later.

It was a short trip to the Ward farm the following morning. They arrived before noon to the surprise of Marjorie Ward, Miss Jean's sister-in-law. She had expected them, but not until the end of summer. Shocked to hear of Jim's death, she greeted them warmly and sent her daughter to the fields to tell her husband that his sister was home. Watching the reception Miss Jean received, Will was satisfied that she was truly welcome. Since this was really his only concern, he was eager then to be on his way. Even though Marjorie insisted that he surely must stay for supper, Will lingered only long enough to meet Henry junior when he came from the fields. Not one to normally turn down the offer of a good meal, he somehow felt a little awkward in the sad reunion. He was no longer a part of Miss Jean's life, so he respectfully declined the invitation, got his pack saddle from the wagon, and took his pick of the wagon team to use as a packhorse. Miss Jean caught him as he was about to leave.

"You're not getting away from here without giving me a hug, Will Tanner," she declared. He grinned and accommodated her. "Thank you for taking such good care of me," she said. "Take care of yourself just as well, you hear?"

"Yes, ma'am, I will," he said, and stepped up into the saddle. Touching his forefinger to the brim of his hat, he bid a final farewell to a woman who had been such a big part of his life. Then he turned the buckskin toward the road that led back to Fort Smith.

CHAPTER 2

Approaching Fort Smith, Will decided that he had earned a drink of whiskey and maybe a good supper, but first he needed to take care of his horses. So when he came to a stable on the east side of town, he pulled up and dismounted. "How do," the owner greeted him when he led his horses toward the corral.

"Howdy," Will returned. "I'm needin' to put my horses up for the night. Whaddaya charge?"

The man looked at the two horses, then took another look at Will. "Tell you what I'll do. I charge fifteen dollars a month to stable a horse, but since you're just wantin' to stay one night, I'll let you have the monthly rate. That'd be fifty cents for the night." He paused to check Will's reaction. When Will didn't protest, he said, "Course, that's for each horse. Since you've got two, that'd make it a dollar."

"How 'bout with a portion of oats?" Will asked.

"Dollar and a half."

"How much if I sleep in your hay barn?" Will asked.

"Two dollars and a quarter."

"Hell," Will said. "How come you charge me more

'n you charge my horse? I ain't gonna eat any hay—I'm just gonna sleep on it."

"Two dollars even," he said, and waited for Will's response.

"All right," Will said, reaching into his pocket. It seemed a little steep to him, but he thought maybe prices for everything in Fort Smith might be high. He counted out two dollars and handed them to the owner.

"Yes, sir. Thank you, sir," he said when he had money in hand. "My name's Vern Tuttle. This here's my livery stable. You in town for the Fourth celebration?"

"Nope," Will said. "I'm just passin' through, I reckon. Thought I'd stay over and get me a good meal and maybe a drink of whiskey. You got any recommendations for either one?"

"Sure do," Vern replied. "Mornin' Glory Saloon for both of 'em. You can't go wrong there. They got a cook there that's every bit as good as any of them in the hotel dinin' rooms, and it's in easy walkin' distance from here."

"That sounds like what I'm lookin' for," Will declared. "Think I'll give it a try as soon as I put my horses away."

Vern pointed up the street. "The Mornin' Glory's right up there. You'll see the sign. Come on, and I'll help you settle your horses and show you where you can put your saddle and stuff." He turned to lead him into the stable. "What's your name, young feller?"

"Will Tanner," he answered.

"Glad to know you, Will. If you ain't ever been in

Fort Smith before, I'll just give you a little advice. This is a bad town to raise hell in." He paused. "Not sayin' you look the type, but just thought you'd like to know. We got more law in this town than we know what to do with. We got a sheriff and deputies, but Fort Smith is the headquarters for the Western District of Arkansas U.S. Marshals Service, too. So there might be a dozen deputy marshals in town at any one time."

"Thanks for the information," Will said, "but I just want a drink and a meal."

"Just sayin', that's all. No offense."

"None taken," Will said.

The Morning Glory Saloon was a little longer stretch of the legs than Vern had said, but Will didn't mind. It was good to work his legs a little after so many days in the saddle. The saloon's sign was not as obvious as Vern had promised, either, but that may have been because of the fact that the nails had evidently backed out of one end of it, causing the sign to hang vertically. Judging by the weathered boards on the facade of the building, Will figured it must have been one of the oldest drinking establishments in town. That notion was further strengthened by the obvious fact that most of the newer buildings seemed to be centered more to the north of town. *But there are a few horses tied at the hitching rail out front, so somebody must think it's as good as Vern says*, he thought.

"Howdy, stranger," bartender Gus Johnson greeted him cheerfully when he walked up to the bar. "What'll you have?"

"Howdy," Will returned. "How 'bout a shot of whiskey to settle the dust?" While Gus reached for a bottle to pour his drink, Will took a moment to look the room over. The large barroom was about half-full. There were a couple of customers at the end of the bar, but most of the crowd were seated at the tables arranged around three sides of the room. As Will casually scanned the tables, he took note that only a few of the patrons were eating supper. That could be good or bad news, but better than no one eating, he decided. His gaze skipped quickly over a table in the back corner of the room, then was drawn back for a second look. One man sitting at the table had his back to the wall. He was one of the diners. A large man, judging by the width of his shoulders, he hovered over his plate of food, which seemed to have captured his full attention. He was drinking coffee, but there was a bottle of whiskey on the table as well. The sound of a shot glass on the bar brought Will's attention back to his drink of whiskey.

"Here you go, young feller," Gus said as he poured. "I ain't ever seen you in here before."

"Reckon not," Will said. "I'm just passin' through."

"On your way to where?" Gus asked.

Will hesitated before answering. When he did, he almost surprised himself. "Damned if I know."

Thinking that Will might have found him too nosy, Gus quickly explained, "It ain't none of my business. I was just makin' conversation. I figured maybe you were in town to watch the hangin' tomorrow."

"No problem atall," Will quickly assured him. He chuckled then and confessed that he really wasn't sure where he was going. He tossed his drink back and waited a few moments to get over the burn before continuing. "I didn't know there was a hangin'."

"Yep," Gus said. "Judge Parker sentenced a young boy named Troy Gamble to hang for shootin' a feller over in the Nations."

"Is that a fact?" Will responded, not really interested. "Vern, over at the livery stable, told me I could get a decent supper here. Is there any truth in that?"

Gus laughed. "You bet there is. We got us a dandy cook, and she's cooked up one of her specialties tonight, cowboy stew."

"Well, I reckon I'm lucky I came in on a night she cooked her specialty," Will said.

"Yes, sir," Gus went on. "What makes Mammy's cowboy stew so good is because she makes hers with real cowboys instead of beef." He laughed harder than Will, obviously enjoying a joke that he had told countless times before.

"Well, I don't reckon I can pass that up," Will said.

"You won't be sorry," Gus assured him.

Will heard a soft voice behind him, and turned to meet a solemn-looking woman, almost as tall as he was. "Evenin', cowboy. You lookin' for some company?"

"No, ma'am," Will said. "Thank you just the same, though."

She immediately turned away. "That's Lucy Tyler," Gus said. "She's one of our regulars."

"I'll have one more shot of that whiskey," Will decided. "That last one didn't quite cook my whole throat." He watched Gus pour his drink. "Who's the big feller sittin' at the back corner table? I noticed a couple of your other customers speakin' to him when they walked by."

"Him?" Gus replied. "I expect about everybody in town knows him. That's U.S. Deputy Marshal Fletcher Pride. He always takes supper here when he's in town." When Will didn't appear to recognize the name, Gus continued. "Pride's the oldest and best-known deputy marshal in the territory. Matter of fact, he's the one brought Troy Gamble in to be tried by Judge Parker. You ain't never heard of Fletcher Pride?"

"Nope, I can't say as I have."

"Where are you from?" Gus asked, incredulously.

"Texas," Will said.

"Well, I'm surprised you ain't heard of him down there 'cause I'm sure he slips over into Texas from time to time."

"Reckon I just ain't been breakin' the law," Will said.

"Reckon not," Gus agreed. "Set yourself down at a table and I'll tell Mammy to bring you a plate. You want coffee with it?" Will nodded.

Picturing Mammy as a rather large woman, Will was surprised when a small, fragile-looking woman with stringy gray hair brought him a plate heaped high with stew. Two thick slices of bread rested on top. *Reckon she doesn't eat her own cooking,* he thought. "Was you the one wantin' to eat?" she asked before setting the plate on the table.

"Yes, ma'am," he replied.

"I'll bring you some coffee," she said. "You want some sugar with it?"

"No, ma'am," he said.

She returned shortly with a large cup of coffee. She set it down on the table, nodded toward his plate, and asked, "Is it good?"

She seemed genuinely interested in his opinion of her stew, so he said, "Yes, ma'am, it surely is." This was in spite of the fact that he thought it a little too greasy. But it sure beat what he would have cooked for himself had he decided to camp by the river instead of sleeping in the hay barn. She gave him an approving nod and returned to the kitchen. Will resumed his assault on the cowboy stew, with no notion that his peaceful supper was about to be interrupted.

Three riders pulled up to the hitching rail of the Morning Glory, dismounted, and looped their reins over the rail loosely, in the event they might find it necessary to make a hasty departure. "How we gonna do this, Pa?" Orville Gamble asked. "Are we just gonna walk in and kill him?"

"No, dammit," his father said. "I want him to know why we killed him, and who it was that done it. So don't neither one of you pull a trigger till I start the shootin'." Luther Gamble was an angry man. He and his three sons had always operated outside the law in their home state of Kansas. After a bank holdup in Wichita, during which a teller was shot, he and his boys slipped over to Oklahoma Indian Territory to lie low for a while. It was purely bad luck that his youngest, Troy, got into a little scrape with a Cherokee policeman and had to shoot the son of a bitch. Maybe Troy was a little hotheaded, but he didn't deserve to be hanged for killing an Indian.

Luther was determined to kill the man who tracked Troy down and brought him to the gallows. He knew he had no chance of saving his son, because of the army of lawmen that guarded every hanging in Fort Smith. But he could put a bullet in Fletcher Pride's head to even the score. He looked at his two surviving sons, Orville and Simon, and felt a sense of satisfaction in knowing they were as mean as their old man. "Let's go have a visit with Deputy Fletcher Pride, boys," he said, and stepped up on the narrow porch.

Busy working on his supper, Will paid little attention to the three men who walked in the door of the saloon. He continued to ignore them until they walked past his table, moving toward the back of the room, and he took a good look at them. He decided then that they had to be a father and his two sons, for there was a definite resemblance—all three appeared to have the same mean streak showing. Spread out, and walking in a single line, they advanced slowly on the big deputy marshal at the corner table. All three were resting their hands on the handles of their pistols. Will suddenly realized the scene that was about to unfold, as did most of the other customers in the saloon. There followed an exodus of most of the men seated at the tables, anxious to avoid being caught in a hail of gunfire.

Pride glanced up from his plate when he realized the three men, with pistols now drawn, were advancing toward him with the clear intention of doing him harm. He made no sudden moves, but studied the three as they silently came to a stop some five paces from his table. He slowly put his knife and fork down beside his plate and dropped his hands in his lap. His heavy, gray eyebrows arched slightly as his gaze went from one man to another, settling on the older man who bristled with anger. "You'd be Luther Gamble, I reckon," Pride said. "I never had the pleasure. I heard you've been pretty busy up in Kansas, though."

"Never mind who I am, you son of a bitch," Luther spat back. "I know who you are, and that's a piece of bad luck for you."

"And these must be your other two sons," Pride went on. "Fine-lookin' young men. I bet you're proud of 'em. Too bad about Troy, though. I reckon that's why you're in town, to see Troy hang, so these other two sons will see that crime don't pay."

"What are we waitin' for, Pa?" one of the boys blurted anxiously. "He's talkin' crazy."

"Shut up, Simon," Luther growled. "He's tryin' to talk his way outta the grave. But that ain't gonna work, lawman," he shouted at Pride. "It's eye for eye. You mighta brought my boy in to hang, but by God, you're gonna go with him."

"That don't make a lotta sense," Pride said, still calm, "when you've got all these guns aimin' right at you and your boys."

"What?" Luther started, looking right and left, seeing no one. "What guns?" He feared for a moment that he might have walked into a trap. "There ain't nobody but you, and I'm tired of hearin' you talk."

"Maybe you better listen to what he's tellin' you," a voice behind him said.

Startled, Orville reacted immediately, spun around, and fired at Will, his bullet tearing a chunk out of the table Will had taken cover behind. Before he had time for a second shot, a bullet from Will's .44 smashed into his chest, driving him several steps backward to collapse on his back. Before Luther could react, a bullet from the .44 in Pride's lap cut him down. Caught in the confusion that had suddenly exploded, Simon Gamble couldn't decide which gun was the most critical. He turned to shoot at Will, only to be cut down by a second bullet from Pride. After the explosion of gunfire, the room was suddenly silent until Pride called out, "You all right, partner? You didn't get hit, didja?"

"No," Will answered, "but I lost half of my supper when I turned the table over."

Pride chuckled as he got up from his chair. "We'd better check these fellers, make sure there ain't no more bite in 'em." It took only a minute to determine there was no longer any threat from Gamble and his sons. Simon was dead, as a result of Pride's bullet to the head. The other two were still alive, but sinking fast. "Best just let 'em lay," Pride said as he kicked their weapons out of their reach. Then he looked toward Gus, who had just surfaced from behind the bar. "Gus, send somebody over to get Doc Peters." Bringing his attention back to Will again, he extended his hand. "Partner, I'm sure glad you joined the party. I was in a tight spot there, and I doubt I coulda got out of it without at least one of 'em puttin' a bullet in me. Are you one of the deputies from up Kansas way? I heard a couple of you fellers might be here for the hangin'."

"No," Will said. "I ain't no deputy. I just came in to get a drink and some supper."

"Well, I'll be . . ." Pride started. "You ain't a

lawman?" Will shook his head. "If that don't beat all," Pride exclaimed. "Then I reckon I really owe you my thanks. Hell, everybody else ran out the door."

Will shrugged modestly. "It just didn't seem like a fair fight, and you bein' a lawman and all." He paused to look at the three men on the floor. "What would you have done if I hadn't been here?"

"Died, I reckon," Pride said with a laugh, then on a more serious note, he confessed that he wasn't sure what he would have done. "I knew for sure that I was gonna get the old man, and maybe one of the boys."

"I reckon it's a good thing they didn't just come in blazin' away before you had a chance to do anything," Will said.

"As soon as I looked up and saw who it was, I figured I had a chance," Pride said. "I knew the old man would wanna see me sweat a little and make sure I knew why he was killin' me. So I tried to talk him up as long as I could to keep him from pullin' the trigger—thought maybe he wouldn't notice I was cockin' my pistol."

"You always eat with your pistol in your lap?" Will asked.

"Not always, but I thought it might be a good idea today, with the hangin' goin' on tomorrow. Trouble is, I got into Mammy's stew too deep to see what was goin' on. If I'd seen those three when they walked in the door, I'da had my piece out and cocked before they got this close."

With the shooting over, the frightened patrons crowded back inside to view the bodies and talk about what a close call they had just had. Gus was happy to give them his accounting of the gunfight as first one and then another leaned close over the victims to get a better look. Pride snorted, amused. "It was kinda hard to see hunkered down behind the bar, I expect. Wasn't it, Gus?"

Having hidden in the pantry as soon as she heard the shots, Mammy came out then to clean up the mess Will had made when he turned the table over. "I'm right sorry, ma'am," Will said as he tried to pick up the coffee cup and plate. "It was real good. I'm sorry I didn't get to finish it."

Overhearing, Pride spoke up. "Fix him another plate, Mammy, and put it on my bill. I'll set down with him and have another cup of coffee." He looked at Will and grinned. "I figure I sure as hell owe you that much."

"It's on the house," Gus chimed in at that point.

"Why, thank you kindly," Will said. "I did work up a little appetite."

Mammy stood for a moment, holding a tray with the dirty dishes she had picked up, until the table was set upright again. Then she spun on her heel and headed toward the kitchen, muttering in disgust, "Men and their guns."

"I ain't never known Gus to give anything away before," Pride teased. "What if Clyde finds out you're givin' away his profits?"

"Clyde might be the owner," Gus replied, "but I'm the one behind the bar when the bullets were flyin'." He turned to take another look at the three bodies. "I expect we oughta drag them out of the middle of the floor."

"Hell," Pride snorted. "They ain't in anybody's way—might as well leave 'em lay till Doc gets here."

"Yeah, but they're bleedin' all over my floor," Gus complained. "I wish they'da waited to jump you outside."

One of the interested spectators, bending low over Luther Gamble's body, declared, "Ain't nothin' Doc can do for this one. He's dead. Best send for Edward instead."

Dr. Peters walked in the door in time to hear the comment. Only slightly irritated to be called away from home at suppertime, he said, "Might as well examine them, just in case." A quick examination confirmed the customer's diagnosis, and by the time he got to the other two, they were gone as well, so he said that Edward Kittridge could come for the corpses. He looked at Gus and said, "It's gonna cost you a drink of whiskey for my services."

Gus had some of the men help Pride and Will drag the bodies outside to wait on the porch for the undertaker to come for them. Pride relieved the bodies of their weapons and anything of value, explaining to Will that he hoped they had enough on them to pay for their burial. He explained that if a deputy marshal killed a felon, he had to bear the cost of his burial. When he was satisfied that he was compensated, they went back inside to finish their supper.

Pride was interested to find out more about this Good Samaritan with a gun, so he questioned Will so intensely that Will was driven to ask a question of his own. "Are you thinkin' I'm an outlaw or something?"

Will's response brought forth a lusty chuckle from the big lawman. "Well, no, I ain't, but since you brought it up, are you wanted for a crime somewhere?"

"No, I'm not," Will said, "unless you're fixin' to arrest me for shootin' that feller just now."

Still grinning broadly, Pride assured him. "Nah, that was in self-defense. Besides, I officially deputized you to help me arrest them outlaws. I just forgot to tell ya." He paused while Mammy brought out a fresh pot of coffee and filled their cups, then he continued. "So you ain't been doin' nothin' but punchin' cows all your life?" Will nodded, and Pride went on. "Things were happenin' fast back there, but I couldn't help noticin' you were pretty handy with that Colt you're wearin', and pretty cool in the middle of all that shootin'."

Will shrugged indifferently. "I reckon I didn't have much time to think about it," he offered.

"Practice a lot with that Colt, do ya?"

"I don't reckon I practice with it at all," Will said, thinking the man must really have a deep interest in firearms. "Shoot a snake with it now and again. That's about all."

"Well, now you've shot a man with it," Pride reminded him. "How do ya feel about that?"

Will shrugged again. Now the conversation was getting a little strange. "I don't know how I feel about it," he said. "'Bout the same as shootin' a snake, I reckon. Tell you the truth, I hadn't thought about it one way or the other. I didn't go to kill anybody, but the feller shot at me, so I shot him."

"He had it comin', right?"

"I don't know if he did or not," Will said impatiently. "But he shot at me, so I shot him."

Pride sat back in his chair, pleased with his impression of the young stranger. "From what you've been sayin', I take it you ain't sure you're headin' back to drivin' cattle again." As before, the comment was met with a shrug from Will. "You consider workin' for the U.S. Marshals Service?"

"Shoot no," Will said at once without having to think about it.

"Why not?" Pride pressed. "You said yourself you ain't got no place in particular to go to. So what are you gonna do? I wouldn't have even mentioned it to you, but I ain't ever seen a man with better makin's for a deputy marshal than you—and I ain't known you for longer than about an hour. Do me—and yourself—a favor and think about it. The Marshals Service needs men that think fast and ain't scared when bullets are flyin'." He sat back in his chair again and drained the last of his coffee while he watched Will, who was obviously thinking the proposition over. Pride had refrained from telling his potential recruit one of the main reasons he had been trying to sell him on the service. The mortality rate for deputy marshals was high. His boss, Marshal Daniel Stone, had just been bemoaning the fact that he had lost two deputies in the last month, both victims of ambush by outlaws. He thought about sharing that information with Will, but he had gotten the impression that it would not have been a deciding factor for the young man. On the other hand, it might have been, so why mention it?

"I don't know, Fletcher . . ." Will paused. "That's right, ain't it? . . . Fletcher?" He was sure that was the name Gus told him. Pride confirmed it with a nod, so Will continued. "I sure as hell never thought about being a lawman. I don't know anything about it."

"You don't worry about that," Pride assured him. "We'll take care of that."

"Like I said, I don't know," Will hedged. "Let me think about it for a while."

Thinking that if he had him on the fence, it wouldn't take much to pull him on over, so he asked, "Why? Back there when that Gamble feller shot at you, you didn't have to think about it for a while. Whaddaya say you meet me right here in the mornin' and we'll go talk to U.S. Marshal Daniel Stone? It'll mean a steady paycheck and a few extra bonuses from time to time."

"Wouldn't hurt to just talk to him, I reckon," Will conceded, since he didn't have any plans for the next day. Pride gave him one firm nod, as if putting a period on the conversation, leaving Will to wonder if he was making a smart decision for himself. He finished his coffee and said good night after promising to return in the morning. He thought about the prospect of becoming a U.S. Deputy Marshal, still not finding it a natural job for him. He had never had any desire to protect the people and punish the lawbreakers. But he honestly did not want to return to driving cattle all his life. This thought brought to mind the three men he had left at the J-Bar-J, Shorty, Slim, and Cal. He wondered if he was letting them down, and immediately told himself that he was not. They knew how to manage cattle. They didn't need him to tell them how. As far as possibly building the operation into something closer to the way it was when Jim Hightower ran it, Shorty had a good head on his shoulders. He was as likely to make it successful as Will was, and Will had told him to run it as if he wasn't coming back. If he didn't return, the ranch would be his free and clear. *Hell*, he thought, *what am I worried about it for?*

He slept that night on his bed of hay, his horses fed and watered, and his stomach filled with a good meal. Tomorrow might mean a major change in his life. He wondered what Jim and Miss Jean would think about it.

CHAPTER 3

"Heard about your little party at the Morning Glory last night," Daniel Stone said when Pride and Will walked into his office over the jail. There was another man standing near the window. He said howdy to Pride and gave Will a nod. "I suppose you're gonna tell me what that was all about," Stone continued.

"Ain't much to report," Pride drawled. "Old man, Luther Gamble, and his two sons came in to register a complaint about Judge Parker hangin' his youngest boy today. I reckon they weren't up to snuff on the proper way to complain. But with the help of my friend, here, we were able to give 'em what they came for, and the issue got settled to everybody's satisfaction."

Stone glanced at the man standing by the window, and they both shook their heads incredulously. Back at Pride then, he said, "You're gonna have to do some paperwork on that little shindig. Gamble and his boys are wanted in Kansas, and we'll have to let them know they're dead." He shifted his gaze to Will. "Who's this you got with you?"

"This here is Will Tanner," Pride announced grandly. "And if it wasn't for him, you wouldn't have the pleasure of my company this mornin'. Will, this is Marshal Daniel Stone. The feller by the window with the sour look on his face is Deputy Ed Pine." Will returned a single nod from each man with one of his own. "Will is thinkin' about pinnin' on a deputy's badge if you're interested, and I wanna say right off that he's damn-sure qualified." He went on then to relate the details of the action that took place in the saloon the night before, emphasizing Will's quickness and accuracy with a handgun. "When those three buzzards pulled their guns out, everybody in the saloon ran for cover except him. And he saw it his duty to help an officer of the law in trouble," Pride said, and when he had finished, he was gratified to see that Stone definitely looked interested.

"Well, Mr. Tanner," Stone addressed him. "Looks like we owe you our thanks." He cocked an eye in Pride's direction. "Although I don't know if it speaks well for your record by saving Fletcher Pride's neck. We've been trying to get rid of him for eight years."

"Nine years," Pride corrected him, "come this fall."

"Seems longer," Stone deadpanned. Back to Will, he began his questioning. "Have you got a good horse?"

"Yes, sir," Will answered. "I'm ridin' a buckskin gelding, little over four years old, and I've got a sorrel packhorse, maybe a little older."

"Pride says you're pretty good with that .44 you're wearing. I expect you've got a decent rifle, too."

"Yes, sir," Will replied, "a Winchester 73."

Stone studied the young man carefully. He liked

what he saw. Tall and lean, yet it appeared to be a powerful lean, and he had already been tested in the altercation at the saloon. Since he had just lost two deputies recently, he needed replacements, but he thought it fair to warn Will of the dangers involved. "If I hire you, you'll be working almost all the time in Indian Territory, and that's not a particularly healthy country for deputy marshals. Pride can tell you that, if he hasn't already. How well do you know that country?"

"Some," Will said.

"Well, I expect you'll get to know it better, if you last long enough," Stone said, aiming not to sugar-coat it. He wanted to know before he made a final decision if Will was inclined to be cautious. He had the look of a man with quiet confidence. Stone hoped he had a brain under that sandy hair. *Well, we'll soon find out*, he thought. "All right, you're hired," he said. "I'm gonna assign you to work with Pride, so you can get a little training on the job. You can go along with him as a posseman, but you'll get a deputy's pay. That's fair, ain't it?"

"I reckon so," Will replied, surprised that there wasn't more to the process. "Ain't there no swearin' in, or somethin' like that?"

"No, I'm sure you know what the job is. I'll tell Judge Parker I've hired you, and he'll officially commission you as a U.S. Deputy Marshal. So I'll just say welcome to the service. I hope it suits you and you suit the service." He offered his hand, and after they shook on it, Ed Pine stepped forward to shake hands as well. Stone continued. "Pride can fill you in on all the procedures and responsibilities, as well as the pay schedule for mileage to and from picking up prisoners. All you need now is a badge." He winked at Ed Pine, still standing by his desk, and opened his desk drawer. "I oughta have two or three in here." Picking out the one he wanted, he held it out to Will. "This is a badge that was worn by a deputy that ain't with us no more." Then he pretended to notice something on it after Will took it in his hand. "Whoa," he said, "I didn't clean this one up very well. I'll get you another one."

Puzzled, Will looked at the badge and saw at once what Stone was referring to. It was rather obvious. The tip of the badge had flecks of red on it resembling dried blood. "This one'll do," he said, and scratched the flecks off with his fingernail. "Looks like the last feller that wore it must have been paintin' somethin' red."

"Damn," Stone swore, disappointed. Then he and the other two deputies had a good laugh at the unsuccessful attempt to jape the newcomer.

That concluded his official hiring as a deputy marshal. The job was a simple one, catch lawbreakers and bring them to Judge Parker's court to be tried by whatever means necessary. In the wide and wild Oklahoma Indian Territory, his authority would be unlimited.

Once the hiring was done, Stone wasted no time before handing them their first assignment. "This oughta be a good training job for our new man," he said. "We just got word from the Texas Rangers on a bad bunch coming our way. They've been chasing a bank robber and murderer named Max Tarbow. There's four more of them in his gang, and they've been robbing banks in small towns for the past two weeks down there. They're pretty sure they've headed up into Indian Territory, because they lost them near Denison on the Red River. So they most likely followed the Seminole Trail, or the Potawatomi Trail up into the Nations."

"They sure as shootin' ain't the first outlaws to use those trails," Pride remarked. "At least we know where to start lookin'."

"Mind you watch yourselves, Fletcher," Stone warned. "The word I got from Texas was these boys are a mean bunch. They left a couple of people dead in one of those banks. All I can tell you is the leader is Max Tarbow. His brother, Billy, rides with him, and I don't know the names of the other three."

"You know me, Dan," Pride said. "I'm always careful. I'll round up Charlie Tate, and we'll get a wagon loaded up with supplies and maybe pull outta here tomorrow."

"Good hunting," Stone said as they left his office.

"Who's Charlie Tate?" Will asked when they got outside.

"A cook," Pride replied.

"What do we need with a cook?"

"We gotta eat," Pride said. "There ain't no tellin' how long it's gonna take to run this Tarbow bunch to ground." He could see the question in Will's face. "You didn't think I was plannin' to hunt game and live off the land, didja?"

"I reckon I did," Will said. "I didn't think you'd wanna be slowed down by a wagon."

"We won't be wastin' time tryin' to run down antelope or deer. This is a huntin' trip, all right, but not that kind." He changed the subject abruptly. "Where are you stayin' here in town?"

"Last night, I slept in Vern Tuttle's hay barn," Will said. "Reckon I can stay there tonight."

"You're gonna need to find you a more permanent place here in Fort Smith. I'll take you over to Ruth Bennett's boardin' house. That's where I stay, and I know for a fact Ruth's got a vacant room, right next to mine. Old man, Heck Tilden, lived in that room for a good while after his wife died, and now he's dead. So I know she's lookin' to rent that room out."

"Sounds just right for me," Will said, thinking about the failed "bloody" badge trick. *Might as well take a room some old man just died in.*

"She sets a fine table, too," Pride boasted. "You can't get no better food anywhere in town."

"That right?" Will asked. "How come you take supper at the Mornin' Glory?"

"Ruth don't serve no whiskey," Pride said, "and I need it for my digestion. How much did Vern Tuttle charge to keep your horses?"

"Fifty cents each, and a quarter for grain," Will said.

"We'll fix that, too. He can give you the same price he charges me, 'cause it's on a more permanent rate."

"This is the young feller I was tellin' you about," Pride said to Ruth Bennett. "He'd like to take a look at that room next to mine."

"Will Tanner, ma'am," he introduced himself, since Pride neglected to.

"Nice to meet you, Mr. Tanner," she said with a pleasant smile. "I see you're already wearing a star."

"Yes, ma'am."

"Come on, and we'll go upstairs to look at the room," she said. "Like Mr. Pride said, it's right down the hall from his room. We hated to lose Mr. Tilden. He was such a kind old gentleman. There are still a few of his things in the room. He didn't have any family to give them to, but we'll get them out if you decide you're gonna stay with us. Most of our guests are older. It would be nice to have a younger guest."

It didn't take Will but a few moments to decide to take the room. It was a sizable room with a large window facing the street, and the rate she offered was more reasonable than he had anticipated. She explained that she gave Pride a reduced rate because there were so many days when he was not in town, and that meant less work to maintain the room. She gave Will the same rate. Back downstairs, she showed him the washroom, a small room at the end of the back porch with a pump, basin, and tub. In the event he wanted to take a bath, she said, he could heat some water on the stove. Will was well satisfied. The arrangement was certainly high-class.

"Will you be taking supper with us tonight, Mr. Tanner?" she asked when she showed him the dining room. "I'm having pork chops, mashed potatoes, string beans, and fresh-baked biscuits."

"Yes, ma'am, count me in," Will said at once. "And please, call me Will."

"That sounds mighty good," Pride declared. "You can count me in, too."

"Well"—she beamed as she said it—"we should be

honored to compete with the Morning Glory." Will was certain he saw the big man flush slightly.

"We've got some things to do to get ready to leave in the mornin'," Pride said. "So I reckon we'll see you back here at suppertime."

The rest of that day was spent getting everything ready to roll in the morning. They visited three saloons before they found Charlie Tate to accompany them the next day to buy the supplies they would need for the trip. Along with the flour, coffee, salt, sugar, dried beans, potatoes, bacon, beef, and grain for the horses, Pride loaded a long chain on the wagon they picked up at the wagon sheds behind the stable. When Will asked about the purpose of the chain, Pride explained that it was to shackle prisoners. Charlie assured them he and the wagon would be right on time to meet them at eight in the morning. Will wondered why the late start, since his days normally started at sunup. Pride explained that he wanted to eat breakfast at the boardinghouse before starting out. "After you try some of Charlie's cookin', you'll understand why," he said.

A little before noon, they joined almost all the other citizens of Fort Smith who had gathered at the gallows, located in a small courtyard behind the jail. Close to the stroke of noon, two guards walked Troy Gamble up the twelve steps to the platform, his hands tied behind his back, and a defiant sneer on his face. His guards led him to a bench at the back of the platform and sat him down to await the reading of his sentence. Standing alone at the side of the platform, the hangman stood patiently waiting. Pride informed Will that his name was George Maledon and he had earned a reputation as the Prince of Hangmen. Seeming disinterested then, Pride left them and began to casually make his way through the crowd of spectators, leaving Will and Charlie still watching the execution. He stopped behind a woman wearing a black bonnet when the court clerk finished reading the sentence and stepped aside for the guards to bring Troy to stand on the trap. The hangman stepped forward to adjust the noose. Unnoticed by all but a few people standing close by, Pride caught the arm of the lady in the bonnet when she pulled the revolver from her skirt and tried to raise it. "Now, Mrs. Gamble," he calmly said, "you don't wanna do somethin' like that. It ain't gonna bring your boy back, and it'd just bring you a barrelful of trouble."

Caught up in her grief, Effie Gamble collapsed as Maledon sprang the trap, sending her youngest to join the rest of the men in her family to the accompaniment of a chorus of gasps from the fascinated spectators. She would have fallen had not the massive deputy locked her in his arms. Completely defeated, she made no effort to resist when Pride took the revolver from her hand and stuck it in his belt. With tears streaming down her face, she could stand only with Pride's support, so he stood with her for a while until she seemed to regain some strength. Will and Charlie watched, astonished by the big deputy's actions, still unaware of what had taken place. They followed when he walked the grieving widow away from the gallows and back toward the front of the courthouse, catching up in time to hear his quiet conversation. "I know it's hard," he told her, "but this chapter's done and gone. You've got to get on with the rest of your life. Now, if you'll promise me you'll go straight back to Kansas, or wherever you came here from, I won't arrest you and I won't tell nobody about this. All right?" She didn't answer right away, so he pressed. "All right? I gotta have your promise." Finally, she nodded, but he insisted. "I gotta hear you promise."

"I promise," she finally muttered, barely above a whisper.

"All right, then," Pride said. "You got a place to stay in town?" She said she had a room in the hotel. "All right," he repeated, "I'll stand right here and watch you go. I'm sorry 'bout your loss. You go along now, and you won't be in no trouble."

"What in tarnation was that all about?" Charlie asked.

Pride pulled the revolver from his belt and held it up for them to see. "That was Troy Gamble's mama," he said. "She was fixin' to shoot somebody with this here pistol. The clerk, the hangman—I don't know if she knew. She most likely couldn'ta hit what she was aimin' at, even if she pulled the trigger." He cocked an eye in Will's direction. "She didn't know it, but it was me or you she shoulda been aimin' at."

"How the hell did you know who she was?" Charlie asked.

"Well, I warn't sure," Pride admitted. "But she was the only woman in the crowd wearin' a black dress and a black hat and veil, so I figured I'd just stand by her to see if she might be thinkin' about doin' somethin' crazy."

"You think she knew about what happened to her husband and her other two sons last night?" Will asked.

"I don't know," Pride said. "I don't know for sure if she even knew they were in town, but she most likely knew they were comin' after me." He shook his head, thinking about her. "I hope she did, 'cause if she didn't, it's liable to kill her when she finds out."

"Did you tell her you was the one that brought Troy in?" Charlie asked.

"Hell, no," Pride blurted.

There was no doubt in Will's mind that the veteran deputy marshal had been anticipating the possibility of a grief-stricken member of the Gamble family showing up at the hanging, with an intent to take revenge on the authorities. It was something he would keep in mind after this. He decided there was much to learn about his new job, beyond shoot-outs with bank robbers, murderers, and horse thieves.

With the excitement of the hanging over, the three men returned to their preparations to leave town the following morning. Since the wagon was stocked, Charlie prepared to drive it to his cabin east of town to park it overnight. "Don't make me come lookin' for you in the mornin'," Pride warned him, fully aware of Charlie's weakness for whiskey.

"Don't worry 'bout me," Charlie retorted. "Just be sure you're ready to go when I get here." They parted then, and Will and Pride headed back to Ruth's.

They arrived back at the house with a little time left before Ruth rang the supper bell. So Will decided he'd take advantage of the washroom facilities. Pride said to go right ahead; he had just taken a dip in the Poteau River a week ago and hadn't sweated all that much since. "Don't be late for supper," he advised. "You don't wanna be the last one to get to the pork chop platter." Will laughed, said he'd be quick, and went upstairs to his room. He put away in the bureau the few possessions he didn't need to take with him, taking up less than half of one drawer. He pulled off his boots, socks, and shirt; threw the towel provided around his neck; picked up the washcloth, his bar of soap, and his razor; then headed down the back stairs to the porch. He walked across the porch to the small washroom, only to find the door locked. He gave it another firm tug, in case it was just stuck and not locked.

"I'll just be a minute," a feminine voice sang out cheerfully from inside.

"Sorry," he quickly apologized, and stepped back from the door.

After a few minutes, the door opened and a young girl came out. Astonished, for he was under the impression that all Ruth's guests were older people, he jumped back a couple more steps, sliding his bare foot on the porch floor and picking up a splinter in the process. "Ow!" he blurted while he fumbled with his towel in an effort to cover his bare torso.

She couldn't help laughing at his reaction. "I'm sorry I startled you," she said, still smiling broadly.

"I was just cleaning up the room a little." She paused while he limped aside to give her room to pass. "You must be our new guest," she said. He nodded, wishing she'd just go, so he could pull the splinter out of his foot. "My name's Sophie," she said. "My mother owns the house."

"Pleased to meet you," he said. "Will Tanner."

"Welcome to our home, Mr. Tanner. May I call you Will?"

"Yes, ma'am, please do." *You can call me jackass if you want, pretty as you are,* he thought.

"Well, let me get out of your way. I'd best go help Mama get supper on the table. Don't be late—we're having pork chops tonight."

"No, ma'am, I won't," he assured her, then hurried inside, closed the door, and immediately sat down on the floor and went after the splinter that had halfway imbedded itself in the pad of his foot.

After a basin bath and a quick shave, he returned to his room, where he put on his clean shirt and pulled his boots back on. It was only a few minutes after that he heard the cheerful ring of Ruth's little dinner bell. Halfway expecting to hear a stampede of running feet and slamming bedroom doors, he was surprised by the casual response by the other guests. There were only three, all male, and he almost bumped into one of them when he came out of his room. The man, a short, frail, little gray-haired gentleman, paused and politely signaled Will to precede him. Will couldn't help thinking that it was strange surroundings for two unrefined lawmen like him and Pride. He could hear Pride's booming voice from downstairs already.

"I met your friend on the back porch," Sophie said to Pride, who was already seated at the table. "Mama said he's a deputy marshal like you."

"That's right," Pride replied.

"I noticed that he walks with a limp," Sophie said. "Is that from a wound he received in the line of duty?"

"Huh?" Pride blurted. "I never noticed him walkin' with a limp. And he just signed on this mornin', so he ain't been wounded in the line of duty." Hearing someone coming through the parlor into the dining room, they both turned to see Will and the old gentleman he had met in the hall. Will wondered why the two seemed to stare extra hard at either him or the old man. Sophie returned to the kitchen to help with the serving.

The meal lived up to Pride's promise of excellence, and Will could understand why Pride wanted to have one more shot at Ruth's table in the morning. Ruth introduced her new boarder to the other guests and they welcomed him warmly. He already felt at home by the time the meal was finished. Afterward, he and Pride retired to the front porch with two of the other boarders to let the pork chops and potatoes digest. Pride rolled a cigarette, and they rode the rocking chairs while he explained some of the obligations of a deputy's job, and the various ways he could be paid additional fees while apprehending criminals. This was all interesting to Will, so he was disappointed when the discussion was interrupted by the arrival of a young man driving a buggy. He pulled up before the front gate of the house and stepped down. When he walked up the steps to the porch, he wished them all a good evening. "Garth Pearson, ain't it?" Pride asked.

"Yes, sir, that's right," the young man said, surprised that the deputy remembered his name. "I work for Judge Parker."

"I remember," Pride said. "If you've come for supper, you're too late. I think the women are already cleanin' up the table."

"Oh no, sir," Garth said. "I didn't come for supper. It's such a nice evening, I just thought I'd stop by to see if Miss Sophie might enjoy a ride in the buggy."

"She might at that," Pride said. "Go on in and ask her."

Leonard Dickens, one of the two other boarders on the porch, got up from his chair. "I'm goin' in. I'll tell Sophie you're here," he said. The old man he had been talking to decided to go inside, too.

"Have a seat, young feller," Pride said. "They'll find Sophie for you."

"I'll just stand here," Garth replied.

"Suit yourself," Pride said. "If I was a young feller like you, I'd sure be callin' on Sophie, myself. She's a fine-lookin' little filly, and that's a fact." Garth forced a faint smile, obviously not wishing to discuss the young lady with the coarse deputy marshal. A silent witness to the conversation, Will had already decided he didn't like Garth Pearson, although he was not sure why.

In a few minutes, Sophie came to the front door. "Hello, Garth," she greeted her caller, her voice almost musical.

"Good evening, Sophie," Garth responded politely,

then seemed hesitant to explain his purpose, obviously uncomfortable with an audience of the two deputies.

Amused by the young man's awkwardness, Pride got up from his chair. "Come on, Will, let's give 'em the porch." Will reluctantly followed him inside.

Will lay awake for some time after he crawled into the bed. His first day as a deputy marshal was quite a day. He thought about the days to come and wondered if the job of a lawman suited him. He had decided on it pretty quickly, without a great deal of thought. It occurred to him that he should have sent word to Shorty and the boys. *I guess after a while they'll figure it out*, he thought. Before he drifted off to sleep, his mind went back to the incident on the front porch, and he realized that he envied Garth Pearson. He seemed so groomed and proper in his high collar and necktie and his evening coat. He was the kind of man who would impress someone as pretty and sweet as Sophie. *It doesn't matter to me*, he thought. *I sure as hell ain't in her class.* But it took him a while to go to sleep.

Always a light sleeper, he was awakened sometime later in the night by a squeaking sound from someone walking on the floorboards. It struck him as odd in the otherwise silent house. The sound seemed close by, maybe from Pride's room next door. He started to turn over and go back to sleep, but then the thought struck him of the possibility that someone up to no good might be stalking the big deputy. In the dead of the night, his imagination needed little inspiration to come up with the possibility that

Troy Gamble's mother might still be looking to avenge her dead. She might have hired someone to seek out the deputy who brought her son to the gallows. *Nah*, he thought, *go back to sleep*. But he was already wide-awake, so he decided to have a look to be sure.

As quietly as he could, he got out of bed, drew his .44 from his holster on the chair, and moved silently to the door. Very slowly, he turned the knob and eased the door open just far enough to permit him to look down the darkened hallway. In the glow of a single candle, he recognized Ruth Bennett tiptoeing out of Pride's room. She closed his door quietly behind her and tiptoed down the hall to the back stairs. *Well, I'll be . . .* he thought, and eased the door shut again.

CHAPTER 4

Ruth served breakfast from six o'clock until eight, because some of her guests were not early risers. Will was sitting, drinking coffee before the first platters of scrambled eggs were delivered to the table. Sophie had greeted him with a good-morning smile and brought him a cup before the bacon was finished frying. "You're an early riser," she said cheerfully. "It won't be long, though." She turned to look at the clock. "It's not even six yet."

"I reckon I've been gettin' up at daybreak for so long I can't break the habit," he said. He glanced toward the door then, hearing the heavy tread of his partner coming in. "Mornin'," he said to Pride.

"Mornin'," Pride returned. "And good mornin' to you, missy," he said to Sophie. "How 'bout gettin' me a cup of that coffee?" She picked up his cup and went to the kitchen to fill it. "Ain't she a right pretty little filly?" he asked.

"She sure is," Will agreed. "You act like you're in a good mood this mornin'. You musta slept good."

"I reckon," Pride said. "I tossed and turned a little

at first, but I finally went to sleep about eleven or eleven thirty."

"That's funny. I woke up about that time, thought I heard some little squeakin' noises," Will said.

"Mice," Pride replied at once. "House is full of 'em. Ruth oughta do somethin' about all them mice."

After breakfast, Pride told Ruth they would probably be gone for three or four weeks, depending on how their luck ran. She wished them a safe trip and asked them to be careful. Pride said they would, then he and Will went to the stable to get their horses. They found Charlie waiting for them. "It's about time," Charlie complained. "I thought I was gonna have to go to that fancy boardin'house you stay at and root you out."

Pride didn't answer him; he looked at Vern Tuttle instead. "How long's he been here, Vern?"

"He rolled in about a minute before you got here," Vern said.

"What I figured," Pride said. "That's your first lie of the day, Charlie." He smiled at Will and informed him, "He'll tell about a hundred a day." Changing the subject, he commented, "That's a fine-lookin' buckskin you're ridin' there, Will."

"Yep," Will replied. "He's the best one I've ever owned. Good stamina and determination, good hard feet, and he don't like to come in second."

"What's his name?" Charlie asked.

"Buster," Will said.

"Buster?" Charlie responded. "What'd you name him that for?"

"No reason." Will shrugged. "I just called him that

one day right after I got him, and he didn't seem to mind, so it stuck."

"I believe like the Injuns do," Pride declared. "I think a man's horse oughta be named to honor his bloodline and the spiritual part he plays as the man's partner."

"Is that a fact?" Will replied. "What'd you name that dun you're ridin'?"

"Goat," Pride said. They all laughed.

So that's the way it seemed on Will's first official assignment as a U.S. Deputy Marshal, as if they were setting out on a Sunday picnic. In fact, they were starting on a journey that would take them seven and a half days, just to reach a starting point in their search.

Following a trail between the Sans Bois Mountains and the Winding Stair Mountains, they rode south-west until striking the Missouri-Kansas-Texas Railroad, locally known as the Katy. The Deadline, Charlie called it. When Will asked why, Charlie explained that the Katy marked the fringe of civilization. And when a lawman crossed the Deadline, he took his life in his hands. "You can ride on almost any trail leadin' into that country on the other side of the railroad," Charlie said, "and you'll find little cards stuck on trees with a lawman's name on it. That's a promise that he'll get shot if he keeps comin'."

"A card?" Will asked, thinking Charlie might be exaggerating the threat. "Outlaws write deputies' names on little cards."

"Ask Pride," Charlie replied. "He's found some

with his name on 'em, and that's just from the ones that can write."

Will turned to Pride for confirmation, and Pride said, "It's a fact. I've found three of those little cards."

"Maybe you'd better turn around and go back to Fort Smith," Will joked. "Charlie and I can go find Max Tarbow."

"I might at that," Pride said, also joking. He got serious then. "I'd say we're about twenty miles north of Atoka. We might as well follow the railroad down there and find Jim Little Eagle—see if he's heard anything about Tarbow's gang around there. Hard to say where that bunch is headin', but there's a general store there. Maybe they needed some supplies, and if they did, they mighta stopped there."

"Who's Jim Little Eagle?" Will asked.

"Indian policeman," Pride replied. "He used to ride with the Choctaw Lighthorse when the Five Civilized Nations all had their own police. A few years back, the government ordered all the nations to be consolidated and they formed one outfit to head up all the police for the Five Nations. Jim's a good man. Me and him's worked together before, and if this bunch we're lookin' for has showed up anywhere in his territory, Jim'll know it."

"It'd help a helluva lot if we knew what these men looked like," Will said.

"The only descriptions Stone had was for the Tarbow brothers," Pride said. "Max is a good-sized man with a full beard—ought not be hard to spot— wears an eye patch over his left eye. The story is, he lost his eye in a knife fight. His brother, Billy, ain't got a hair on his head—his face, either. Supposed to have had some kinda fever when he was a baby that left him bald as an onion. Stone didn't have any description of the three ridin' with Max and Billy."

"Well, that's something," Will allowed.

"We gotta rest these horses before we go much farther," Charlie reminded them. "We might as well camp here and go on down to Atoka in the mornin'.'"

"I expect you're right," Pride said. So they followed the trail beside the railroad tracks for about a mile, stopping to make camp when they came to a sizable creek.

Dixon Durant glanced up from the back counter when the five men walked in the front door of his general merchandise store in the little settlement named for his father. His first thought was that he was about to be robbed, for they were a villainous-looking group of men. From time to time, his store had been visited by men he was certain were outlaws, but they had never caused him mischief. For the most part, the many outlaws who sought sanctuary in the Nations pushed farther west and north of Durant and the railroad. Now, as he looked at these strangers, he feared his luck had run out. A large man, who would seem to be the leader, walked into the center of the store and stood there, glancing around him as if checking the shelves and their contents. He was a frightening man in appearance, with a full beard of coarse black hair and wearing an eye patch over one eye, akin to a pirate with his crush-crowned hat pulled down low on his forehead. One of the men, a smaller man than the imposing pirate, stepped close to him and said, "I want some molasses. Ask him if he's got any molasses."

The large man stared at Dixon then. "You heard him. You got any molasses?"

"Yes, sir," Dixon mumbled, "I've got a barrel that's half-full."

"Well, wheel it out here, then," Max Tarbow said. "We ain't got all day."

Dixon looked quickly to Leon Shipley, his clerk. "Get the gentleman some molasses," he said. The expression on Leon's face told Dixon that he was of the same opinion as he in regard to their guests, so he moved at once to maneuver the barrel out from behind the counter. In the meantime, the other men went straight to the shelves on both sides of the room, pulling articles that struck their fancy and placing them on the counters. Most of the items were standard supplies needed to set up a camp for an extended period. When at last they finished, there were items stacked high on the counters. "That it?" the menacing brute asked.

"Ever'thin' I can think of," one of the men answered.

"Chewin' tobacco?" Tarbow asked.

"Yep," the young one with no hair answered him.

"Well, I reckon we're done, then," Tarbow said, and turned back to Dixon and his clerk. Staring the frightened man in the face, he paused for a long moment before blurting, "You got all this added up?"

"Ah, no," Dixon stammered, having feared it wouldn't be necessary. "Just take me a minute or two."

"Well, hurry up, man," Max Tarbow commanded. "We've got ground to cover before dark." He was smart enough to know that, although they had outrun the Texas Rangers, the Rangers would certainly notify the Marshals Service in Fort Smith. So the sooner he and his men left the railroad behind them and disappeared into the wilds of the western part of the Nations, the better. This was not the first time he had fled to Indian Territory to hide out until things cooled off, so he was heading to a place he knew well.

"Yes, sir," Dixon replied and hurriedly began to list the items and their prices, still not completely convinced they would depart peacefully. When he had totaled the purchases, he slid the bill across the counter to Tarbow, wondering what the big man's reaction would be. To his amazement, Tarbow pulled out a large roll of money and counted out the full amount. They were more than able to pay for their purchases since they still had almost all the money they had robbed from three different banks in Texas. But that was not the primary reason Tarbow willingly paid when it would have been just as easy to simply take what they wanted. He reasoned that there was no sense in having the store owner alert the Indian police and the U.S. Marshals Service of the gang's presence in the territory. He handed the bill to one of the other men. "Here, Jesse, you're the one that went to school. You figure what ever'body owes me for their part." Back to Dixon then, he said, "We could use a little help loadin' this stuff on them packhorses out front."

"Yes, sir," Dixon exclaimed eagerly, finding it hard to believe he and Leon were still standing. They both willingly pitched in to carry the merchandise outside, where a couple of the men were loading it on three packhorses.

"How the hell do you expect me to tie that barrel on a packhorse?" a tall, bone-thin man complained when Leon wheeled the molasses barrel out on the porch.

"You're the one that was braggin' about how good you are at loadin' a packhorse," the young bald man said, and an argument soon ensued.

"What are you two squabblin' about, Whip?" Max Tarbow wanted to know when he came out of the store.

"Billy's dang molasses," Whip Doolin answered. "There ain't no way to balance that big ol' barrel with the rest of the load. You need another barrel to balance it."

Billy, seeing his older brother hesitate, insisted. "I want that molasses, Max. We ain't run across none in a coon's age, and it's mighty good on a biscuit."

Dixon Durant, seeing the possibility of a return of the molasses, was quick to offer a solution for their problem. "We can fix that in a minute," he offered. "I've got some large fruit jars that'll hold a half gallon. We can pour the molasses in jars and you can balance your packs any way you need to, then."

Max gave Dixon a grin and said, "There you go, boys. Now, let's get to it." The horses were soon packed and the band of five outlaws pulled out of Durant, heading northwest, on the trail to Tishomingo, much to the satisfaction and great relief of Dixon and Leon.

* * *

It was approaching dusk by the time the gang guided their horses down along the banks of the Blue River to a shabby little trading post run by one Lem Stark. Hearing his old hound barking when their horses pulled up out front, Lem walked to the door to see who his visitors might be. "Max Tarbow," he announced. "I thought you was dead. I ain't heared nothin' 'bout you in about a year. And Billy, I see he's still with you, but I don't recall seein' them other three."

Tarbow grinned. "Lem Stark, you old coot, I'm surprised the marshal, or the army, ain't sent somebody out here to run you outta the territory." He nodded to the men behind him. "You remember Billy. Say howdy to Jesse Becker, Whip Doolin, and Tom Blanton." Howdies were exchanged all around. "You better have some of that bootleg whiskey, 'cause I'm in sore need of a good belt. We've been ridin' for quite a few days." He felt like relaxing now that they had reached Tishomingo. They were far enough over the Deadline that he felt he was now in territory that belonged to the outlaw. He would be happy to welcome any deputy marshal fool enough to venture this far into the Nations.

"I got all you want," Lem said. "My boy, Jeb, brought half a wagonload up from Texas two weeks ago. This ain't moonshine. This is genuine sour mash store-bought. I'm glad you boys showed up to drink some of it up." He received an enthusiastic response from his visitors. "You fixin' to set up camp in the Arbuckles again?"

"Yeah, I reckon," Max replied. "That's as good a place as any, if I don't find some wolves or Injuns has took it over since we left. I'm thinkin' 'bout holin' up in those mountains for a good spell, till the dust settles a little from the bank jobs we pulled back in Texas. We'll set up camp here on the river tonight, maybe tomorrow, too, if you ain't lyin' about that sour mash whiskey. We ain't in no hurry."

"Well, go ahead and get your camp set up and come on in the house when you're finished. I'll have Minnie cook up some supper for ya," Lem said. "Won't be no charge for the supper." He figured it would be a small investment on his part for a chance to part Max and his men from some of that bank money.

"That's right sportin' of you, Lem," Max said. "We're much obliged." He had already figured to get a supper out of Lem, knowing the old man would be speculating on how much he could sell him. "So you still got that little Chickasaw woman cookin' for you, huh?"

"Yep, Minnie's still here," Lem said. "She ain't got no place else to go, or she'da most likely already been gone." He laughed when he said it. "I know what you're thinkin', but she don't do nothin' but the cookin'. I'm too old to think about anything like that, anyway. These days, I get more pleasure outta a good bowel movement."

Max threw his head back with a loud guffaw. "I hear you sayin' the words, but I know you're lyin' now. All right, we'll ride down there below that stand of willows and set us up a camp. Then we'll be back to see if Minnie Three Toes can still cook like she used to."

* * *

At about the same time Max Tarbow and his gang arrived at Lem Stark's store, two U.S. Deputies and a cook pulled up before a modest cabin resting beside Muddy Boggy Creek, north of the Atoka train depot. Choctaw policeman Jim Little Eagle opened the door a crack and peered out. Seeing the imposing figure of Fletcher Pride astride the big dun gelding, he opened the door wide and stepped outside. "Fletcher Pride," Jim announced heartily. "What brings you to this territory?"

"Jim," Pride greeted him. "How you makin' out? It's been a while since we worked together."

"About a year," Jim confirmed. "I thought maybe you'd retired."

"Can't afford it," Pride returned.

"I see you brought a wagon and a posseman," Jim said. "You goin' to pick up some prisoners?"

"Fact is, I'm lookin' for some outlaws that might be headed this way, and I'm hopin' maybe you mighta got wind of 'em."

"What'd they do?" Jim asked.

"They robbed some banks down in Texas and murdered a couple of bank tellers," Pride said. "Supposed to be a real bad bunch. I figured it was a good chance they mighta come up your way."

Jim stroked his chin thoughtfully. "No, I haven't seen any sign of them, and nobody's told me about seeing any strangers. You and your men step down and come sit on the porch. I'll have my wife make some coffee." His wife, Mary Light Walker, was standing at the door. She turned at once and went to the kitchen.

"That would sure be to my likin'," Pride declared,

threw his leg over, and stepped down. Will followed suit. Pride made the introductions then. With a wave of his hand in Will's direction, he said, "This is Will Tanner. He's a new deputy marshal, and that's Charlie Tate settin' on the wagon seat." Jim walked over to shake hands with Will and Charlie as Pride continued. "Jim and me have been workin' together for a long time," he said to Will. "He's a good man to know in this territory." Back to Jim then, he said, "It's gettin' a little late in the day, so I figured on campin' here tonight, maybe up the creek a ways."

"You know you are always welcome," Jim Little Eagle said.

"Good," Pride continued. "We appreciate it, but tell that little wife of yours we didn't come for supper. We've got plenty of food on that wagon, so we'll ride on up the creek a piece and unhitch the horses and let 'em water. By that time, that coffee you mentioned oughta be ready."

Pride and Will followed the wagon about fifty yards upstream where Charlie picked his spot to camp. After they had taken care of the horses, Charlie wanted to know if he should stay and start preparing their supper. "No, not yet," Pride said. "If I've got it figured right, Jim's wife is gonna cook up somethin'. She'll figure it impolite if she don't. So grab a sack of that flour and some of them coffee beans, and maybe some of that salt pork. We'll take her a little somethin' for her trouble."

As Pride had predicted, Mary was busy slicing bacon to fry with some beans she had simmering on the stove. She was outwardly pleased by the gifts of food the lawmen brought with them. "Sit down, drink coffee," she said in her broken English. "Food cook soon."

"What's been goin' on in your district?" Pride asked Jim as Mary handed him a cup of coffee. "You ain't seen no new faces at all?"

"Nope," Jim replied. "It's been quiet for a good while. I think maybe if the men you're looking for came up through Durant, then they most likely struck out farther west, maybe up toward Tishomingo. There's been two or three gangs of Texas outlaws that have hid out in the Arbuckle Mountains over the last two or three years. Maybe these outlaws you're looking for are going back there. If I was you, I'd ride down to Tishomingo first. If these outlaws are thinking about the Arbuckles, or going on up into Osage country, they'd most likely go through Tishomingo. I'd bet on it."

"You might be right," Pride said. "Anyway, it's as good a place as any to start lookin' for these boys. Is that crooked little sidewinder, Lem Stark, still up there on the Blue River? If they went through there, they most likely stopped there."

"He's still there," Jim said. "I've been meaning to ride down there myself—I've had a few reports that he's been selling whiskey to my people again. By treaty, I can't arrest him unless I can catch him in the act of selling to an Indian, and he knows it."

"Yeah," Pride said. "The government's got you tribal police's hands tied when it comes to dealin' with white people. But I think we'll start out for Tishomingo in the mornin' and have a little talk with ol' Lem."

Will said very little as supper went on, but he was

rapidly getting an overall view of the situation in the territory of the Five Civilized Nations when it came to law enforcement. What it amounted to was, the Indian police were empowered to arrest and punish lawbreakers, but only those who were members of the tribe. There was little wonder, he realized, that Indian Territory was a haven for wanted outlaws from Texas and Kansas, especially if they behaved themselves while hiding out here. The Indian policemen would not bother them.

The federal lawmen said good night to their hosts early in the evening. They thanked Mary for the supper and retired to their camp by the creek. When Jim Little Eagle got up the next morning, they were gone, already started on the thirty-five-mile journey to Lem Stark's little store on the Blue River.

"Well, well," Lem Stark crowed, "if it ain't Fletcher Pride himself." The wily little storekeeper walked out to meet the party pulling up just as the sun was settling into the prairie to the west. "I didn't expect to see you over this way again." He paused to take in the wagon driver and the rider on the buckskin horse. "Looks like you came plannin' on catchin' a wagonful. Don't recall ever seein' them fellers before." Unconcerned with Charlie, driving the wagon, because he figured him to be no more than a cook, he asked, "Who's the feller on the buckskin, a posseman?"

"He's Deputy Marshal Will Tanner," Pride answered.

"Deputy, huh? Who you chasin'?"

"You tell me," Pride replied. "They were here for a day or two, I expect."

"Who was?" Lem responded. "You're the first people I've seen in over a week." He knew Pride was bluffing.

Likewise, Pride knew Lem was lying. On the long day just ended, he had given a lot of thought to the possible places Max Tarbow might go. Since he didn't follow the railroad straight north toward the Cherokee Nation, it made sense that he headed west toward the Arbuckle Mountains. That mountain range was a favorite place for outlaws to hide out. There were hundreds of springs and caves in those mountains, places hard to find and easy to defend. This could turn out to be a long trip. "How's business, Lem?" Pride asked. "You sellin' plenty of whiskey?"

Lem's whiskers parted to allow a slow grin. "Why, Deputy Pride, you know it ain't legal for me to sell alcohol. I wish I had a little for myself. Why, hell, I'd offer you boys a drink if I had some."

"I'm sure you would," Pride said. "Now you can tell me how long Max Tarbow and his gang were here and how long's it been since they left."

"I don't believe I've ever had the pleasure of meetin' nobody by that name," Lem said. "Like I said, I ain't seen no strangers in over a week. Now, you fellers need any supplies, I'd be glad to have the business, but I don't know nothin' 'bout no outlaw named Max Tarbow. I'd invite you boys to eat supper, but my woman's come down with somethin', and she's so sick she can hardly stand up."

"Is that so?" Pride replied. "Well, we're sure sorry

to hear that. I sure hope she'll be feelin' better soon."
He could see her standing just inside the door, watching them. "Where's that youngest boy of yours? Jeb,
ain't that his name?"

"Yep," Lem said. "Jeb's his name. I don't know
where he is—most likely off somewhere huntin'."

"Too bad we missed him," Pride said. "What about
your older boy, Eli?"

"Hah," Lem grunted. "You know Eli ain't been
around here in a year or more. I reckon he's up in
Montana country somewhere."

"Is that a fact?" Pride replied. "I figured he mighta
got homesick to see his old daddy." When Stark only
grunted in response, Pride said, "I guess we'd best
get along now while there's still a little light to make
camp. Thanks for all your help." He signaled Will
and Charlie, and they turned their horses back
toward the river road.

When they were back up on the road, Will asked
Pride, "What about this younger son of his? Is he a
young boy?"

"No, Jeb's a grown man," Pride replied. "He lives
there with Lem, and he's about as worthless as his pa.
I expect he'll turn out to be as big an outlaw as his
brother. Eli has a downright mean streak in him,
seems to enjoy killin' people. I was on his trail for
about three weeks a little over a year ago, but I lost
him when he went up in Kansas. So far, ain't none of
the tribal police reported seein' him around these
parts again. Ol' Lem acts like he don't know where
Eli is, but those Starks were always a tight bunch. One
of these days Jim Little Eagle or one of the other

Indian policemen might find out Eli's back in the territory. And when he does, I'll be on his tail again."

They only traveled far enough to get out of eyesight of Lem's store before making camp by the edge of the river. The horses needed rest, especially the two pulling the wagon. They had covered thirty-five miles since leaving Jim Little Eagle's cabin. Will's buckskin and Pride's dun could have gone farther, but that was a long trip for a wagon. As soon as the horses were taken care of, Charlie built a fire and started cooking a quick supper. Will was curious about something he'd noticed back at Lem's store, so he said he was going back to take another look. Before anyone had a chance to question him, he slipped off into the growing darkness along the riverbank. Pride looked at Charlie and shrugged.

Since they had made their camp no farther than a mile from the store, Will went on foot, thinking that for his purposes, he was better off on foot, anyway. In about ten minutes' time he was close enough to watch Lem's store, so he found himself a spot close to the corral behind the small barn next to the store. He just had a hunch, and he wanted to satisfy his curiosity about it. Before, when he and Charlie were sitting quietly, listening to Pride talk to Lem, he had counted four horses in the corral. Sitting there behind a clump of chokecherry bushes, he counted them again. The same four horses were still in the corral, so he knew nothing had changed since they left. If Lem was in as tight with Max Tarbow as Pride said, and Lem was lying about his son being gone, then Will thought there was a small possibility his hunch might be valid. In the next few minutes, he was proven right. The darkness at the rear of the store was suddenly penetrated when a man was revealed, standing in the open door, holding a lantern. *That would be Jeb*, Will thought. The man paused for only a moment before stepping outside and heading for the barn.

Will stared hard in anticipation, waiting for the man to come from the barn. As he had suspected, Jeb came out carrying a saddle on his shoulder. Will waited patiently while a horse was being saddled. When it was done, Jeb put his lantern out and led the horse out of the corral. Stepping up into the saddle, he wheeled the horse and loped up from the barnyard and struck out to the west, away from the river. Moving as fast as he could, Will ran after him to make sure of the direction Jeb had taken. When he was certain, he looked around for something to mark the trail. There were two oak trees tilted in opposite directions, forming a V several feet from the place where the horse had loped over the bluffs. This is where he would find the trail in the morning.

Pride looked up at him when he returned to the camp. "What was you wantin' to see back at the store?"

"I just had a notion that I was curious about," Will said. "Some fellow just came out the back door of that store, saddled up a horse, and took off like he was in a big hurry. It wasn't Lem Stark. This fellow was a younger man, near as I could tell, and I'm bettin' it was Lem's son Jeb."

Pride shrugged, not sure why that was of such interest to the new deputy. "I expect it mighta been, all right. What are you thinkin'?"

"I'm thinkin' we need to do a little trackin' come

sunup. If Max Tarbow and the four men with him camped here recently, we oughta be able to find that camp. If we do, then we should be able to see which way they went when they left here."

"Well, I reckon," Pride answered. "I was plannin' to do just that, but what's Jeb ridin' off got to do with it?"

"Maybe nothin'," Will said, "but if his trail leads in the same direction as the Tarbow gang's, then there's a possibility he took off to warn Tarbow that we're on his trail. And that means we'd best make sure we don't ride into an ambush somewhere between here and the Arbuckle Mountains. I don't know about you, but I've got a strong feelin' that that's exactly where Jeb Stark is headin'—and I'da damn sure gone after him, if our horses hadn't been rode so hard all day."

"That's somethin' to think about, all right," Pride said. "I think you might be right, and I was hopin' that bunch wouldn't know we were lookin' for 'em. If they do, it's gonna be a whole different game."

When morning came, it didn't take long to find the spot where Tarbow and his men had camped, and the tracks told the lawmen that they were still relatively fresh. "Two or three days ago," Will said when Pride asked his opinion.

"I agree, and when they left, they headed out straight yonder way," Pride said, turning to peer off toward the northwest. "Arbuckle Mountains," he muttered, thinking of the difficult job ahead. "There's a thousand places to hide in those mountains."

Will nudged Buster lightly with his heels, and the buckskin started at a lope toward two oak trees that formed a V on the edge of the bluff. In the morning light, the single line of hoofprints were also easily found. Will looked out along the trail they left and was satisfied to see that it would intercept the trail left by the party of five riders and their packhorses. He nudged Buster again and followed the tracks until they crossed Tarbow's trail, then turned to go in the same direction. He sat there and waited for Pride and the wagon to catch up to him. "Looks to me like they're all goin' to the same place. I'd guess they're headin' someplace where they've been before, and Jeb's headin' there, too. When he left here last night, it was too dark for him to see their tracks, especially as fast as he was ridin'. But these tracks show he cut back close to the trail they left. He knows where they're goin', and if we don't lose this trail, it oughta take us right to 'em."

"No argument from me," Pride said. "Let's get goin'."

They followed an obvious trail for half a day before stopping by a small stream to rest the horses and test some more of Charlie's cooking. They could now see the Arbuckles in the distance, rising no more than about five hundred feet above the surrounding terrain. Running approximately thirty-five miles east to west, the range appeared inviting to the hunter or trapper, with its densely forested slopes and gentle foothills. Pride knew all too well, however, that the mountain range was a Jezebel with a thousand springs and caves to hide robbers and murderers on the run.

When the horses were rested, they set out again,

following a trail that was still easy to see until they struck the Blue River again, and the trail led into the water. "Looks like they decided it'd be a good idea to try to hide their trail," Pride said. "I was hopin' they wouldn't do that. I reckon Jeb Stark musta caught up with 'em and told 'em about us, so they took to the river."

"I don't think so," Will said, studying the hoof-prints on the riverbank. "There's some tracks from a single horse that didn't go in the water with the rest of 'em. I'm thinkin' these are Jeb's tracks, and if they are, that means he's headin' straight for the place he thinks Tarbow's goin' to."

"Well, now, that does make sense, don't it?" Pride responded. "Couldn't be nobody else's tracks but Jeb's—save us a lotta time tryin' to find where Tarbow came outta the water."

They left the banks of the river and followed the single set of tracks leading toward the middle of the mountains. Reaching the foothills as the sun began to sink behind the mountains still before them, the tracks of the single horse became more difficult to follow. Finally, as they drew closer to the edge of the mountains, they lost the tracks altogether. When they came to a spirited stream flowing down from the mountains, they stopped to talk it over. "Looks like that damn horse musta took wings and flew," Charlie said, still perched on the wagon seat.

"He mighta took off up through the trees back there, and we just missed it," Pride speculated.

"Maybe," Will allowed. "Maybe he just rode up this stream. Might be he's thinkin' 'bout coverin' his tracks now."

"Well, this is about as far as I'm goin'," Charlie said. "I can't drive this wagon up in those mountains."

"We're about through for the day, anyway," Pride said, looking up at the sky. "We'll set up our base camp by this stream, where we've got good water. Charlie, you can back that wagon up in that little ravine, so it'll be a little harder to see. In the mornin', me and Will can start scoutin' these hills." At this point, he couldn't help wondering if they had bet on the wrong set of tracks, although he wasn't ready to express it. It still made sense, but the fact was they had not seen any sign of the gang's tracks intersecting Jeb's trail.

Will was thinking the same as Pride, so he expressed the possibility. "You know, there ain't no guarantee that Jeb's headin' to the right spot. Tarbow mighta decided to hole up somewhere else."

"I've been thinkin' about that," Pride admitted. "I reckon we'll find out in the mornin'." There were a couple of places on his mind that might make good hideouts on this side of the range. Tomorrow, they would just have to start combing these mountains.

Chapter 5

With their base camp established by the stream in the foothills, Charlie left the horses unhitched and hobbled them. Will and Pride would range out from there in search of Tarbow's hideout. "Well, boys," he said when they saddled up the next morning, "good huntin'. I'll mix you up some pan biscuits for your supper." He had made them a hearty breakfast because he didn't expect to see them for a noon meal.

"Whaddaya say we split up?" Pride proposed. "I know a spot about a mile back up between those two mountains yonder where some outlaws built a cabin a couple of years ago. It ain't all that easy to find, sits at the bottom of a waterfall. I ran across it one day when I followed a game trail around the mountain. I'm guessin' that's where these boys went, since that trail was headed this way till we lost it."

"If you're feelin' pretty sure that's where they are," Will asked, "then why split up?"

"Well, I'm thinkin' about what you said about Jeb maybe ridin' up the stream," Pride said. "If I know about that cabin by the waterfall, most likely other people know about it, too. So they might have found a new place that nobody knows about yet."

"Fair enough," Will said, "but what have you got in mind if one of us finds 'em?"

"Come back and get the other one," Pride said. "We'll do the right thing, give 'em a chance to surrender, but we'll need the two of us to even think about that."

"I reckon so," Will agreed. "It's hard to surround five men by yourself."

Pride grinned at him. "I don't want you gettin' yourself shot on your first assignment. So come on back and get me if you find 'em. I think we can handle Mr. Tarbow and his gang." They both checked their rifles to make sure they were loaded and ready. "Let's get to it, then," Pride called out, and they parted ways. He headed for the valley between the two mountains, and Will started out along the stream.

It had been a while since he had found the waterfall and the log hut beside the pool at the bottom, but Pride recognized the stream that had led him to it when he was there before. To confirm it, he discovered some recent hoofprints on the game trail leading up the mountain. Certain the outlaws had taken over the old cabin, he started to go back to wait for Will, but hesitated when the thought occurred to him, *What if it's somebody else and not Tarbow? Better make sure I'm stalking the right game before I pull Will off that stream.* So he continued up the trail until he heard the sound of the waterfall above him. Dismounting then, he pulled his rifle from the saddle sling, led his horse over into the trees, and looped the reins in the branches of a laurel bush.

Thinking it a bad idea to stay on the game trail, he moved through the trees, to his left, making his way up the slope to come out beside the small pool at the bottom of the falls. As he inched his way up closer, he could hear voices in coarse conversation coming from outside the cabin. As he peered through the branches of a large fir tree, he knew at once that these were the men he searched for. There was a large fire burning near the front of the cabin, and the men were gathered around it. Facing him, a large man with a full beard, wearing an eye patch, was dominating the conversation, while the others laughed or swore in response. Without question, he knew from the description he had been given it was Max Tarbow. He counted the men around the fire—there were five. They were all there and completely vulnerable. He knew that he had told Will not to act alone if he found them, but he had all five of them sitting unsuspecting, like ducks on a pond. He decided he could not miss the opportunity to capture them while they were caught at a disadvantage like this.

With his Winchester held hip-high and cocked, he moved slowly down past the fir tree, managing to come within twenty yards of the circle of men before one of them looked up to discover him. "Uh-uh," Pride warned when the man bolted upright at the sight of the big lawman. "It'll cost you your life," Pride threatened. "Just sit right there, and don't give me no cause to kill anybody. I'm a U.S. Deputy

Marshal and I'm arrestin' all of you for bank robbery and the murder of two bank tellers in Texas."

Stunned by the sudden appearance of the lawman, the outlaws found themselves unable to react immediately. When one of them started to reach for a handgun rolled in a cartridge belt on the ground nearby, Pride cautioned him. "Mister, I'll cut you down before you reach it." Then he warned the others. "I'll take you back to Fort Smith for trial if you're peaceful, but if you want to give me trouble, I'd just as soon take your sorry carcasses back."

"I'm bettin' you're Mr. Fletcher Pride," Max Tarbow snarled sarcastically. "I've heared of you down in Texas."

"Then you know I mean it when I say if you boys give me any trouble, it's gonna be mighty hard on you." Pride said. "Let's start by you three wearin' the gun belts easin' those pistols out of the holster, one by one. Do it real slow with just two fingers on the handle, and drop it on the ground. You first." With the muzzle of his rifle he motioned toward Tarbow. "I know what you're thinkin', but you ain't that fast, I can guarantee you."

Tarbow did not make a move. Neither did any of the others. Instead, they all continued to stare at him as if frozen. Empty seconds ticked slowly by before a smug smile stirred the heavy beard covering most of Tarbow's face. Puzzled for a moment, Pride started to threaten him again when he heard the cocking of the .44 right behind his head. "Now, s'pose you drop that Winchester before I blow a hole in the back of your head," Whip Doolin growled.

Fletcher Pride's brain was immediately caught in

a whirlwind of thoughts, all within the space of mere seconds. He had come to the end of his trail because of a stupid, careless mistake, realizing only then that he had forgotten to count Jeb Stark. There were six, not five, to be accounted for, and now he was going to pay for that mistake. He had secretly feared for some months before that he might be too long in the service and that a day like this might be approaching when he made a fatal mistake. He had lasted longer than most, but there was a time for every man, and he knew his time was now. Fully aware that he was a dead man whether he dropped his rifle as ordered or not, he decided to take at least one with him. "Go to hell," he bellowed, and pulled the trigger. Anticipating such a move, Whip pulled his trigger at the same time, killing the big deputy marshal instantly.

The sudden explosion of shots sent the men sitting around the fire diving for cover and reaching for their weapons. Tom Blanton, who had been sitting next to Max, rolled over on the ground with the slug from Pride's rifle in his shoulder. "I'm shot!" he cried, but no one came to his aid until they were all sure Pride was dead. Realizing after a moment that he was in no mortal danger, Blanton pulled his bandanna from his neck and stuffed it against the wound, and complained. "Damn it, Whip, what was you waitin' for? Why didn't you shoot him when you first came up behind him?"

Whip grinned. "I just wanted to hear him squeal when he found out his bacon was fried."

"To hell with that," Max blurted. "Where the hell's that other one?" His pistol in his hand now, he was looking all around, expecting shots from Pride's partner. "Spread out and make sure he ain't hidin' somewhere." They scrambled to do his bidding. "You did say there was another deputy with him, didn't you?" Max grabbed Jeb Stark by the arm.

"That's right," Jeb said, "another deputy named Will Tanner and a feller drivin' a wagon."

"What about me?" Blanton moaned. "I need some help."

"You ain't hurt bad," Max said. "Just a little ol' bullet in your shoulder, but you better get up from there before you get shot again. Go on in the cabin and take care of it yourself. We ain't got time to fool with you now. I wanna know if that other son of a bitch is sneakin' around here somewhere."

While Blanton withdrew to the cabin to try to tend his wound, the other five scouted the ridges on both sides of the pond. After a thorough search, there was no sign of another deputy. Billy Tarbow, leading Pride's horse, came up from below the pond. "I found him tied up behind them firs on the trail up to here," he announced. "Warn't no sign of another horse, just this 'un."

Max paused to consider the situation. If there was another deputy, where was he? Maybe he was here, but hightailed it when Whip got the jump on Pride. Most likely he had sense enough to know he was bound to get the same as Pride, so he turned tail and ran. He'd be a fool not to, seeing as how he was one against six men. *Well, one against five and a half,* he thought. *Still bad odds.* Thinking that a likely possibility, he acted quickly to retaliate for the attempted arrest. "Saddle up!" he ordered. "They musta set that wagon up somewhere below here for their camp.

And if they followed us from Tishomingo, then it's most likely somewhere along the valley trail leadin' between this mountain and the one next to it. The jasper drivin' that wagon ain't nothin' but a cook, and as soon as he finds out ol' Pride is dead, he's gonna hightail it, too." He paused for a moment, but his anger was growing by the second, fueled by the thought of what might have been if Whip hadn't gone up in the bushes to take a crap. "By God, they come up here in Injun Territory, lookin' for us," he bellowed. "We need to teach 'em a lesson they ain't likely to forget." He started to run for his saddle, then another thought struck him. "And a couple of you throw that big son of a bitch across his saddle. We're takin' him with us." Caught up in his enthusiasm, they all ran to saddle up. Like Tarbow, they were eager to strike a blow against the U.S. Marshals Service for invading what they considered their territory.

Having followed the stream all the way up near the top of the mountain to its source, where it seeped up through fractures in the limestone bedrock, Will had been left staring at the spring it created. His notion that Jeb could have ridden up the stream had been a poor one. There was no outlaw camp on that side of the mountain. Rather than turn around and ride back the way he had come, he climbed all the way to the top to look around for other likely sites. From there, he had a view of several deep gulches, but one looked ideal to defend if there was a camp at the end of it. He decided to ride over to the neighboring mountain to satisfy his curiosity.

When he got to the entrance to the gulch, he knew at once there was no camp there because he could find no tracks indicating anyone had ridden in or out. *It would make a good one,* he thought. *It just ain't the one I'm looking for.* It was then that he heard the two shots fired, one from a pistol, another from a rifle, from the sound of it. Though clearly gunshots, they were muffled because of the distance, for it seemed they had come from the far side of the mountain next to the one he had just left. *Pride found them,* he thought at once, but he was puzzled because there were only those two shots. It was hard to speculate what had taken place. Maybe neither of the shots came from Pride. They had agreed to take no action on their own, but to return to the wagon to decide their plan of attack. Whatever, he knew one thing for sure—he had to find out where the shots came from, so he wasted no time heading in that direction.

Crossing two mountains over, he came upon a strong stream and decided to follow it down the mountain. He had not ridden far when he found himself at the edge of a cliff where the stream formed a waterfall that cascaded over to fall some seventy feet to a pond in a canyon below. When he dismounted and walked to the very edge, he saw a log cabin below, tucked back in against the face of the cliff. It had to be the hideout they searched for. He remained there for a short time, watching for any sign of activity around the cabin. He saw no horses nearby, causing him to wonder if the cabin was occupied. There was no question but that he had to make sure. The problem facing him, however, was the difficulty in reaching it from where he now stood. To reach the cabin, it would be necessary to back-track a couple hundred feet to a ravine that looked like it might lead down the backside of a ridge that formed one side of the canyon. It would take time, but there appeared to be no quicker way to reach the canyon floor.

He had guessed right on the ravine. It led down to the base of the mountain, with a high ridge between him and the waterfall. On foot now, he led Buster up through the trees to the top of the ridge. As he had figured, the cabin was now below him. He dropped down on one knee to study the camp. There was still no sign of anyone about, but there was a small corral with four horses inside on the other side of the cabin. He had not seen that from the top of the falls. Then he noticed the ashes of a fire in the small yard in front of the cabin. They were still smoking. The fact that he had heard gunshots remained to cause him concern, so he decided he had to determine if there was anyone inside the cabin before he did anything else.

With Buster tied to the branch of a tree, he made his way cautiously down through the firs, watching the door of the cabin constantly, in case someone suddenly appeared. There was only one door and two small windows, one in front and one in back. His plan was to make his way to the back window, hope-fully to get a look inside. It was possible to use the trees as cover until reaching a point about fifty feet from the cabin where there was an open space with nothing but stumps. Evidently they had provided the logs from which the cabin had been built. He crouched at the edge of the trees and listened for a few minutes before making a quick dash through the patch of stumps to the back of the cabin. Edging up to the side of the window, he cautiously eased an eye over far enough to peek inside. When there was no immediate response from inside, he took a longer look into the dark interior. With light only from the open door and the two small windows, it took a moment for his eyes to adjust. Then he saw the man lying on a pallet next to the side wall.

At first he thought the man was asleep, but then the man groaned when he turned onto his side, and Will could see that he was favoring a wound in his shoulder. *That explains one of the gunshots*, Will thought. His concern now was the result of the other one. He already assumed that this was no doubt the hideout he and Pride were looking for, and the wounded man was one of the Tarbow gang. Right away, his mind was filled with possible explanations for what he had discovered. None of them seemed favorable to him. The most likely he came up with told him that Pride had shot the man he was now looking at, and the second shot must have either wounded Pride or driven him off. Either way, it didn't look good for Pride, because it was his guess that the rest of the gang were not here because they were after him. *They'll be heading for the wagon*, he thought, *and Pride and Charlie are gonna need my help.* He took another look at the wounded man and decided, *To hell with him. I've got to get going.*

Without even considering the possibility that the man lying inside the cabin might get up and take a shot at him, Will ran across the clearing in front of the cabin. As he passed the dying remains of a large campfire, he suddenly spotted something on the ground that caused him to stop short. He took a closer look at what appeared to have been bloody spray, now dried, and what appeared to be pieces of bone and maybe brain matter—he wasn't sure. It served to make him even more apprehensive, and he set out running again, only to stop abruptly. *Gunshots!* Far off in the distance, there was a series of a dozen or more, and then there was nothing. They came from the direction of the ravine where they had left the wagon. Up through the trees on the ridge, he raced to his horse.

Buster's hooves thundered over the worn surface of the game trail leading out of the canyon as Will called for everything the big buckskin had to give. He was afraid that the picture he had in his mind, as to what had happened back at that cabin, might be the true story. He hoped he was wrong. It seemed that it was taking forever to cover the ground back to their base camp, but he was soon going to have to rein the buckskin back, or he was going to finish him. On foot now, he let Buster blow, as he walked him down the floor of the canyon, ever cautious, lest he suddenly confront Max Tarbow's murderous band returning to the cabin. His caution paid off, for he heard the sound of men and horses as he approached a sharp turn in the canyon trail. With no time to spare, he ran toward a thicket of young pines off to his left and led Buster into the middle of them. He dropped to one knee and drew his rifle up to his shoulder and waited. He saw them then: five riders, a heavyset man with an eye patch, leading them. It had to be Max Tarbow, based on the description they had been given. Will laid the front sight of the Winchester on the big man's back as they rode by, unaware of the rifleman in the pine thicket. About to pull the trigger, he hesitated when he saw the big dun gelding and the empty saddle. *Goat!* he thought, *Pride's horse!* He wasn't sure he could believe they had killed Pride. It was something he could not think possible. The big deputy was invincible and would always come out on top in any fight with an outlaw. He brought his mind back to the gang of murderers passing before him. Taking aim again, he was confident that he could get Tarbow, and maybe one other before they scattered, but he wanted to get them all. He pulled the rifle down, deciding he'd best find out if they had attacked the wagon, and if Pride was all right. If he took the shot, all hell would likely break loose, and it might be some time before he could get back to Pride and Charlie. They had a better chance of capturing at least some of the gang if the two of them were working together. *Besides*, he told himself, *I know where I can find Tarbow and his men*. He led his horse back out to the trail and continued to lead him back toward the wagon.

He saw him from a hundred yards away, near the mouth of the little ravine that Charlie had backed the wagon into. From a lower limb of a big oak tree, they had hung his body so that it could be easily seen by anyone happening to ride that trail. He was stunned by the sight of the big deputy marshal, a rope knotted around his neck, his huge body hanging awkwardly in death. His shirt had been stripped away to reveal the underwear he wore year round. As Will walked closer, he understood why. It was so the message printed across his chest could be more easily read. LAWMEN TAKE WARNING, it said, and it had obviously been written with blood. He looked toward the wagon where Charlie Tate's body lay facedown in the dirt, then shifted his eyes to the grassy meadow on the other side of the stream, where two dark humps told him of the horses' fate. He returned his gaze to concentrate on the body hanging in such brazen contempt for the law, the once broad, jovial face shattered by the impact of a .44 slug. He could feel the fury building up inside him when he realized that they had killed Pride back at the cabin, from behind, by the look of the broken face. And then they brought him back here to blatantly display their evil work.

He forced himself to relax when he realized that he had been clinching his fists so tightly that his fingernails had drawn blood from his palms. The time he had ridden with Fletcher Pride was brief, yet he felt that he had known the man for so much longer. And the picture of him hanging there would burn an image in his memory that would never be dulled. What he could not know was how it would change him from this day forward, as he sought justice for Fletcher Pride, and vengeance from men like Max Tarbow. Tarbow would pay for this murderous act. There were no thoughts of capture and returning the prisoners to Fort Smith for trial. Will had already given them their trial, and their penalty was death.

It sickened him to see Pride hanging there, so he started to cut him down to bury him and Charlie. To reach the rope, he would have to get up on his horse, and he was in the process of doing that when he hesitated and thought about how he would take his vengeance against Pride's killers. Evidently, Pride had tried to arrest all of them at one time, and there was a good possibility that he might suffer the same fate. So instead of cutting Pride down, he decided it improved his odds if he left him to hang, thinking it better to let them suspect that he had taken flight. Most likely, some of the gang would pass by the ravine in the next few days. It was best that they see the bodies undisturbed. He apologized to Pride for not cutting him down right away, but felt that Pride would understand. "When I'm done," he said to him, "I'll give you a proper burial."

He went to see what was left of the contents of the wagon, pausing to take a look at the corpse that was once Charlie Tate. Poor Charlie was shot full of holes. *It's a damn dirty shame*, Will thought. *He wasn't even a lawman.* Will felt great sympathy for the simple cook, but not the passion for revenge he felt for Pride. Aware of the possibility that his retaliation against the outlaws might last for days, he searched the wagon. As he expected, any supplies that were easily carried on horseback were taken. Extra ammunition and firearms were also gone. Luckily, he had taken an extra cartridge belt with him when he rode up the stream to look for the hideout. The only food left in the wagon was a sack of beef jerky. Evidently, the outlaws' sense of taste was too refined to consider the jerky, he thought. He took that and an ax that Charlie had strapped to the side of his wagon, the outlaws apparently having overlooked it.

Promising once again to come back to bury them, he rode away from the cruel scene. His first objective in the war he had declared on Max Tarbow was to establish a base from which he could work, one that would ensure the safety of his horse, for he was already of the opinion that much of his combat would be on foot. The canyon he had searched two mountains to the north came to mind at once. He remembered thinking that it would be a good place for a hideout, so he decided to make that his base while he attempted to work away at reducing his enemy's advantage in numbers. He had no plans to take prisoners. Justice would be served, and the world a better place, if the murderous scum that rode with Max Tarbow were removed from it.

Leaving the ravine behind, he rode up the same creek he had followed that morning when he and Pride had decided to split up to search. *I wish to hell I had never suggested that Jeb might have ridden up this damn creek*, he thought. *Things might have turned out differently*. As much as he tried to tell himself that things just turn out the way they're supposed to, he couldn't put it out of his mind that he had not been there to back Pride up. Maybe it wouldn't have mattered, and the result would have been both of them dead. *I swear they won't go unpunished*, he silently promised the big lawman.

This time, when he followed the stream up the mountain, he knew that Tarbow's camp was on the far side. His intention was to return to the top of the waterfall where he could once again look down on the outlaw camp, and he could not afford to waste time in reaching it. The day was already wearing thin.

Soon it would be sundown, and he didn't like the idea of riding Buster over unfamiliar mountain terrain in the dark. He nudged him gently and the big buckskin, rested now, sprang to obey.

When he reached the top of the mountain, he tied Buster close by the stream, then he proceeded down the stream to the edge of the cliff and the top of the waterfall. This was the same spot from which he had watched the cabin before. They were all there. He counted six, so Jeb Stark was with them. The fire outside was burning brightly, and a couple of the men looked to be cooking something in a pot over the fire. He was too far away to see their faces clearly, but he studied their bodies in an attempt to memorize the way the different men moved, the husky ones, the slim ones. From the sound of their voices, they seemed to be in a celebratory mood. He could not understand the words, but it was obviously boastful, punctuated by occasional outbursts of individual crowing. The scene served to stir his anger to the point where it was difficult to control his urge to take up his rifle and start shooting as rapidly as he could. But he knew he would probably hit no more than one or two before they were able to scramble for cover. And then he would have alerted them to be cautious. For him to be able to clean out the entire rat nest, it was important that they think he had fled, until he was ready for them to find out they were wrong.

He was counting heavily on the assumption that they would stay put for a while. It stood to reason that this cabin was their destination when they fled from Texas, so it was also reasonable to assume they planned to stay awhile. By his count earlier, there were three extra horses in the corral, which meant they had arrived with three packhorses carrying supplies. Now they also had what supplies they had taken from the wagon. He was counting on them to settle in for a long stay, at least long enough for him to do what he planned to do.

As darkness settled in over the canyon, he decided it safe to move in closer to the circle of men sitting around the campfire. So he led Buster down the backside of the ridge as he had the first time he paid the cabin a visit. This time it was a good deal slower descent because of the darkness. When he reached the spot where he had left the horse before, he tied the buckskin to a tree limb and climbed up over the ridge to work his way in closer. When he got to a large tree, about forty yards from the fire, he decided it best not to risk trying to go farther. Using the tree for cover, he dropped to one knee and listened, undecided what he was going to do. A jar of whiskey was making numerous rounds around the circle by the fire, and the men seemed in high spirits, recounting the assassination of Fletcher Pride. They were still six hardened gunmen against his lone rifle, and if he simply started shooting, he could not guarantee how many of them he might get before their numbers forced him to retreat. *I need to reduce their six-to-one odds if I can,* he thought. *Without them knowing about it would be even better.* That seemed impossible at the moment, but as he listened to them talking, he decided to stay where he was and see if an opportunity presented itself. The odds were against it, but he figured that there was always a possibility when men like these were celebrating with a generous amount of whiskey. And it appeared they had plenty of it with them. *Maybe,* he thought, *I'll wait them out, and hope some of them drink themselves into a stupor.* That might give him enough time to knock off most of them before they could respond. At the moment, it seemed the best plan.

CHAPTER 6

"That ol' boy sure looked funny when we came up behind him and caught him bendin' over that fire," Jesse Becker blustered. "He liked to fell in the middle of it when he saw us."

"I thought he was gonna fill his drawers when Whip shoved Pride's body off the horse," Billy Tarbow said, laughing. "What was it you told him, Whip?"

"Here's your daddy, come home for supper," Whip Doolin repeated. Then they all laughed, recalling Charlie Tate's fright. "He took off for that shotgun on the wagon, though," Whip went on. "I think he mighta made it, if he hadn'ta got shot so full of lead he couldn't tote it all."

"I'll tell you what, though," Billy said, "the ol' boy made some pretty good pan biscuits. Maybe we shouldn't have shot him till he showed Tom how to make 'em like that."

"Ain't nobody said you gotta eat my biscuits," Tom Blanton responded, his arm in a makeshift sling. "I don't see any of 'em left after I make a batch. Ain't that right, Max?"

"Yeah, I s'pose," Max answered, his thoughts on a more serious plane than those of his men. "What I'm wonderin' is what became of that other deputy marshal? I don't know for a fact that he ain't still around here somewhere." His comment served to dampen the jovial mood around the campfire somewhat.

"I don't know, Max," Billy said. "If he was with Pride when he sneaked up here, he sure didn't try to help him. And he wasn't down there at the wagon with that other feller when we got there. I'm bettin' he mighta been close enough to see what happened to Pride and figured it weren't good for his health to stick around."

"That's what I think," Jesse seconded. "I bet that child is headin' back to Fort Smith as fast as a horse can carry him."

"Maybe," Max allowed, but not enthusiastically. "I'd like to know for sure. Might not be a bad idea for one or two of us to ride back down to that wagon in the mornin' and see if he's been back there snoopin' around."

"I'll go," Jeb Stark volunteered immediately, thinking it an opportunity to impress Max, and maybe an invitation to join Max's gang.

"I figured you'd be headin' back home," Max said.

"Ain't nothin' there I'm interested in," Jeb replied. "I was just there visitin' Pap for a spell. Tell you the truth, I wouldn't mind joinin' up with you boys. I'm pretty handy with a six-shooter."

"Is that a fact?" Max asked. "You'd have to be better 'n pretty good to ride with us." He winked at Billy. "You'd have to be damn good."

"I'm damn good," Jeb replied.

"I reckon we'd find out pretty quick," Max said. He had no objection to having Jeb join them, figuring there was safety in numbers. And he had to give him credit for riding up from Tishomingo in the middle of the night to alert them that the deputies were following them. "All right, you ride on down there in the mornin' and look around that wagon real good—see if anybody's been back there since we left. Right now, pass that whiskey back over here."

"If they have, I'll know it," Jeb boasted. "I'm pretty good at trackin'."

"There you go again, just pretty good," Whip couldn't resist japing.

"Better 'n anybody here," Jeb responded with a show of temper, a little irritated at what he perceived as a dose of hazing.

"Whoa!" Whip whooped in mock alarm. "Got your back up a little, didn't ya, boy?"

"I ain't no boy," Jeb replied.

Not inclined to let up on him, Whip kept pressing to see how far he could push him. "Around here, you gotta prove you're a man before you walk around brayin' like a donkey."

"Who you callin' a donkey?" Jeb flared up.

"Take it easy on the kid," Max said, stepping in. "Ain't no need to get him all riled up. You've had your fun."

"All right," Whip said. "I was just funnin' with him." He shrugged and chuckled. "I believe he was about ready to call me out, so I reckon I'd better let him be."

"I expect you'd better," Jeb blustered, thinking

Whip was backing down. "Maybe I am thinkin' about callin' you out. I don't take no japin' from nobody."

Everything suddenly got quiet around the campfire until Max said to Jeb, "Be careful what you say, boy. You don't wanna call Whip out. Just settle yourself down."

But Jeb had already gone too far, and being called boy again, this time by Max, he couldn't stop his mouth from making a contract he couldn't complete with his .44. Looking Whip straight in the eye, he said. "We'll forget the whole thing just as soon as you tell me you're sorry about ever'thin' you said."

"Shit," Whip drawled out contemptuously, no longer in a playful mood. "It'll be a cold day in hell before I say I'm sorry to you, or anybody else. Now, you just set down over there and keep your mouth shut before you start somethin' you can't finish."

Jeb's ears were burning, and he felt as if he had been shamed and left with no alternative except to call the arrogant gunman out. The only other option would be to slink away and sit down as Whip had ordered, and then every one of them would feel nothing but contempt for him. "I'm callin' you out," he finally said, barely over a mutter.

"What did you say?" Whip demanded.

"I said I'm callin' you out," Jeb declared, this time with more conviction.

"Well, you're a damn fool then," Whip said. "But if you're lookin' to die young, then I'll sure as hell accommodate you." He got to his feet, walked several paces toward the corner of the cabin, and turned back to face the fire while he shifted his pistol belt to a comfortable position on his hip.

As Jeb got to his feet to face him, everyone else backed away from the fire to give them room. Aware then of the smug confidence reflected in the older man's smiling face, Jeb suddenly realized his opponent was not at all worried about the outcome of the contest. He shot a quick glance in Max's direction, but Max gave no indication of interfering, figuring he had warned the young fool, and the rest was on Jeb's shoulders. Also, like the other men, Max was curious to see the outcome, knowing how fast Whip was with a gun, faster than any man he had ever seen, in fact. Maybe the brash young kid was fast himself, he thought. *We'll know in about three seconds*, he told himself. "How you wanna do it, Whip?" Max asked. "Wait for the first to move, or count to three?"

"I didn't know there was any rules to it," Whip replied. "I'll just leave it up to him. Just go for it when you feel lucky, boy."

The two combatants stood poised, staring each other down, while the amused spectators watched in anticipation of an outright assassination at the hands of the older gunman. All participants were totally unaware of the lone rifleman in the trees at the edge of the clearing, his Winchester steadied on a limb of a large oak tree.

"You wanna call it off, boy?" Max asked after several tense moments passed. It was at that moment that Jeb suddenly made his fatal move. He was quicker than anyone expected, clearing his holster with the Colt .44 he wore, but not before Whip's first shot tore into his belly. Already on his way down, he still tried to shoot, managing to get off two harmless shots before he crumpled to the ground. In answer, Whip pumped two more shots into him. The spectators were stunned an instant later when Whip stumbled backward a couple of steps before collapsing, a fatal wound in his chest.

"What the hell . . . ?" Billy Tarbow blurted amid cries of disbelief from the others. Everyone stood frozen for a second before suddenly rushing to crowd around Whip.

"I never saw that comin'," Jesse muttered.

"That was nothin' but bad luck," Max declared. "One of those wild shots hit Whip right in the chest—pure luck." He bent low to get a closer look at the dying man. His throat already filling with blood, Whip was unable to speak, his eyes wide in confusion as he made a feeble attempt to cough the blood from his windpipe. They all stood around him until he finally stopped struggling and lay still. No one bothered to take a look at Jeb. There was no need to.

"If that don't beat all I've ever seen," Tom Blanton declared. "Killed by a shot from a dead man, 'cause that boy was dead before he even pulled the trigger." He thought about it for a moment more. "Them shots even sounded different." He turned to Max and asked, "Didn't you think them shots had a different sound to 'em?"

Max shrugged, having not really given it any thought. "Just the echo down in this canyon, I reckon," he said.

"You reckon we oughta bury 'em?" Tom asked.

"You can if you want to," Max said. "Me, I don't feel much like diggin' a grave. It sure ain't gonna make no difference to Whip. Dead's dead—I expect he's more worried about goin' to hell right about now. Might as well see what they got in their pockets and check their saddlebags and stuff, and we'll split it up. Then just drag their carcasses over beyond that ridge and let the buzzards take care of 'em." He walked back to the fire then and poured himself another cup of coffee. "I still want one of us to ride back down to that wagon to see if there's any sign of anybody sniffin' around there," he called back.

"I'm kinda gonna miss ol' Whip," Jesse said. "He was fast with a gun—not as fast as I thought, though."

"I wish he had bigger feet," Tom said. "I've always admired them boots of his."

The shadowy figure in the darkness of the forest pulled his rifle down from the oak limb and moved back deeper into the trees, being careful not to make a sound. The opportunity had come as a complete surprise and it had worked to his satisfaction. He had expected at least one of them to realize the shot that killed Whip had come from behind Jeb, and was from a rifle. *I reckon I can thank corn whiskey for that*, he thought. His opposition had been reduced by two, and they were still unaware of his presence. He would be waiting near the wagon in the morning, hoping to further cut the odds against him. On the backside of the ridge again, he untied his horse and led him down the mountain, waiting until he reached the mouth of the canyon before ejecting the spent cartridge from his rifle.

* * *

He was ready and waiting early the next morning, although he didn't expect anyone from the cabin to make an early appearance. His horse was saddled and tucked out of sight in a small clearing about a hundred yards from where he sat in a berry thicket a dozen yards from the wagon. From his position, he could see the gruesome spectacle that Max Tarbow had left as a warning to lawmen, as well as the crumpled body of Charlie Tate. Will had been in place when the sun first began to probe the darkness of the valley, and the eerie image of Fletcher Pride's body, hanging grotesquely from the limb of the tree, was gradually backlighted by the rising sun. The sight of it served to enrage the very blood in Will's veins and renewed his determination to finish the grim task he had vowed to complete. There was still no feeling of guilt on his part for his simple plan of assassination. Being honest with himself, he realized there was very little chance of his arresting the Tarbow gang and taking them back for trial. And he rationalized that the outlaws' crimes would certainly call for the death penalty. With circumstances being the way they were, it was nothing more than swifter justice if he performed their executions himself. He asked himself if he could live with that on his conscience, and he answered that he could. His thoughts were interrupted then by the sound of a horse's hooves plodding along the bank of the stream.

Before he approached the body hanging at the end of the rope, Jesse Becker reined his horse to a stop while he looked the eerie scene over. Everything appeared to be just as he had last seen it, but to satisfy Max, he nudged his horse forward to take a closer look. Stepping down, he dropped his reins on the ground and studied the tracks before the wagon. He felt sure they were tracks that he and the others had left before. No one else had been there, he decided, so he walked over to the wagon, just to see if there was anything useful that they might have overlooked. Walking around it to stand at the tailgate, he was unaware of the grim figure stepping out into the open behind him. He remained unaware until the metallic sound of a rifle cranking a cartridge into the chamber suddenly sent an icy chill down his spine. A man of violence, he reacted automatically, spinning around while reaching for the .44 at his side. Will's shot slammed into his chest before he could turn to face him. He staggered from the impact, then tried to raise his arm to fire, but sent a harmless round into the ground when Will cranked a second shot into his chest. Knowing he was finished, he dropped to his knees and stared at his grim assassin. "You've kilt me, you son of a bitch," he muttered weakly, as the pistol fell from his hand.

"I reckon," Will replied. They remained where they were, the outlaw still on his knees, the lawman staring into his eyes, still wary. Even had there been second thoughts about executing the man, he had been given no choice except to shoot before he was shot. He continued to watch Becker carefully, their eyes locked, until Will realized that the spark of life in Becker's eyes was gone. Only then did he relax his grip on the Winchester. He walked up to him, raised his boot, and kicked him over on his side. He glanced at the foreboding body hanging from the limb then. "That's three of 'em, partner."

He rolled Jesse Becker's body over and pulled the cartridge belt out from under him. Replacing the pistol in the holster, he hung it over the saddle horn on Becker's saddle. The outlaw had ridden a red roan. It would now serve as Will's packhorse. The three remaining outlaws should soon be on their way to investigate. The shots just fired could be heard at the cabin. It was now a question of how soon they would come, so he prepared to be ready for them. He looked around him and decided that the little ravine the wagon had been backed into offered him the best position to defend, if the outlaws were cautious enough to come at him from three directions. His concern then was protection for the horses, so he led Becker's horse to the clearing where he had left Buster. When he was satisfied that they were as safe as he could make them, he positioned himself behind the wagon and laid his weapons and cartridge belts on the wagon bed before him. Checking his Winchester to make sure he had a full magazine, he then did the same for the rifle he had gained from Becker's death, a Spencer cavalry carbine. There was nothing left for him to do but wait for the three remaining outlaws.

His stomach reminded him that he had eaten nothing since the day before, so he took a couple of strips of beef jerky from the bag he had recovered and chewed the tough repast, wishing that he had some coffee to wash it down.

"That don't sound too good," Billy Tarbow said when they heard the faint sound of shots from below the cabin.

"Three shots, sounded like to me, weren't it?" Tom Blanton asked.

"That's what I heard," Max agreed. "Like two rifle shots and one pistol."

All three men paused to remain dead still, listening for additional shots. When no more were heard, Blanton wondered aloud, "Whaddaya s'pose he was shootin' at?"

"Who knows?" Max replied. "I'd say a buzzard or a coyote or somethin', but it seems kinda funny they weren't all from the same gun. Whatever it was, I expect it'd be a good idea to find out. Jesse ain't one to waste bullets on buzzards. Let's saddle the horses and take a ride down there."

While they saddled their horses, Max was still concentrating on the three shots they had just heard. Two from a rifle, one from a pistol, and he was reminded of the casual comment made about the odd sound of the gunfire the night before. Thinking about it now, it caused him to wonder. The exchange of shots between Whip and Jeb had occurred almost at the same time. Max couldn't help wondering if the shots they just heard had been closer together, might they have sounded the same as those the night before? It was enough to make him question their assumption that one of Jeb's wild shots had struck Whip. And, when he recalled, that shot had nailed Whip dead center in his chest. The possibilities that thought provoked were troubling. Had they been too careless in figuring that other deputy had hightailed it? But if Whip Doolin had really been shot by the deputy, why didn't he take another shot? They were all standing around, easy targets. It didn't make sense that he'd shoot Whip and then back off. *Unless,* it occurred to him, *he was set on picking us off one at a time without us knowing what he was up to.* That way, he wouldn't have to go up against all of us at the same time. *Damn!* he thought, anxious now to find out if Jesse was all right, at the same time deciding to take extra caution in doing so.

When they were all ready, Max casually rode up beside his younger brother's horse and took hold of his bridle to hold him back, so Tom Blanton could lead them down the narrow trail beside the stream. When Billy gave him a puzzled look, Max shook his head, and when Tom was out of earshot, he cautioned his brother. "I got a funny feelin' about them shots," he said, almost in a whisper. "Let Tom lead out, and when we get close to that ravine where that wagon is, let him get on ahead." He nodded once for emphasis, and added. "And Billy, keep a sharp eye."

They followed the stream down into the foothills, and as they approached the narrow ravine where the wagon had been left, Max and Billy reined their horses back cautiously. Max reasoned that if everything was as it should be, they would have probably met Jesse on the trail, coming back to the cabin. It shouldn't have taken him long to take a good look around, if nothing had changed.

Unaware of the gradually growing gap between him and the two Tarbow brothers behind him, Blanton rode into the mouth of the narrow ravine. He pulled his horse to a complete stop when he looked toward the tree where Pride's body was still hanging, but there was no sign of Jesse Becker. He wheeled his horse around to declare his concern, only then to find he was about forty yards ahead of them. "He's gone!" he called back. "Jesse ain't here!" The thought struck him at that moment that Max and Billy were hanging back for a reason, so he drew his rifle from the saddle scabbard and wheeled his horse back around to face whatever threat they anticipated. A single shot rang out from the ravine, knocking him from the saddle, mortally wounded.

"I thought so!" Max bellowed. He and Billy both had their rifles drawn right after Tom first called out the warning, but they were not sure where the shot had come from. "The wagon!" he yelled then, thinking that the likely place, and the two of them started firing toward the wagon as fast as they could. Rapid return fire snapped like angry hornets all around them, first from a Winchester, then from a Spencer. "Run for it!" Max shouted as he wheeled his horse, not waiting to see if Billy did the same.

"What about Tom?" Billy yelled.

"To hell with him!" Max shouted back. "He's dead! Save your own ass!" Flogging his horse relentlessly for more speed, he galloped back the way he had just come, with Billy following. He didn't have to see a body to know that Jesse was dead, and now Tom. This demon lawman had killed all but Billy and him, and it was damn apparent that he wasn't interested in arresting anybody—he was an assassin. As his horse began to falter, he looked back over his shoulder, expecting to see someone in pursuit. He could see no one behind Billy, whose horse was showing signs of fading as well. Reluctant to let up on them, but knowing they would be in worse shape if their horses failed, Max finally reined his back when they reached a particularly steep part of the trail. He and Billy stepped down, looking anxiously behind them.

"I don't see nobody yet," Billy exclaimed breathlessly as they walked as fast as they could while leading the horses. "You reckon there's more 'n just one man? Some of them shots came from a different rifle—like a Spencer."

"Maybe," Max said. "Maybe just one man with two rifles. I don't know."

"You think we oughta stop up the trail a ways, find us a good spot, and ambush him?" Billy asked. "Hell, there's still two of us, and one of him."

"I still ain't sure he ain't got some help somewhere," Max said, worried. "Might be one of those Injun policemen with him. We'd be better off gettin' to the cabin, right now. Can't nobody come up that trail without us seein' 'em. Then we'll decide what we're gonna do."

Behind the two outlaw brothers, Will admonished himself for springing the trap too soon, but he hadn't seen that he had much choice. He had not counted on two of the outlaws lagging so far behind the other. And when they turned to run, he had to take the only good shot he had. With his horses back in the clearing so far behind him, he couldn't get to Buster before the two men would have a considerable lead. He was not overly eager to chase recklessly up that narrow mountain trail, anyway, only to blunder into an ambush. His best bet to finish the task he was sworn to do was to wait until darkness, so he could move in close to that cabin and look for an opportunity to strike again.

Since it was not even noon yet, he figured he could go up the backside of the ridge again and return to the ledge above the falls, where he could keep an eye on the cabin. Although he could not move directly on the cabin until he had the cover of darkness, he might get a chance to take a shot from up above them. But there was one obligation he had that he should satisfy now, while he had time to do it. He silently apologized to Pride for leaving him swinging at the end of a rope for so long. "I can at least put you and Charlie in the ground," he said aloud. Before starting to dig, however, he brought the horses up to the wagon in case he was surprised before he completed the burial and had to make a run for it.

It would be a hell of a job to pick the huge deputy up and lay him across the saddle. So Will decided to dig his grave right under the tree, instead of moving the body somewhere else. He untied the rope from the limb Tarbow's men had secured the free end around. It was a hard knot, but he soon got it untied, and lowered the already stiffened body as gently as he could to the ground. Fortunately, Tarbow's men had no use for Charlie's shovel, for it was still in the wagon, so at least he had that. He would have to do without a pick. Aware of the time this grave digging would cost him, he nevertheless felt he owed Pride and Charlie a decent burial, and he figured now might be the only opportunity he had. He couldn't predict what might happen on the next encounter with the notorious brothers. He was certain that the two remaining outlaws were, in fact, the Tarbow brothers, this based on a simple process of elimination. None of the men killed so far fit the description of Max, with the heavy beard and the eye patch. Likewise, none fit the description of Billy, the slighter of the two, with a total absence of hair on his face or head.

He began digging the grave right beside Pride's body, working away at the hard ground with his shovel. It was slow going without a pick to break up the heavier areas, but he did have the ax to cut away the roots he ran into. Halfway through his task, he was suddenly startled by a sound in the trees behind him, causing him to drop the shovel and snatch up his rifle. It was only Blanton's horse returning after having bolted when the shooting started before. Will tied the horse with the others, then went back to his work, stopping often to look around him for uninvited visitors. When he was finished, he had a single grave, wide enough to accommodate both men. A thought struck him as he worked. *You might be the only deputy to take your cook with you to hell, or wherever you end up.* Then it occurred to him that Pride and Charlie were probably getting a helluva hoot watching him struggle with that hard ground.

When he had finally finished digging a hole he felt suitable, he removed the badge from Pride's underwear, where his killers had pinned it after ripping his shirt away. Then he rolled Pride's body over the edge to drop to the bottom of the shallow grave. Charlie was not the challenge Pride had been. A man slight of built, Charlie's stiffened body was easily propped up so Will could get a shoulder under him and carry him to the grave, where he took his place beside Pride. Will then went to work filling in the grave. "That's about the best I can do for you, boys," he said in parting. He was certain there was a hell of a lot more he could have learned had he been given more time to ride with the big deputy. But there was a good bit he had picked up in the short time he had known him. Anxious to be done with this bad-luck camp now, he gathered the extra weapons and ammunition from the two dead outlaws and loaded them on the roan and the sorrel that Tom Blanton had ridden. Stepping up into the saddle then, he turned Buster toward the trail he had ridden before, up the backside of the ridge.

"Whaddaya wanna do, Max?" Billy fretted as they finally led their spent horses into the clearing by the pond. "You reckon he's comin' after us? Whaddaya think we oughta do, hole up in the cabin and wait for him?" Max had always told Billy what to do, and he needed to be told what to do now. "He mighta got some of them Injun policemen to come help him, them Lighthorse Injuns. How'd them deputies know we was up here in the first place? You reckon that damn Lem Stark told them we was up here?"

"Damn it, Billy, shut up a minute!" Max bellowed. "I can't think with you runnin' your mouth like that."

"Well, we need to be doin' somethin' before that deputy shows up here," Billy persisted. "I thought when we killed that big 'un that'd be the end of them lawmen snoopin' around. And we ain't even laid eyes on the son of a bitch that's killed off ever'body but me and you."

"Ain't nothin' special about him," Max said. "He's just like every other lawman that's tried to run us to ground. He just had a little luck go his way." His statement was primarily for Billy's benefit, to try to calm his brother down. But truthfully, he was a little worried about the unseen deputy, who had methodically reduced his gang down to Billy and him. He wasn't sure he liked the idea of being holed up in the tiny cabin, afraid to venture outside in the daylight. He lifted the patch over his left eye and rubbed the empty socket while he thought about their situation. "Right now, let's get these horses watered and put 'em in the corral." He couldn't escape the feeling that he was being watched by several sets of eyes around them in the trees, even though his common sense told him that they'd be shooting at them if that was the case. He had never been really spooked before, but there was something unnatural about this lawman tightening his noose around them. He wasn't a lawman like the others. He was an assassin, plain and simple. *And nobody but a damn fool would wait around here until he comes after you,* he told himself.

Too impatient to wait for his brother to think, Billy pressed for an answer. "What are we gonna do, Max?"

"I'm thinkin' Injun Territory ain't a healthy place for us right now," Max finally decided. "Them damn marshals and the Injun police have got to workin' together too much, and now ever' one of 'em knows about this hideout, so we ain't safe here no more. So we're gonna get outta here before they have a chance to trap us up here on this mountain."

That sounded good to Billy. "Yeah, Max, that's what we'll do. Let's get outta here before they surround us." He stopped to think then. "Where we gonna go, Max, farther west?"

"There ain't nothin' west of here, unless you wanna live like an Injun," Max said. "No, the best place for us is to go back to Texas where them marshals outta Fort Smith can't touch us. We can ride straight south from here about fifty miles and strike the Red River. Cross that, and we're in Texas, and good-bye, deputy marshals and Injun police."

"Yeah, but what about the Texas Rangers?" Billy asked. "They just chased us out of Texas."

"That's the reason we'll be better off in Texas," Max said. "The Texas Rangers think they chased us on up into Injun Territory, and that would be the last they'd see of us. They'll figure we're the marshals' problem now." The more he thought about it, the more he convinced himself that it was the smart thing to do. "What we gotta do right now is load them packhorses and get the hell outta here before dark. We'll go around this mountain till we find a good place to go down. Once we get to the valley, we'll head south and be long gone while that deputy and his Injuns are sneakin' around this cabin. I'm thinkin' we oughta strike the Red not too far from Mendoza's place," he said, referring to a small trading post on the river that was a favorite outlaw hangout. "Mendoza will know if there's any Ranger business goin' on around there. We can lay up there for a while till we decide what we wanna do." In an attempt to break the tenseness of their situation and appear confident, he gave Billy a wink and said, "Ol' Mendoza will be glad to help us spend some of that bank money."

"I expect so," Billy responded with a weak grin.

They wasted no time in packing up, taking only what they thought they couldn't do without from the ample supplies they had packed in on three horses. The first thing they did was switch their saddles from the two horses they had worn out in their forced escape up the mountain. In the event it came down to having to make a run for it, Max didn't want to risk having to try it on two spent horses. Since they still had eight horses, counting Fletcher Pride's dun, they loaded the fresh horses the heaviest, with light loads for the other two. As soon as they were loaded and ready to go, they led the horses up the ridge that formed one side of the gulch where the cabin was nestled. Over the top, they descended halfway around the mountain toward a deep ravine that looked as if it would lead all the way down to the valley. Once they reached the ravine with no shots fired at them, they felt they had successfully made their escape.

CHAPTER 7

There were many thoughts running through Will Tanner's mind as he guided Buster up the narrow game trail beside the stream. Most of them were troubling. He had become little more than a government assassin, a role he wasn't comfortable with, but he could not honestly say that he had been given a choice. There were now only two of the Tarbow gang left alive, and he had made a solemn commitment to Pride's spirit that he would kill them all. Now he questioned his right to do so. When he had accepted his appointment to enforce the law, it was with the understanding that he would make every attempt to bring a criminal to justice. And that meant taking them in to stand trial for their transgressions. After all that had happened on this ill-fated assignment, he was not certain that he would not be requested to turn his badge in—if he ever did return to Fort Smith. As soon as he had that thought, he knew he was obligated to go back to tell Marshal Stone what had happened to Pride and Charlie. He also knew that he had to decide if he wanted to continue working as a deputy marshal if Stone gave him that option. Max and Billy Tarbow were the leaders of the Texas gang that had staged a series of bank robberies. Arresting them would serve to show other outlaws that their lawlessness would not be tolerated if the Tarbows were tried and sentenced to hang. Finally, he gave in to his conscience and told himself, *I'll arrest them if I can, and I hope Pride will understand.*

He continued up the backside of the ridge to the point where he had crossed over the night before, when he had shot Whip Doolin. The sun was already getting low in the sky. Soon it would drop below the mountaintops. It was unfortunate that he had taken so long to reach the cabin, but he had felt that he had to bury Pride and Charlie, because he was not sure when he would be able to return to do it. Now anxious to take advantage of what daylight he had left, he tied his horses in the trees as before, and made his way down close to the clearing where the cabin sat.

When he reached the position where he had fired the fatal shot at Doolin, he paused to look the clearing over. He knew at once that they had fled. There were no horses in the corral and the cabin sat deserted. Even so, he had to make sure it was not a trap, waiting for him to spring it. They could have hidden the horses and were waiting in ambush in the trees beyond the pond. *Only one way to find out,* he thought, even though his gut told him they were gone. He cranked a cartridge into the chamber of his rifle and made a dash for the cabin, ready to answer any shots fired. As he expected, there were none.

He pulled the door open and stepped inside the

one room of the cabin. In the middle of the dirt floor, there was a quantity of various supplies, scattered haphazardly. Sacks of dried beans, even some coffee beans, salt pork, salt, sugar, flour, lard, molasses—all left behind by the outlaws in their hurry to flee. He even found a frying pan and a small pot, but no coffeepot, which was the thing he needed most. Feeling certain that the outlaws had deserted the cabin, he walked outside and stood in the clearing for a few minutes, looking around him, wondering in which direction to start looking for a trail. He considered the possibility that they would come back, maybe hoping to catch him there, but he discarded the idea. If they had planned to come back, they would not have loaded up their supplies and taken the packhorses with them. And he felt sure they had loaded the horses, because of the state of the supplies left behind. The sacks and boxes were strewn this way and that and scattered about, as they would be if someone was hurriedly searching through them. They had brought in supplies for five men, planning to stay for some time, so it was not that unlikely that some would be discarded. *Well, I appreciate it*, he thought, *because I've got nothing but half a sack of beef jerky.* In addition to the supplies, he also had a generous amount of money that he found in the saddlebags of the two men he had shot that morning. It was obviously money stolen from the Texas banks, but he didn't know how much, because there had been no time to count it.

While there was still ample light, he went to the corral to see if he could determine in which direction the two outlaws set out. It was an easy trail to find, tracks of eight horses, all carrying a load, and it started up a ridge where there had been no trail before. On foot, he followed the obvious trail up through the brush and trees to the top of the ridge. He stood for a few minutes, looking at the tracks leading down through the trees, before turning around to return to the cabin. Glancing up at the sky, he knew that soon there would not be enough light to follow the trail down through the thick forest. He would have to wait for morning, but he was not discouraged. He had time, for no matter how long it took, he promised himself that he would catch up with Max and Billy Tarbow.

With food to cook for a change, he built a small fire in the ashes of the one the outlaws had made. There wasn't time to soak the dried beans, but he cut some slices of salt pork and mixed up some flour, lard, and water in an attempt to come up with some version of pan biscuits. He never fancied himself as much of a cook, but he ate the doughy balls that resulted. After crushing some coffee beans between two rocks, he used the small pot to boil his coffee. It wasn't much of a supper, but it beat another meal of jerky. When it was time to bed down for the night, he decided not to take any chances on a return of the Tarbow brothers, so he spread his bedroll near the back of the corral, where he could keep an eye on his horses. While he waited for sleep, his thoughts returned to the money he now carried in the saddlebags, and what he should do with it. He supposed the right thing to do was to give it to Stone and let him take the proper steps to return the money to the banks that lost it. He still had not counted it, but it was only part of the money stolen. Max and Billy had the rest. *I'm going to use any of it I need to pursue those two,* he thought. *Whatever I've got left, I'll turn in.* With that settled, he went to sleep.

He was up with the first rays of sunlight that found their way through the branches of the trees behind the corral. He saddled all three horses and rigged up some crude packs for the two extra horses he had picked up, using some rope and the saddles that came with them. There was no telling where the trail he was set to follow would lead, or how long it would take, but he hoped to trade the extra saddles for pack saddles somewhere along the way. Once he was loaded up and satisfied that his makeshift packs would ride all right, he led Buster up the ridge to follow the trail he had found the night before.

Will had always been skillful at tracking. Even though his skills were honed by tracking deer and elk and other game, they came in just as handy when called upon to track men on horses. In this case, at least starting out down the mountain, it didn't require a great deal of tracking ability, for it was difficult to lead eight horses through the thick brush on the mountainside without leaving a broad path.

Because of the steepness of the slope, Will had to remain on foot, leading his horses along a trail that made its way around the mountain until starting down a deep ravine. The ravine led him all the way down to the bottom of the mountain, where he was able to step up in the saddle and ride. The tracks of the horses he followed were the only ones on the valley floor, and so were easily followed. Judging by the pattern of the tracks, he decided that the Tarbows had pushed their horses to lope along the long, narrow valley. Will followed suit, nudging the buckskin gelding with his heels, until reaching the mouth of the valley, where it was crossed by a wide stream. This was the first attempt the outlaws had made to hide their trail, for he found no tracks leaving the stream on the other side. They had taken to the water, but in which direction? He looked upstream and down, and decided to gamble on downstream, because upstream would lead them back up into the mountains.

There was no sign that they had left the water, even after following it for what he estimated to be about a mile, where it emptied into a creek. Before setting out to search both sides of the creek, he decided he might have been wrong, so he turned around and rode back to the point where their trail had gone into the stream. Following the stream with his eyes, he was faced with the mountains again, and questioned the outlaws' intention to go back there. He rode only a few dozen yards up the stream before stopping to reconsider. If they had it in mind to ride west, deeper into Indian Territory, as he was prone to assume, they would have ridden downstream. He decided to turn around again, but was stopped by something that caught his eye at the edge of the stream—a single hoofprint. One of the packhorses they led must have gotten too close to the bank. *They're heading back up in the mountains*, he thought, the opposite of what he would have figured.

Riding back through the foothills, he kept a sharp

eye on both sides of the stream until he finally found
their tracks where they had left the water. They led to
the east, through a series of low mounds, toward the
rolling plains beyond, instead of going back into the
mountains. It didn't figure, because on this course,
they were heading back toward the more populated
part of the Choctaw Nation. He continued on until
he crossed a common wagon trail that ran north and
south, and he pulled up suddenly when he realized
the tracks did not continue on the other side of the
road. He dismounted and checked the many tracks
in the road to make sure. The fresh ones he found
confirmed his findings. They had turned south on
the trail, and it struck him then. *They were heading back
to Texas!* That was the last place he figured they would
run to. But the more he thought about it, the more
sense he saw in it. Their intention was to escape Oklahoma Territory marshals, who were more dangerous
to them now than the Texas Rangers. If they slipped
back into Texas, they would be out of the Oklahoma
marshal's jurisdiction. And the Rangers would no
longer be looking for them in Texas, thinking they
were in Indian Territory. *It makes sense,* he thought,
*except for one thing. This deputy marshal doesn't give a shit
if they're over the line or not.* He climbed back into the
saddle and turned Buster's head south, following the
common trail to Texas.

As the morning worked its way along toward
noon, Will saw what looked to be a sizable creek up
ahead, judging by the line of trees that snaked across
the prairie. The horses were due a little rest, so he
decided he would take advantage of the chance to
water them. When he got a little closer to the creek,

he spotted a rough structure of weathered boards sitting between two large cottonwoods on the creek bank. When he got even closer, he determined that it was a trading post of some kind. But it was not until he stopped at the edge of the water to let his horses drink that he noticed the gray-haired little man standing at the corner of the tiny porch, watching him. He also noticed the double-barrel shotgun leaning conspicuously against the corner post. "Howdy," Will called out.

"How do?" the little man answered.

He seemed a bit cautious, so much so that Will was prompted to ask, "You open for business?"

"I surely am," the man answered, still cautious. "What are you needin'?" He peered suspiciously at the two horses with empty saddles and the bundles tied to them with ropes.

Will dismounted. Leaving the horses to drink, he walked across a narrow footbridge and approached the store. "I'm needin' a few things," he said. "You ain't by any chance got a coffeepot for sale, have you?"

That somehow served to break the guarded attitude of the storekeeper, that and the first notice he took of the badge on Will's shirt. "You a deputy marshal?" he asked.

"I am," Will answered.

"Well, I reckon you're in luck, Deputy, 'cause I just happen to have one." He grinned big then. "My name's Elbert Gill. This here's my establishment."

Will nodded toward the shotgun. "Is business so bad that you need to hold a shotgun on your customers to make 'em buy something?"

"Just about," Elbert said, laughing. "I would ask you what you're doin' down this way, but blamed if I don't think I know why. You wouldn't be lookin' for two sidewinders leadin' a string of packhorses, would you?"

"Matter of fact, I am," Will replied. "Did they stop here?"

"Not for long," Elbert said. "They stopped to water their horses late yesterday evenin', and they came in my store lookin' for whiskey. I told 'em I didn't have no whiskey, told 'em it's against the law in Injun Territory. They acted like they didn't believe me, and I was worried there for a minute, I wanna tell you. One of 'em especially, he was a big ol' feller with a bushy black beard, wore a patch over one eye. They didn't want nothin' but whiskey, so they moved on after the horses were watered. They 'peared to be in a hurry, and I was glad of it. I heard one of 'em—little feller, head as bald as a boiled egg—tell the other 'un they could still make a little more time before hard dark."

"Last night, huh?" Will asked, thinking about the time he would have to make up to catch them. "How far is it from here to the Red River?"

"Twenty miles," Elbert said.

"Twenty miles," Will repeated, thinking how far he had pushed the horses already that day, and considering whether or not he should ask for twenty more miles. Max and Billy Tarbow should have already crossed over into Texas, and tracking them might prove to be a little more difficult on the other side of the Red, for he would no longer know where they were heading. "Well," he decided, thinking he might as well be patient, because it might take some time before he tracked them down. "I reckon I'll ride on for another five or ten miles, then I'll be done for the day."

"What about that coffeepot?" Elbert reminded him.

"Lemme see it," Will said.

Elbert led him inside the store and hurried to a shelf behind the counter. He pulled a small coffeepot from behind a sack of coffee beans and wiped the dust from it with his shirtsleeve. "It's a dandy," he said. "Just has this one dent on the side of it." He held it up for Will to see. "Won't hurt the coffee atall. Feller I got it from said it come from the time a Chickasaw woman he was livin' with bounced it off the side of his head. He said he didn't blame her a bit. He'd been drinkin' a little and tried to climb in bed with her sister. 'Cause of that dent, I can let you have it for a dollar."

"I expect I coulda bought it when it was new for a dollar," Will said. "But I'll take it, and maybe that sack of coffee beans it was hidin' behind."

"Yes, sir," Elbert said. "The feller said it made good coffee. You know, you could camp here by the creek tonight, if you want to. My woman will cook up a good supper, wouldn't cost you but a quarter. I bet you ain't had a good supper in a while."

"Thanks just the same," Will said, "but I reckon I'll ride on a ways before dark. If I get back this way again, maybe I'll take supper with you then." He paid Elbert for his coffee and pot, walked the footbridge back across the creek to fetch his horses, and set out again toward Texas.

After a ride of approximately twelve miles, he came to another creek. This one was smaller than the one

Elbert Gill's store was on, but obviously a frequent campsite, for there were several remains of old campfires. He figured he might as well camp there, too. After taking the saddles off his horses, he hobbled them to graze in the short-grass meadow beyond the trees that lined the creek. Before building his own fire, he took a close look at the ashes of the other fires, curious to see if the outlaws he followed might have camped here, as well. As he halfway expected, he found ashes that appeared to be from a more recent fire. He could not be sure, but he figured it a strong possibility that he was camping at the same spot Max and Billy had. It was of little importance other than to suggest that he was locked on to their trail.

As a precaution, before he built a fire, he moved down the creek far enough so that he could not be so easily seen from the road. The simple fare he had prepared the night before seemed to have remained on peaceful terms with his stomach, so he fixed the same supper, thinking that he really had a craving for some fresh game. Eager to try out his new coffeepot, he went to the water's edge to fill it with water, planning to rinse it out beforehand. When he opened the lid and peered into the pot, there appeared to be some small pieces of dirt in the bottom, so he shook them out on the ground. They looked a little odd, so he picked up one of the particles to take a closer look. It occurred to him then what it was. *Mouse shit*, he thought, sure of it then. His new pot must have been a home for a mouse at one time. "Huh," he grunted, and rinsed the coffeepot in the creek a couple of times before filling it with water to make his coffee. *That oughta take care of it*, he thought, *especially when I put it on the fire.*

Mice—the house is full of 'em . . . The phrase popped into his head. It had been said by Fletcher Pride the morning after Will had seen Ruth Bennett sneaking out of Pride's room in the middle of the night. Recalling it brought a moment of sadness when he thought about the late deputy marshal, lusty and seemingly larger than life. It would be his sad duty to tell Ruth that the brawny deputy would not be returning to his room in her house. How deep was her affection for Pride? He hoped that it was no more than a casual arrangement of convenience for two lonely people in need. Thinking of Ruth naturally led him to thoughts of her daughter. "Sophie." He pronounced her name softly while recalling her radiant face. "There's some mischief in those eyes," he said. In a moment, he found himself wondering what it would be like to be married to a girl like Sophie. *It wouldn't be much of a life for her if she married a man in this business*, he thought. With no wish to linger there, he turned his mind back to the business of making his coffee. After he ate his simple supper, he went to the meadow to bring his horses back close to his camp, and tied them to a rope stretched between two trees.

Off to an early start the next morning, he planned to eat his breakfast in Texas while he stopped to rest the horses beside the Red River. Since he had no way of knowing which way the Tarbow brothers intended to go once they reached the border, it was critical that he could follow their tracks. So far, that had been fairly easy, since it appeared they were intent upon heading straight for Texas. So he continued south until he finally struck the Red, the border between Oklahoma Indian Territory and Texas. For him, it was the border between official business and personal business, because he had no authority on the other side. The road led right down to the river and a ferry crossing. On the other side of the river, in Texas, he saw what appeared to be a store beside the landing, and the ferry tied up to the bank. He didn't see anyone on the Oklahoma side of the river until he rode down to the landing, and then a boy of about twelve or thirteen emerged from a tent on the bank. Smoking a corncob pipe and wearing what looked like an old powder horn on a cord hanging around his neck, the boy walked up to meet Will.

"You fixin' to swim 'em across, or you lookin' to ride the ferry?" the boy asked. "It'll be twenty-five cents for you and your horse, and fifteen cents apiece for them other two horses."

"I'll be ridin' the ferry across," Will said, and stepped down. He reached in his pocket and pulled out some silver. Then he counted out fifty-five cents into the boy's outstretched hand. The boy put the money in his pocket, then turned toward the river, put the powder horn to his lips, and blew a loud, screeching signal out across the river. Buster and the two packhorses, startled by the unfamiliar sound, jerked back in reaction until Will calmed them down. "That's a right shrill horn you got there," he commented.

"Yes, sir," the boy replied as he jammed his pipe back in his mouth. "Pa's gettin' a little deef, so he's got where he don't hear that whistle I used to use, 'specially if it's windy. He'll bring the ferry across to get you."

"Are you and your pa gettin' much business lately?" Will asked.

"Some," the boy answered. "Most of it goin' the other way, from Texas to Oklahoma."

"You mighta seen two fellers leadin' some pack-horses sometime yesterday," Will said. "Maybe they took the ferry across."

"Matter of fact, they did," the boy said. "It was pretty near the same time of mornin'." He looked at the badge Will wore and asked, "Are you after them fellers?"

"I would like to catch up with 'em," Will said. "Do you know which way they headed when they got across?" Thinking it might not be a good idea to be wearing a deputy marshal's badge in Texas, he took it off then and put it in his saddlebag.

"I knew them two looked like outlaws," the boy said. "One of 'em didn't have a hair on his head. I don't know which way they headed. Pa might, though. What did they do?"

"They did a lot of bad things," Will said, then quickly changed the subject. "I'd best get my horses down to the landin'. Looks like your pa's already halfway across." He took Buster's reins and led him down closer to the water to watch the boy's father guide the ferry to the landing. The boy moved in position to catch the rope to secure it when his father threw it.

As the ferry grounded to a halt, the man pulled the tiller up out of the water and went to greet his passenger. "Good day to you, sir. My name's Bob Tucker. We 'preciate your business. That young feller there is my son, Jack." He held his hand out to Jack for the money and quickly counted it when the boy gave it to him. "Just bring your horses right on up on the ferry, and I'll have you across in a jiffy. Lead that buckskin up to the other end—plenty of room—and we'll get goin'."

When Will had his horses aboard and settled down, Tucker raised the ramp, picked up a long pole, and proceeded to push the ferry back away from the bank. Once the boat was free, he dropped the tiller in the water again and began working it with the current to steer the ferry to the opposite shore. "Looks like you lost somebody," Tucker said, eyeing the two empty saddles.

"Nope," Will replied. "Just got a couple of saddles I'm lookin' to sell, and this is just a good way to tote 'em. Matter of fact, I'm tryin' to catch up with a couple of fellers. Your boy, Jack, said they rode the ferry across yesterday, said you could tell me which way they went after they got on the other side."

"Mister, I can tell you which way they were headed when they left my place," Tucker said. "They headed west. It ain't none of my business, but I don't know why in the world you'd wanna catch up with those two. Runnin' this ferry, I've seen outlaws comin' and goin' across this river, and that pair had a look of hellfire about 'em that I usually see headin' the other way, up to Injun Territory. And the Texas Rangers are usually not far behind 'em."

"Well, Mr. Tucker, I have to give you credit for havin' a good eye," Will said.

"Like I said, it ain't none of my business, but are you a lawman, or did those two do some harm to your family, or somethin'?"

"I'd have to say both, I reckon," Will confessed. "Those two killed a man that I had a lot of respect for, and I am a lawman." He paused before continuing. "At least I was, but I won't be as soon as I set foot on the other side of this river."

"Oklahoma, huh?" Tucker asked. "U.S. Deputy Marshal?" Will nodded, so Tucker continued. "Well, mister, you ain't the first federal marshal to slip over into Texas, chasin' some lowdown, murderin' outlaw. About a year ago, I had the pleasure of meetin' a helluva hard-ridin' deputy out of Fort Smith. The murderin' son of a bitch he was after had a Colt .44 in my face, demandin' the money outta my cash drawer when that deputy walked in. I'll never forget that big ol' lawman—Fletcher Pride was his name. You know him?"

"I reckon. At least I did," Will said softly. "The two men that just passed through here killed him. That's why I'm chasin' 'em."

Tucker was visibly shocked by the news. He didn't say anything for a few moments before declaring, "I'da shot 'em myself if I'da known that." He paused again to think about the seemingly indestructible lawman he had admired. Then, eager to help in any way he could to bring Pride's killers to justice, he said, "I know where they might be headin'. Like I said, they struck out to the west when they left here, and I wouldn't be surprised if they weren't headin' to Turtle Creek. That's about twenty miles straight west from here. There's a Mexican feller has a tradin' post on Turtle Creek where it empties into the river. At least, he calls it a tradin' post. A saloon is what it really is, and a hangout for every outlaw in this part of the territory. His name's Mendoza, and I expect a good portion of the bootleg whiskey that gets up in Indian Territory goes through Mendoza's place."

Tucker was prone to continue talking nonstop, especially since Will appeared to be interested in what he had to say. He was still talking, even when he was busy with the ramp as he guided the ferry to ground. He paused only a moment to throw a rope to another boy standing there waiting. This one was younger than Jack. "Ain't just whiskey that slips across at Turtle Creek," he said. "There's many an outlaw that takes that trail up into the Nations at that spot. I wouldn't be surprised if that was where that gang of bank robbers, that Tarbow gang, crossed into Indian Territory before the Rangers could catch 'em." He dropped the ramp and yelled to the boy, "Go ahead and tie it off, Bobby."

Will paused before leading Buster onto the bank. "The Tarbow gang crossed over the river down below Durant."

"Is that a fact?" Tucker replied. "I'm just happy they didn't cross over here. I heard they were a pretty mean bunch. They say ol' Max Tarbow ain't got but one good eye—wears a patch like a pirate."

"Kinda like that feller you rode across the river

yesterday, I reckon," Will said, wondering if he should enlighten Tucker or just let it ride.

He saw by the stunned expression on Tucker's face that the thought hadn't occurred to him until that moment. His mind was working hard to remember everything about the men, horrified to think he had not even suspected they were part of the Tarbow gang. "But there weren't but two of them," he exclaimed, still finding it hard to believe.

"That was Max and Billy Tarbow that came through here yesterday," Will said. "They're all that's left of the gang."

"Good Lord help us all . . ." Tucker drew out, realizing then how close he had come to what might have been a dangerous situation for him and his family. "I never even thought about that one wearin' a patch over his eye." Thankful that the danger was past, he tried to recall the pair's features. "Folks said he looks like a pirate. He looked more like a one-eyed grizzly to me." Then another thought struck him. "Is that where those two empty saddles came from—two of that Tarbow gang was ridin' those horses?"

"That's a fact," Will said, wishing now that he had not enlightened him.

It was too late by then, however, because Tucker's brain was already thinking about the possibility of exploiting the opportunity. "Mister," he said, "would you be interested in sellin' one of those saddles? 'Cause I'd be interested in buyin' one of 'em, or better 'n that, I'd be interested in buyin' the horse and saddle." He hesitated a moment. "Those *are* the horses Tarbow's men rode, ain't they?"

"Yeah," Will said. "They belonged to Tarbow's men." He couldn't understand why anyone would want the horse and saddle of a dead outlaw, but he supposed that they would seem a curiosity to some folks, and the Tarbow gang was well known in this part of Texas. His first reaction was to say no, but on second thought, he hesitated. He wouldn't mind getting rid of one of the horses, since it would be easier to manage just one packhorse. And he felt no obligation to return to Fort Smith with any horses he captured. Thinking about the possibility of his returning, if in fact he was successful in his mission, he realized that he would likely not be paid mileage for his entire trip if he came back with no prisoners. With that in mind, maybe he should take advantage of the spoils of his assignment. Looking into the eager face of Bob Tucker, he said, "All right, we'll talk about it while my horses are gettin' watered and rested. I'm gonna eat some breakfast, anyway. I wouldn't mind droppin' one of those horses, but I ain't of a notion to give one away."

"Oh, I'll make you a fair offer," Tucker replied excitedly, already envisioning folks making special trips to his store to see the horse and saddle of one of the notorious Tarbow gang. "Can you tell me the names of the outlaws who rode 'em?"

"No, I can't," Will said. "I didn't know their names. I just know they were ridin' with Tarbow. One of 'em burned his initials in his saddle, *T. B.* That's the best I can do for you."

"Don't matter that much," Tucker said, still keen to make the trade. "Which one's got the initials on it?"

"The sorrel," Will answered.

"You say you ain't had your breakfast yet," Tucker suggested. "Take care of your horses and come on up to the store. My missus can cook you up somethin' to eat and we'll work out a deal while you're eatin'."

"That sounds to my likin'," Will said. He led his horses down the bank a little way and unloaded them. He was hoping that Tucker had a rig for a pack saddle for the one horse he intended to keep, so he could load the horse more efficiently than the arrangement he had fashioned with rope.

After a hot breakfast of coffee, eggs, grits, and sausage, and his horses rested and watered, Will set out again, riding a trail that generally followed the Red River. With a proper rig now for his packhorse, his supplies were packed more efficiently on the red roan. He ended up selling Tucker both of the extra saddles as well as the horse that Tom Blanton had ridden. There was no question that Tucker had certainly gotten the best of the trade, but Will didn't care. He was free of the bother of the extra horse, and he loaded his packs with most of the .44 cartridges that Tucker had, along with any provisions he thought he could use to sustain him on what might prove to be a long hunt, plus a reasonable amount of cash. So he rode away satisfied with the results of the trade, leaving Tucker to explain to his skeptical wife the sensibleness of acquiring the horse and two saddles they didn't need. "It'll bring more customers in to the store," Will heard Tucker say, pleading his case. He couldn't hear what the little lady said, because she spoke in a tiny voice, but the tone sounded deadly. Will couldn't help smiling. He figured that she was probably asking her husband the same question that was in Will's mind, *Where the hell would these customers come from?*

The trail he followed was well defined, and as Tucker had told him, ran close by the Red River, leaving it only when the river took one of its many turns, striking it again when it returned to the trail. Tucker said it was twenty miles to Turtle Creek and Mendoza's place. That would put him there around midday.

CHAPTER 8

"Hey, Mendoza," Max Tarbow blustered, "have that woman of yourn fix us up some grub. I need to put somethin' in my belly besides this poison you call whiskey." He winked at his brother, sitting across the table from him. "Ain't that what you say, Billy?"

"Damn right," Billy replied. "Fix us somethin' to eat." Like his brother, he was feeling full of himself again, smug in the celebrity status they enjoyed with the small-time outlaws who frequented Mendoza's saloon. His mood was further strengthened by the added feeling of safety, now that they had crossed back over into Texas, and that relentless deputy could no longer hunt them down. It was too bad about Becker, Doolin, and Blanton, but the important thing was that he and Max had gotten away safely. He was confident that Max would soon build a new gang of men to follow him, and they would be back in business again.

"Keep your shirt on," Mendoza replied. "My woman's fixing something. She make you a fine dinner. I get you another bottle." He intended to get as big a portion of that bank money as he could, knowing they were probably still carrying a lot of it. "You smart coming back to Texas, Max. Them Rangers, they think you up in Injun Territory. They don't look for you no more in this part of Texas. You stay here awhile, rest, eat, drink whiskey." He gave Max an impish grin. "Maybe you spend some time with Gracie. Make you feel better."

"Huh," Max grunted and cast a critical eye in the direction of the sullen-faced woman sitting alone at the table next to his. Gracie, they called her. That wasn't her name. She was Mexican, like Mendoza, and his American customers had difficulty pronouncing her real name. "Gracie" was the closest they could come, so that's what she was called. "As temptin' as that sounds," he said, sarcastically, "I ain't that rutty right now." He grinned then. "Billy's the one needin' some female attention. He don't never get enough."

Billy's face lit up at that remark. "That don't sound like a bad idea at that," he said to Gracie. "Maybe we oughta go to your cabin after we get us somethin' to eat. Whaddaya say?" The woman called Gracie gave him an indifferent shrug in response.

Witnessing her response, Mendoza said, "I think maybe you gonna have to buy Gracie a few drinks first. She looks like she need it."

Max grunted again. "Course, you don't mind sellin' more of that rotgut, do ya? If she wants a drink, she can have one outta this bottle I already bought."

Still with a look of complete disinterest, Gracie got up from her chair, picked up a glass, and poured herself a drink from the bottle on their table. With no word of thanks, she sat down again to drink it. Max glanced at Billy, who was gazing at the sullen woman in undisguised anticipation. "You better eat some grub first, or you ain't gonna be able to get your money's worth," Max advised his younger brother. He turned to Mendoza then. "Tell that woman of yours to shake a leg before we starve to death."

In a short time, Maria Mendoza came to the back door of the saloon to tell her husband that the meal was ready. "I put it on the table," she said. "If they want to eat, they gotta come to the kitchen. I ain't gonna bring it in here."

Overhearing, Max grinned wide and announced gallantly, "She's got you on a mighty short rope, ain't she? Well, I sure ain't gonna let the lady's food get cold." He pushed his chair back, causing it to fall over on the floor. Without bothering to pick it up, he strode toward the kitchen door. "Come on, Billy. Let's eat."

Billy got up from his chair, then paused to press two dollars into Gracie's palm. "I'll be down to your cabin soon's I finish eatin'." He hurried after Max then.

"It's gonna cost you more 'n this," Gracie called after him, also aware that the two Tarbow brothers had hit several banks before fleeing Texas.

"You fellows go eat," Mendoza said. "I don't eat now. I watch the store."

Still standing by the door, his wife asked, "Why you don't eat now? Nobody here to bother the store."

"Shut up and go with them," Mendoza growled. "And shut the door behind you." He thought it was an opportune time to get a look inside Max and Billy's saddlebags. So they would not get suspicious, he decided to go out the front door and walk around behind the building to the barn, where they had left their horses. When he got to the door, however, he was stopped by the sight of a lone rider, leading a packhorse, and heading his way. "Shit," he muttered, irritated at missing his chance to search the saddlebags. He remained in the doorway, peering at the approaching rider, straining to see if it was someone he recognized. As the rider came closer, Mendoza realized he was no one he had ever seen before. He walked out on the porch and waited by the front post.

As he guided Buster straight to the hitching rail in front of the porch, Will watched Mendoza carefully. He had taken a good look at the layout of the place while he was approaching, the store with the house built on behind; the barn and corral behind that; a couple of small log cabins about twenty yards to the right of the store, close by the creek. He counted a dozen horses in the corral, but there were no horses at the hitching rail as he pulled up before it. Keeping an eye on the man leaning against the post, he stepped down. "Howdy," he said. "I bet you ain't got no beer in that store."

"Well, you sure enough won that bet," Mendoza said, naturally suspicious of any stranger. "I ain't got no way to get beer around here. I got whiskey. You want whiskey?" He didn't wait for an answer before continuing. "I never see you around here before."

"I reckon not," Will said. "What you got inside?"

"General merchandise. What you lookin' for?"

"I might need a couple of things," Will replied, and stepped up on the porch. "Your name's Mendoza, ain't it? I heard you had a store over this way." He shifted his gaze quickly to the left and right, checking the two windows in the front of the store, but he could not tell if there was anyone standing by them or not. Walking past Mendoza then, he went in the door, his hand resting on the handle of the Colt riding on his hip. The store was empty. He turned around to face Mendoza when he followed him inside.

"Are you a lawman?" Mendoza asked.

"Why do you think that?" Will answered.

"I don't know. I never see you before. I think maybe you're a Texas Ranger."

"Well, I ain't," Will said. He could see that he wasn't going to get any information out of Mendoza, but he thought he might as well try. "I'm hopin' to catch up with a couple of fellers that might be lookin' for some help. I heard they lost some men recently and they might be lookin' for somebody to replace 'em. They said they were comin' by your place. You seen 'em?"

Mendoza shook his head slowly. "No, man, there ain't been nobody like that around here." He was certain now that Will was a lawman, and became immediately anxious to get him out of the store before he discovered who was in the kitchen. "I'm sorry, the store is closed now, so maybe you stop by again sometime, okay?" As soon as he said it, there was the sound of a man laughing from the other side of the kitchen door.

"What's goin' on in the back room?" Will asked.

"Nothing," Mendoza blurted nervously. "A birthday party, my father's birthday party," he said, thinking fast now. "That's the reason the store is closed today. No one but family."

"Oh," Will replied. "Well, I sure wouldn't wanna disturb the party. Tell your daddy I said 'Happy Birthday.'" He turned and walked out of the store. Wasting no time in stepping up into the saddle, he wheeled Buster away from the rail. "See you next time I'm by this way," he said to Mendoza as he rode away. Pretty sure he knew where Max and Billy were now, he fought the feeling that there was a rifle aimed at a spot between his shoulder blades. In spite of that, he held Buster to a slow lope back down the river trail, so as not to arouse Mendoza's suspicions. As soon as he was out of sight of the store, he turned the buckskin back on a line to intercept Turtle Creek about a half mile below Mendoza's store. He crossed over the creek then and rode cautiously up the other side until he could see the store. Pulling his rifle from the saddle sling, he dismounted and tied the horses beside the creek. Then he began to work his way in closer to the store. When he was as close as he thought it safe enough to remain unseen, he knelt in a stand of willows and watched for some sign of the two outlaws.

He didn't have to wait long before the back door of the house behind the store opened and two men ran out to the corral. The broad bearlike body of

Max Tarbow was readily identified even if he was too far away to make out the eye patch below the brim of his hat. Behind him, the thinner figure of Billy Tarbow was close on his heels. It was time to make a decision, because they each led a horse into the barn, no doubt to saddle up. He figured he was about a hundred yards from the barn. That was well within the can't-miss range of his Winchester, so he knew that he could end the whole thing right now with two quick shots. *Should he attempt to make the arrest?* He had labored over the decision ever since following the two fugitives from Indian Territory. The grotesque image of Fletcher Pride hanging from the tree, and the bullet-riddled body of Charlie Tate, came to his mind. It might be the hardest decision he would ever have to make, and he had little time to make it. He hadn't placed his hand on a Bible and sworn an oath to uphold the laws of the U.S. court system. His commission as a deputy marshal had been an almost casual agreement to arrest and escort prisoners back to Fort Smith for trial. *I never swore to bring anybody in for trial,* he reminded himself. "But, damn it, that was inferred when I accepted the job," he scolded himself aloud. "I'll give 'em a chance."

His decision made, he plunged through the willows and ran down along the creek bank, heading for the barn, hoping he would reach it before they had time to saddle up and ride. It might depend on whether or not they took the time to load the packhorses they arrived with, and as far as he could tell, they were still in the corral. That was no better than a guess, however, because he didn't know how many horses were typically in Mendoza's corral. When he reached a point opposite the corner of the corral, he left the creek bank and sprinted across a twenty-yard-wide open area to the side of the barn. With his rifle cocked and ready, he paused there for a few moments to listen. He could hear the excited exchanges between the two outlaw brothers as they frantically hurried to make their escape.

He moved cautiously around the corner of the barn, making his way toward the door at the front of the building. When he reached the door, which was standing open, he inched up to the crack between the door and the doorpost. It was just wide enough for him to see inside, where the two brothers were hurriedly saddling their horses. "What about the packhorses and all our stuff?" he heard Billy ask. "We ain't got time for that!" he heard Max answer. Moving slightly, Will was able to get a little better view of the inside of the barn. He was disappointed to discover an open door at the back of the barn. He would have to be ready to act fast, in case they refused to surrender. It was at that moment that the kitchen door to the house opened. A moment later, the stillness was shattered by a piercing scream from Maria Mendoza when she saw the rifleman crouching behind the barn door.

Will had no time to think. Reacting instinctively, he dropped to one knee as he came out from behind the door, his rifle leveled at Billy, who was closest to the front door. Seeing the rifle aimed at him, Billy reacted immediately, drawing his .44 from his holster and firing a wild shot that ripped a chunk of wood from the door, inches from Will's head. Before he could fire a second shot, a slug from Will's Winchester slammed him in the chest, sending him stumbling backward into his horse's legs. The horse reared up, startled, and jumped back.

Will ejected the spent cartridge as he dived to the ground and rolled over in an attempt to use Billy's frightened horse as cover. When Max couldn't get a clear shot at the scrambling deputy at once, he didn't wait to risk the same as his brother got. With one foot in the stirrup, he flailed the excited gray gelding and fled through the back door, swinging his leg over to land in the saddle on the run. Billy's horse, still frantic, turned and followed the gray out of the barn before Will could stop it. "Damn!" Will cursed upon seeing the horse in full gallop behind the fleeing outlaw. With his horse tied a hundred yards back up the creek, Will would have jumped on Billy's horse to give chase. Since that option was lost, he turned his attention back to the man lying on the dirt floor of the barn, thinking there was still a possibility of getting shot in the back by a dying man. A quick glance told him that there was no threat of harm ever again from Billy Tarbow. He turned his attention then to Mendoza and the two women standing at the kitchen door. Seeing no threat from that quarter, either, he unbuckled Billy's gun belt and pulled it out from under his body. Walking out of the barn, he paused briefly to speak to Mendoza. "Looks like your daddy decided not to stay for the birthday party." He nodded back toward the body lying in the barn. "I reckon you can bury your uncle, back there. There's a half a dozen horses in the corral that don't belong to you. They'd better be here when I come back for 'em. If you take good care of 'em, I might leave you a couple of 'em for your trouble." Even as he said it, he had no idea when, or if, he would ever be back for them. With his business finished at Turtle Creek, he walked back along the creek to get his horses, resigned to another job of tracking ahead of him.

Behind him, two terrified women stood speechless until he disappeared into the trees beside the creek. "Who was that man?" Maria finally felt safe enough to ask.

"I never see him before," Mendoza said. "I think maybe he's the devil's debt collector."

Holding his horse to a full gallop, Max Tarbow sped west across an open plain of brown grassy swales and hummocks, treeless for the most part. He looked back over his shoulder frequently, expecting to see the relentless deputy on his trail. So far, there was no sign of anyone tailing him, but he knew he would be coming. He was convinced that the demon would always be coming, and there was no way to hide his tracks across this open plain. The devil had chased them out of Indian Territory and refused to stop at the Texas border. He knew it was the same man. He had to be crazy, with no regard for the boundaries of the territories, killing his men off one by one, until there was no one left of his gang of five men, but him. When he had the time to think about it, he might mourn the loss of his brother, but right now his only concern was to lose the relentless devil on his tail. And there seemed to be no real cover to hide in, so he held the gray to a killing pace in hopes of reaching a line of hills before him that were partially clad with scrub oak forests. The weary horse was already heaving for breath and starting to falter. He knew he was going to have to let up on it; he couldn't afford to let the horse founder.

Finally, he reined the laboring gray back to a walk, then dismounted, looking nervously over his back trail as he led the horse up the first in the line of low hills, into a patch of trees. He kept moving, hoping to find a way to lose his pursuer in the hills, but every time he looked behind him, he could see the clear tracks he was leaving. In near panic, he ran, leading the tired gray down the slope of one hill and up the slope of its neighbor, until at last he found what he hoped would be his salvation. In the floor of a narrow valley, he came to a busy stream just when he was about to decide that he had no choice but to stand and fight. Gratefully, he led the gray into the stream and started walking north, toward the Red River. A few miles short of the river, he came to a wagon road that crossed the stream. Eager to see where the road led, and hoping to lose his tracks among those on the road, he led his horse out of the water.

Soon, he came to some cultivated fields on either side of the road, and a mile or so farther on, he saw a house and a barn. There was a corral with half a dozen horses in it. Right away, he saw his means of escape, so he started to trot toward the corral, still leading the exhausted gray. Before he reached the corral, a man came out of the barn to greet him. "Howdy," Lester Coble called out, puzzled to see the grizzled stranger suddenly show up on the road to town. Tarbow ignored him and continued on to the corral, where he stood looking over the horses inside. "Howdy, neighbor," Lester repeated, thinking the man must not have heard him. "Somethin' I can do for you?"

"Yeah," Tarbow said, his eyes never straying from the corral. "Me and you are fixin' to trade horses. I like the look of that chestnut yonder. He don't look like he's too old. He might do me just fine." Without waiting for Lester to speak, Tarbow started pulling his saddle off the gray.

"Whoa! Wait a minute, mister," Lester objected. "You can't come on my place and just take your pick of my stock. That chestnut's my ridin' horse. He ain't for sale. Who are you, anyway?"

Tarbow turned to face him then, his one good eye glaring like a hot coal as he locked his gaze on the shaken farmer. Lester knew there was to be no choice on his part, for he had no doubt that he was looking into the eyes of pure evil. "I ain't got time to fool with you," Tarbow said, his voice cruel and threatening. "Get in there and put this bridle on that chestnut, and be quick about it. I'm in a hurry." He pulled his bridle off the gray and handed it to Lester. Realizing the depth of the danger he was facing, Lester took the bridle and went immediately to the chestnut. While Lester put the bridle on the horse, Tarbow watched the road anxiously.

When the frightened farmer led the chestnut out of the corral, Tarbow wasted no time throwing his saddle on it and tightening the girth until the horse flinched. It caused Lester to plead, "Go easy on him, mister. He's a gentle horse. He ain't never been treated bad."

The comment seemed to disgust Tarbow. "I don't give a damn if you made a pet outta him. If he don't do the job for me, I'll shoot him and be done with him. You ain't got no cause to be bellyachin'—you got a good horse for him."

Tarbow started to put his foot in the stirrup when Lester's fourteen-year-old son came out of the barn, holding a shotgun. "You heard my pa!" he commanded. "Sonny Boy ain't for sale!"

"Sammy! No!" Lester yelled, but it was too late. Reacting to the threat, Tarbow drew the Colt he wore on his hip and pumped a .44 slug into the boy before he could think about raising the shotgun. The boy dropped his shotgun and crumpled to the ground.

Tarbow started to put another round into the fallen boy when Lester ran to his son. Seeing no further threat from either of them, however, Tarbow holstered the weapon and stepped up into the saddle. "Sonny Boy," he huffed in disgust. "What kinda sissy name is that for a man's horse?" Feeling more like he was in control again, now that he had a fresh horse, he kicked the chestnut hard with his heels and galloped out of the barnyard. Back on the road again, he held the horse to a gallop for about a mile, solely for the feeling that he was putting more space between him and his pursuer. He reined back to a fast walk then, to avoid repeating the mistake he had made with the gray.

As he rode, he tried to decide what he should do about the relentless stalker behind him. His natural tendency would have been to find a good spot to lie in wait for the deputy and bushwhack him. But that was before he became convinced that he was dealing with a man who was not quite human. He had still never even seen the man, which made him even more forbidding, since the images he formed in his imagination were of the darkest nature. His instincts told him to run and hide, and the question that followed was *where.*

When the road led between two low ridges, Tarbow left it and rode up on top of one of the ridges to look over his back trail. From the summit, he could see for at least two miles, and he was encouraged by the fact that he couldn't see anyone. Looking at the road ahead of him then, he saw a small cluster of buildings on the horizon, possibly two or three miles distant. With one more look behind him, he reassured himself that there was no one in sight, so he descended the hill and continued to follow the road. It was getting late in the day now and it occurred to him then that he was hungry, having been forced to flee Mendoza's just as Maria started putting food on the table. *Maybe I can get something to eat there,* he thought, *if that's a town, and it looks like it is.* He was starting to feel confident again, thinking that he might find a place to hide and wait to surprise this persistent lawman. *Maybe hang him with a sign around his neck, like I did with his partner,* he told himself.

The buildings he had spotted from the ridge turned out to be a small settlement in the middle of a wide stretch of fertile farmland. As Tarbow walked the chestnut along the short street, he discovered a post office, a general merchandise store, a blacksmith shop, and a stable, but no saloon or dining room. Considering the prospects not too promising, he decided to try the general store, thinking that maybe he could buy something to cook. Then he remembered that he had no utensils to cook anything with. He still had plenty of money in his saddlebags, though, so he could damn sure buy him some. Pulling up at the hitching rail, he dismounted and tied the chestnut. Taking another look back toward the way he had come, he was satisfied to see no one behind him still. It caused him to wonder if he might have lost the deputy when he had ridden up that creek. He paused for a moment then, questioning the advisability of leaving his horse tied out front of the store. Then he smiled to himself when it occurred to him that the deputy had seen him ride off on the gray. He wouldn't be looking for a chestnut.

Wiley Monroe looked out the window when Tarbow pulled up before his store. "You ever see that fellow before, Winona?"

His wife walked to the front of the store to see for herself. "No, I can't say as I have, and I believe I'd surely remember if I ever had." They stood at the window to watch the burly, ominous-looking brute as he looped his reins over the rail. "He looks like a pirate out of the storybooks, with that eye patch and his big, black beard," she said, then turned to walk toward the counter so she wouldn't be caught staring at him.

"Good day to you, sir," Wiley sang out cheerfully

when Tarbow walked in the door. "What can I help you with?"

"Don't know yet," Tarbow replied gruffly as he stood in the middle of the store, looking around him. Seeing that the store was divided into two separate sections—a counter at one end, a bar at the other—he asked, "Is that a saloon on that side of the buildin'?"

"Yes, sir," Wiley said. "We tend a small bar for some of our customers in the community."

"Well, good," Tarbow said. "We'll start on that side of the room, then. I could sure use a drink. Whaddaya got?"

"I've got some rye whiskey, shipped in from Dallas, and some bootleg corn whiskey that was made locally," Wiley said.

"Anyplace here to get somethin' to eat?" Tarbow asked next.

"Right here," Wiley replied. "My wife will rustle you up something, if you don't mind having what we're having for supper." He ignored the painful look his wife gave him for telling him. She was clearly not comfortable with the rough-looking stranger. "Winona cooks for a couple of fellows in town who don't have wives of their own—the blacksmith and John Carver down at the stable. We don't charge but fifty cents for supper," Wiley said.

"Is that right?" Tarbow responded. "I'll take a taste of it and see if it's worth fifty cents. How 'bout that?" He didn't plan on paying for it, anyway, or anything else he needed as well. He had the money, but he saw no need to waste it. Who was going to stop him from taking what he wanted? "Now, go pour me that drink of whiskey," he said. Grinning then at a shocked Winona Monroe, he said, "You ain't gonna get no supper cooked if you don't get started."

"Well, I never . . ." she muttered, and retreated to the kitchen.

Will approached Lester Coble's farm, four miles east of there. It was not yet dark as he guided the tired buckskin off the farm road and rode up to the house. He was greeted at the front porch by a man holding a shotgun. "You can just keep on ridin', mister. We ain't got nothin' here you'd be interested in, so just get on back on that road and ride."

Will was hardly in a mood to have a problem with a belligerent farmer. He had already lost too much ground to the outlaw he was chasing. He had not been able to get on Tarbow's trail immediately after he shot Billy Tarbow because he had not been quick enough to stop Billy's horse from bolting. Guessing that Billy had been carrying his share of stolen bank money, Will had no choice but to go after the horse before it wandered too far. He finally caught the sorrel when it stopped at a stream to drink. As Will had assumed, there was a large roll of money in Billy's saddlebags. He had then set out to get on Max Tarbow's trail, leading the sorrel behind him. He made a wrong guess when he came to a creek a few miles short of the farm where Tarbow had decided to hide his tracks. The trail had been easy to follow until he reached the creek, but Will had made the assumption that the fugitive would turn south, going deeper into Texas. Turning the other way would have taken him back into Oklahoma, and that didn't make sense. So now he found himself facing a hostile farmer holding a shotgun. "You folks in West Texas ain't particularly hospitable to strangers, are you?" Will asked.

"Some strangers are welcome, some ain't," Lester said, still suspicious of a second stranger within a time span of several hours.

"Well, I won't bother you any longer than it takes to . . ." He paused then, having just noticed the gray horse standing tied to the outside of the corral, its head and tail still hanging down. "Where's the man ridin' that horse?" Will demanded.

"Gone to hell, I hope," Lester replied curtly. "He left it here and stole my horse, a good four-year-old chestnut sorrel. And that gray's done foundered."

"What's at the other end of this road?" Will asked.

It was beginning to dawn on Lester that this somber-looking man was anxious to catch up with the crude brute who had struck his home earlier, and maybe not because they were friends. "A little town called Bulcher," he answered, then asked, "Are you a ranger?"

"No," Will said. "I'm a deputy marshal out of Fort Smith, Arkansas, and I need to catch the man who stole your horse."

"He shot my son!" Lester blurted.

"Oh?" Will responded. "How bad? Did he kill him?"

"No," Lester said. "He hit him in the shoulder, but it wasn't because he wasn't tryin' to kill him."

"How far is that town?" Will asked. "What was the name of it?"

"Bulcher," Lester repeated. "It's four miles."

"Is there a doctor there?"

"No," Lester said. "It ain't hardly big enough to support a doctor. It there was one, that's where I'd be right now, but my wife's lookin' after my boy. I think he'll be all right." He looked a little sheepish then, as he tried to apologize. "I'm sorry I wasn't very friendly when you first rode up, but I weren't sure you wasn't one of that other fellow's friends. Who is he, anyway?"

"His name's Max Tarbow," Will said.

"Good Lord in heaven . . . !" Lester exclaimed. "I've heard of him! He's the fellow that robbed all those banks down near Fort Worth and Dallas." He was speechless for a few moments then when he thought about the danger his family might have faced. "I reckon we were lucky he didn't cause us worse trouble than woundin' Sammy."

"I'd say so," Will replied stoically, and turned Buster's head back toward the road. "I hope your boy gets along all right." He paused then when a thought struck him. "You say Tarbow took your horse and left you with that gray?" Lester nodded and frowned. "I'll tell you what I'll do. I'll leave you this extra horse, and maybe that'll help make it right."

Surprised, Lester replied, "Why, sure. I mean, that's mighty fair of you. Do you want that gray?"

"Nope," Will said. "You keep it."

"How 'bout the saddle?" Lester asked.

"That, too," Will said. "Soon as I empty the saddle-bags."

"'Preciate it," Lester said. This day was turning out

to be a profitable one after all. He stood watching while Will emptied Billy's saddlebags of money and weapons, eager to tell his wounded son that he was going to be the lucky recipient of a horse and saddle. "Good luck," he called after Will as he rode away. "I hope you catch up with that killer."

The gift of the horse had taken a little extra time, and the rapidly approaching darkness caused Will to rethink his original intention to continue on to the town. What if Tarbow had not gone to Bulcher? In any case, he decided it might be wiser to rest his horses and take up the trail again in the morning.

CHAPTER 9

Max Tarbow felt like he was back in control again. It had been hours since he had galloped away from Mendoza's place, and there was still no sign of the persistent lawman. He was convinced he had lost him, and even if the lawman did happen to stumble on this little settlement, Tarbow was confident that he would be hard put to corner him here. In fact, he almost hoped the deputy would come riding down the middle of the short street. He'd take great pleasure in knocking him out of his saddle.

Looking around him now at the people seated around Winona Monroe's table, he enjoyed the fear he saw in their faces. There was very little conversation except for the boisterous comments he made while the other three men at the table ate hurriedly, their faces almost in their plates. He was purposely a little rowdy, just because he enjoyed watching the men squirm, afraid to tell him he was being disrespectful of their hostess.

"I baked an apple pie, fresh this morning," Winona said when John Carver wiped the last of the gravy from his plate with the last bite of a biscuit and abruptly pushed his chair back from the table. "No dessert?" she asked, surprised. "I thought you were fond of apple pie."

"Yes'm, I am," Carver said. "I reckon I ate too much tonight. My stomach's just too full for dessert. I've got some work to do at the stable before I'm done for the night, so I reckon I'd best get to it." Not in a mood to linger, he immediately headed for the door.

"That's all right, neighbor," Tarbow called after him. "I'll eat your piece of pie." Then he threw his head back and laughed. He had a pretty good idea what had killed Carver's appetite. "I'll be bringin' my horse down to see you when I'm done here."

Barely three minutes after Carver went out the door, Seth Polzer, the blacksmith, finished his supper as well. "Well," he muttered briefly, "I reckon I've et more 'n my stomach can hold, too." He got to his feet. "Them was fine vittles as usual, Miz Monroe. I just can't hold no more tonight."

"Well, if that don't beat all," Winona exclaimed. "You, too? I ain't never known you or John to pass up my apple pie. I'm beginning to think you boys don't like my cooking."

"Oh no, ma'am," Polzer was quick to reply. "Ain't nobody can top your cookin', and that's a fact." He took a nervous glance in Tarbow's direction and noticed the wide grin of intimidation parting the bushy black beard. "I'm just mighty disappointed I can't hold no more right now."

"Don't fret yourself," Tarbow said. "I'll finish off

the pie for you." He guffawed as if he had made a hilarious joke.

"I'll save you a slice of pie," Winona said, ignoring Tarbow's crude behavior. "One for you and one for John, too. You just come by whenever you want it, and you can have a cup of coffee with it."

"Yes'm, thank you, ma'am," Seth replied, then headed for the door. He truly hated to pass up a slice of Winona's apple pie, but he knew he'd enjoy it a lot more after Tarbow had left town. So he left Wiley and Winona to deal with their obnoxious supper guest.

"I'll get your pie for you, Mr. . . . ." Winona paused, realizing that Tarbow had never offered his name. "I'm sorry, you haven't told us your name."

"That's right, I ain't," Tarbow said with a smug grin, and offered nothing more.

Winona waited, but after a few moments with no response, she began to tire of his obvious efforts to intimidate them all. "Well, I guess we'll just call you Mr. Smith." She got up from the table then and went to the counter to cut the apple pie. When she returned, she placed a piece of pie at her husband's place and said, "You'd better not tell me you're too full to eat dessert." It was definitely a threat. Then she placed a piece before Tarbow. "Here's your pie, *Mr. Smith*," she said, emphasizing the alias.

Tarbow chuckled with devilish delight for her purposefully snide remark. "I swear, Wiley, damned if you ain't got yourself a right spunky little woman there. She don't give a damn what she says, does she?" Ignoring the fork she had placed beside the plate, he picked the slice of pie up in his hand, took an enormous bite of it, and gulped it down like a dog might. Three more bites finished the whole slice. "Damn, Wiley, she does bake a good pie—good cook and a feisty little woman, too. *Wiii*-nona," he bellowed, dragging out the first syllable, "You sure you're man enough to handle a woman like that? Maybe I could give you a little help. Course, if I had a little go-round with her, she might kick you outta the bedroom."

"All right," Winona said, having heard enough. "Supper's over, and I've got to clean up my kitchen now. You can pay my husband back in the store." She knew her husband well, and she saw him tensing up. She had to act quickly before he forced himself to defend her honor. "You two get on outta here, so I can finish up sometime tonight." She had no desire to see Wiley confront the obvious bully, for it would be no match at all. "Go on," she prodded when Wiley still sat there with his teeth clenched so tightly that she could see his jawbones pressing out.

The tense moment was passed, however, when Tarbow got up and said, "All right, the boss has done spoke. We'd best get outta here before she starts flailin' us with the broom." He started toward the kitchen door, content with the effect that he had caused at the supper table. He had no interest in Wiley's wife; his sole purpose was to entertain himself with the total discomfort of everyone at the table. "Come on, Wiley, and I'll pay you for the supper. Your wife's cookin' is so good that I think I'll take breakfast with you before I head out tomorrow." Behind him, Winona gave her seething husband a stern look and shook her head slowly, lest he work

himself up to say something. The look he returned
was apologetic, and she smiled and nodded.

Satisfied that there was much more he could take
from the little town than the fifty-cent price of supper,
Tarbow willingly paid Wiley for his meal. Afterward,
he stepped out on the front step of the store and
paused there for a few minutes. Looking from one
end of the street to the other, he was reassured when
he saw no sign of the deputy. *I lost him,* he thought. *By
God, I lost him. And now I've got a whole town that's mine
for the taking.* It was a powerful feeling. *Too bad ol' Billy
ain't here,* he thought then. It was the first time he had
brought his brother to mind since he had ridden
into town. Tarbow was incapable of feeling real grief
for the loss of his brother, any more than he did for
the loss of the three other men who had ridden with
him. It was more a feeling of inconvenience, but
then he really didn't need any help in taking this
small town. He could envision knocking over one of
the three businesses after another, starting with the
general store, cleaning it out of everything of value,
and leaving two silent witnesses as he went to the
next unsuspecting target. He didn't figure the blacksmith for anything of value, but he would take care
of him next, since he looked like he could use a rifle
if he was forced to. If it went like he expected, the
post office wouldn't even know what was going on
until he had already ridden out of town. *Yes, sir,* he
thought, *it was a lucky thing, landing in this little defense-
less settlement.*

He climbed aboard the chestnut sorrel and rode
the short distance down to the stables, where he
stepped down and led the horse inside. He found

John Carver coming out of the last stall. There was no horse in that stall, so he asked, "Whatcha doin' back there?"

"Nothin'," Carver said. "Just cleanin' up some stalls. Are you lookin' to board your horse tonight?"

"I reckon I am," Tarbow said. "Me and my horse, too, since there ain't no fancy hotel in town."

This was not good news to Carver, who had hoped the intimidating brute would be on his way after eating his supper. "Well, you can take that front stall. I just put some fresh hay in it, in case you did decide to stay."

"I think I'll take that back stall," Tarbow said. "What's wrong with that one?" He was thinking that Carver looked kind of sheepish when he came out of that stall. It could be that he was just plain scared to see him, and it could be that the back stall was where he was hiding his operating cash. The latter wouldn't surprise Tarbow. It wouldn't hurt to look around in there a little at any rate.

"There ain't nothin' wrong with the back one," Carver said. "It just ain't as clean as that one up front. I think I got a leak in the roof back there and sometimes the hay gets a little rancid."

"Is that a fact?" Tarbow said. "Well, that don't bother me none. I'll take that one, and you'd best give my horse some grain. I'll just throw my saddle in the corner of the stall and I'll be just fine."

"Yes, sir," Carver replied. "Either one—don't make no difference to me." He attempted to sound sincere, in spite of the fact that he had emptied all his extra cash out of his cash box into a carpetbag. He had just finished burying the carpetbag under the hay piled up in the corner of the back stall when Tarbow came in, almost catching him in the act. He silently berated himself now for moving the bag from its usual place on a hook in the tack room. With Tarbow's insistence on using the back stall, Carver had no choice but to try to appear unconcerned. He stood by while Tarbow led his horse into the stall. Looking the chestnut sorrel over as it was led by him, Carver couldn't help thinking that the horse looked like the twin of Lester Coble's sorrel. "Is that enough hay for you and the horse?" he asked. "If it ain't, I can throw some more down in that corner."

"Looks like plenty to me," Tarbow said. "I'll lay my blanket right on that pile in the corner, make me a good bed." He looked around him then, noticing that all but a couple of the stalls were empty. "You ain't got many customers, have you?"

"Right now, you're the only one," Carver said.

"Ain't hardly worthwhile, seems to me, but you must do enough to stay in business." He was thinking of the slim prospects the stable offered him. "Well, it's time for me to turn in."

"All right, then," Carver said as cordially as he could affect. "I reckon I'll see you in the mornin'." He left the grinning brute and went to the little room next to the tack room where he slept, thinking that Tarbow looked like he knew there was something hidden in that stall. There would be no sleeping for him on this night, not with the likes of Max Tarbow bedding down on top of the little bit of money he had managed to save. He wrapped a blanket around his shoulders and sat down on the floor beside the bed, with his back against the wall and his .44 in his lap, intending to remain awake all night.

Although Carver had no intention of dozing during the night, he was unable to keep his eyes open for longer and longer periods of time, until finally at a little past midnight, he surrendered totally to the urge. It didn't come soon enough for the menacing figure watching him from the tack room door. Tarbow was losing his patience, and just about ready to simply step inside the room and shoot Carver, and risk the shot being heard. When he had realized that there was no one else in the stable but the two of them, he decided to go ahead and be done with Carver, but he wanted it to be done silently. At last the stable owner cooperated.

Tarbow slowly pushed the door open and stepped silently into the room. He stood for a few seconds, grinning at the sleeping man, his chin resting on his chest. *Sixty-five dollars*, he thought, referring to the paltry sum he had found in the carpetbag under the hay. *That's all you're worth, but I've killed for less.* He reached down and carefully lifted the pistol from the sleeping man's lap and stuck it in his belt. Then he drew a long skinning knife from a scabbard on his gun belt, grabbed a handful of Carver's hair, jerked his head back, and brought the knife swiftly across his helpless victim's throat. Carver's eyes opened wide in shock as his killer held a huge hand over his mouth and thrust the cruel blade deep into his gut. The only sound he made came from the sucking of air from his severed windpipe. In a few short minutes, his body relaxed in death. Tarbow wiped his blade on his victim's shirt and put it away. Then he pulled the body down flat from its sitting position and rolled it under the bed. His work finished, he went back to the stall where his horse was, and wrapped up in his blanket to get a little sleep before daylight. "Sixty-five dollars," he grunted contemptuously before drifting off.

Tarbow was up with the first light of dawn. He saddled his horse in case he found it necessary to leave town in a hurry after he relieved Wiley Monroe of all his money. But first he intended to avail himself of the opportunity to enjoy another of Winona Monroe's meals. There would be plenty of time afterward to rob the store. His time frame depended to some extent on who else came to breakfast at her kitchen. Before leaving for Monroe's, he ransacked John Carver's room, looking for anything he might fancy. When he was finished with that, he went into the tack room, looking for a rig for a packhorse, with the intention of taking one of Carver's two horses with him. He chose a sturdy-looking gray gelding with a broad chest, being always partial to grays, and led his two horses up the street to Monroe's store.

Tarbow was tying his horses to the rail in front of the store when Seth Polzer came across the street from his blacksmith shop. "Mornin'," Seth forced halfheartedly, having had to decide if he was too hungry for breakfast to avoid further contact with the obnoxious stranger. He turned to look back toward the stable, expecting to see John Carver on his way to breakfast.

"Good mornin'," Tarbow returned grandly, taking satisfaction from the fact that Seth was not wearing a gun. It would make his job much easier if Polzer lingered too long over breakfast.

Since Seth knew he would feel a good deal more comfortable if Carver was at the breakfast table, too, he asked, "Ain't John comin' to eat?"

Tarbow answered with a smug grin. "Nah, he ain't. He didn't feel much like eatin' this mornin'—got a sore throat and a pain in his belly—musta et too much last night."

"I declare . . ." Seth muttered. "That don't sound like John to miss breakfast."

"Just leaves more for me and you to eat, though, don't it?" Tarbow said. "Let's go on inside and see if Miss Wiii-nona has got our vittles ready." He stepped aside at the door to permit Seth to precede him. Seth walked in, uncomfortable with the menacing-looking outlaw behind him, thinking that he was even more threatening when he purported to be in a jovial mood. He suspected Carver of faking an illness, so as to avoid breakfast with the belligerent visitor.

Inside, they found Wiley standing behind the counter. Like Seth, he found it hard to disguise the disappointment in his face upon seeing Tarbow still in town. He gave them both a curt "Good morning" and said, "Winona's putting it on the table now." When Seth stepped to the counter and placed his money down, Wiley asked, "John's not coming?"

"No, he ain't feelin' like eatin' this mornin'," Tarbow answered for him. He pulled out his money.

"Here. I'll pay you for mine and his, so you and the missus ain't out no money." He peeled a couple of dollars off and tossed them on the counter.

"That's too much," Wiley said. "We don't charge but fifty cents each."

"That's all right," Tarbow said. "I'm fixin' to get a helluva lot more stuff to put on that packhorse after breakfast. Let's go eat." He stood there for a moment, a large grin parting his heavy whiskers, as he watched Wiley open his cash drawer and deposit the money.

To Winona's surprise, their unwelcome guest was not as crude in his remarks as he had been the evening before. In fact, she could almost say he was jovial. Like everyone else at the table, she had hoped he would have gotten an early start and gone on his way without subjecting them to his presence this morning. She decided to attribute his improper behavior at supper to a possible overindulgence in alcohol. Maybe the boorish brute did know how to behave after all.

An equally amazed Seth found that he was comfortable enough to eat his eggs without a constant effort to keep his gaze locked on his plate to avoid eye contact with the one-eyed brute. He even lingered long enough to eat the piece of apple pie that Winona had saved for him. Tarbow, however, decided that breakfast was taking too long, so he informed Wiley that he had to get on his way, and there were a lot of things he needed to buy. "I reckon we've all got to get to work," he said, looking at Seth.

"I reckon you're right about that," Seth allowed. "I'd best get back to the shop. I've gotta repair two bent rims for Lester Coble's wagon before he comes into town tomorrow." He got up and complimented Winona on the breakfast. "When I see John, I'll tell him he missed a good 'un. I'll be back tonight for supper," he said, going out the door.

Tarbow walked out of the kitchen behind him, followed him to the front door, and stood there watching him to make sure he went back to his shop and not down to the stable. When Wiley came into the store, Tarbow turned around, all business then, and started calling off things he needed. He scanned the shelves, pointing out items that caught his fancy, causing Wiley to become excited as the costs piled up. When there was nothing more he could think of, he said, "That oughta do it. Now I need to get this stuff packed up on my horses."

Still beaming over the total he had added up for his biggest sale ever, Wiley was more than willing to help him carry his purchases out and tie them down on the gray packhorse. Before they were finished, Winona came from the kitchen and helped with some of the smaller items. Packed up and ready to go, Tarbow said, "That oughta do it. Let's go back inside and settle up." They followed him into the store again and went behind the counter, then Wiley slid the paper with the total bill across the counter to Tarbow. "I'm gonna need one more thing," Tarbow said.

"Yes, sir," Wiley responded. "What's that?"

"I'm gonna need a sack to empty that cash drawer into," Tarbow said, drew his .44, and aimed it directly in Wiley's face. "And be quick about it. I'm ready to shake the dust of this little shithole off my boots." Wiley was too stunned to move. He just stood there, his eyes and mouth all wide open and speechless. Winona uttered a little gasp of surprise, stunned as well. With no patience for their shock, Tarbow threatened her. "If you don't reach behind you and get one of them sacks, I'm gonna blow a hole in that ugly head of yours." It was enough to break Winona free of her paralysis. She turned immediately and picked up a sack from a stack on the shelf behind her. "Now, Wiley," Tarbow ordered, "pull that drawer out and dump it into that sack."

Still frozen in a state of disbelief, Wiley did not move. Tarbow cocked the hammer back on his pistol, causing Winona to punch her husband on the shoulder and cry out, "Do it!" When he was still unable to respond, she shoved him out of the way, pulled the drawer out, and emptied it into the sack.

"That was a smart thing to do, lady," Tarbow said to her. "'Cause I was just before puttin' a hole in that dumb head of his. I might yet—I ain't decided. Reckon it depends on whether or not you do what I tell you. If you do, we're all gonna be a lot happier when I leave here." He pulled the sack of money over to him. "Now, where do you keep the big money? You got a safe? Where is it?"

"That's all the money we have," Winona pleaded. "We don't have a safe."

Tarbow suddenly reached out and grabbed the collar of Winona's dress with one hand and pulled her halfway across the counter. His other hand still held the pistol aimed at Wiley's face. "Now you're lyin' to me," he blurted in her face. "You think I'm that dumb? I'd just as soon rip your gizzard out as look atcha."

Wiley came out of his frightened stupor then. "Let her go!" he exclaimed. "Don't hurt her! I'll show you where the money is!"

"That's more like it," Tarbow huffed. "You give me any more trouble and I swear I'll kill the both of you."

"Don't give him anything," Winona cried, almost choking from his grip on her collar. "We've worked too hard for that money. We can't stay in business without it." Tarbow gave her a sharp crack across the side of her face for her protests, knocking her to the floor.

"Don't hurt her anymore," Wiley cried out. "I'll get you the money!"

"Well, get it, then!" Tarbow demanded. "I ain't gonna wait no longer."

"It's in the house," Wiley said, "in the bedroom. I'll get it."

"We'll all get it," Tarbow said. "You lead the way." He reached down and grasped the back of Winona's dress and pulled her to her feet. "Come on, darlin', we're wastin' daylight." He herded the two of them into the bedroom, where he gave Wiley a shove that almost knocked him down. "Get it," he commanded. Wiley went directly to the bed and pulled the sheets and blankets loose at one of the bottom corners. He reached between the mattress and the bedsprings and pulled out a bundle of money wrapped in a pillowcase. Tarbow's eye lit up when he saw it. "Gimme it," he said. "How much is in there? I ain't got time to count it."

"Three hundred dollars," Wiley said.

Tarbow snatched the bundle from him and dropped it in the sack with the money from the cash drawer. "Now, what am I gonna do with you two? It'll be a helluva lot easier if I put a bullet in both of you."

"Please," Wiley pleaded. "You don't have to do that. There ain't nothing we can do to stop you. There ain't any sheriff to go to. Just let us be and go on your way."

Tarbow studied the frantic couple for a few long moments before deciding. His decision was swayed heavily by the fact that a couple of gunshots might cause the blacksmith, or possibly the postmaster, to break out their weapons. "Come on," he said, and herded them back into the store. "Fetch that spool of rope there under the shelf." Wiley did as he was told. "Now, both of ya, set down there on the floor back to back." When they did, he handed Wiley one end of the rope. "Hold on to that," he said, then kicked the heavy spool over and started pulling rope from it, causing the spool to roll across the room until bumping into the wall. Then he started winding the rope he had pulled off around and around them, pinning their arms and hands tightly to their bodies. When he was satisfied that they were bound, helplessly unable to move, he took out the knife he had cut John Carver's throat with and sawed the rope in two. He tied the one loose end around Winona's ankles, so they could not loosen it to unwind their rope cocoon.

When he was finished, he took a moment to admire his handiwork. "Well, it don't look like you folks are goin' anywhere anytime soon. I reckon I oughta tell you what a good time I had visitin' with the folks of this fine little town, but I'd best be gettin' along now." Pleased with himself, he threw his head back and laughed. "Yessir, I had a fine time." With that, he headed for the door, his bag of money in his hand.

Out the door he strode, never seeing the backside of the shovel that caught him full in the face, leveling his nose and landing him flat on his back. Dazed, but not unconscious, he struggled to come to his senses, only to be driven back flat again with another blow with the shovel, this one with enough force to split the wooden handle and leave him out cold on the floor. Wasting no time, Will Tanner relieved the unconscious man of his gun belt. Then, while keeping an eye on the prone outlaw, he untied Winona's ankles and began unwinding the rope. "You folks all right?" he asked as he unwound it.

"I reckon we are now," Wiley blurted gratefully, then concerned for his wife, he asked, "You all right, Winona?"

"Yes," she said. Looking wild-eyed at her rescuer then, she asked, "Who are you?"

"My name's Will Tanner, ma'am. I'm a U.S. Deputy Marshal out of Fort Smith, Arkansas. That man lyin' over there is Max Tarbow. I've been chasin' him from Indian Territory. He's a robber and a murderer, and I'm just glad to find you folks alive." He drew his knife then and proceeded to cut the rope he had unwound to that point. "I'm gonna need this rope to make sure Mr. Tarbow doesn't jump up and run off. I'll be right back to get you outta that mess."

He tied Tarbow hand and foot while the huge man was helpless to resist. Thinking it might be handy to have a lead rope on Tarbow's bound wrists as well, he tied a fifteen-foot length securely to them.

Once the outlaw was secure, Will finished unwinding the rope from around the trussed-up couple. "Mister," Winona declared, "you're the most welcome sight I've ever seen. That man is a monster."

"Yes, ma'am, he's as bad as they come," Will said. "I'm sorry I didn't get here a little bit sooner, though. I stopped at the stable first."

The expression on his face caused Wiley to react. "Is John Carver all right?"

"No, sir, I'm afraid not. Like I said, I wish I'da got here sooner. That feller at the stable, John Carver did you say? He's dead. Tarbow done for him." He refrained from describing the condition he found Carver in, with his throat cut and a hole in his gut.

"John dead," Wiley muttered, scarcely able to believe it. He continued to stare at the belligerent bully just now showing signs of life. "Whaddaya gonna do with him?" he asked.

"Well, I'm aimin' to take him back to Fort Smith to stand trial for murder and robbery, unless he gives me too much trouble and I have to shoot him." That last part was for Tarbow's benefit, since he appeared to be recovering his senses. Will could see him struggling against his bonds.

"Why don't you go ahead and shoot him now," Winona suggested, to her husband's surprise. "It wouldn't be any different than shooting a mad dog," she added.

"I've thought about it," Will answered truthfully. "But I reckon I'll try to give Mr. Tarbow his day in court. If you had a sheriff or a judge here, I'd turn him over to 'em, but you ain't, so I reckon he's my problem to deal with."

Seth Polzer walked in then, having become aware of something going on at the store and noticing a couple more horses at the rail. He came to an abrupt stop when he saw the menacing Tarbow tied up in the middle of the doorway, his nose flattened and bleeding. "My word . . ." he gasped. "What happened?"

"He tried to rob us," Wiley said, clutching the bag of cash he had retrieved. "But he ran into Mr. . . ." He paused, looking at Will. "Who'd you say?"

"Will Tanner."

"Right," Wiley continued. "He ran into U.S. Deputy Marshal Will Tanner, here, and that's as far as he got."

"Not before he killed John Carver, though," Winona reminded her husband.

"John?" Seth exclaimed. "My Lord . . . My Lord," he whispered, finding it hard to believe. "John dead?" He shook his head slowly as he let it sink in. "And all of us sittin' at the breakfast table with his killer."

Seth's lament caused Wiley and Winona to reflect on the loss of their friend as well until Will decided he had lingered long enough. "It's a long way from here to Fort Smith," he said, "so I'd best get my prisoner on his horse and get a move on."

"That horse he's ridin' don't belong to him," Seth spoke up then. "That's Lester Coble's chestnut. I don't know how that son of a bitch come by it. Scuse me, Winona."

"I hope Lester's all right," Winona said, ignoring Seth's loose tongue.

"Yes, ma'am," Will said. "He's all right. His boy got shot in the shoulder, but he's gonna be all right, too." He had been thinking so hard on the problem of transporting Tarbow back to Fort Smith that it had slipped his mind that the outlaw had stolen Coble's horse. He hadn't been a deputy marshal long enough to know what the proper procedure was for problems like the ones he was facing here. *I reckon I'll make them up as I go,* he decided. "You're right about the horse," he said to Seth. "So I'll leave the horse here and Coble can pick him up next time he's in town. You reckon you can take care of the stable?" Seth said he could. Will continued to work out the details. "There's another horse in the stable. I'll let my prisoner ride that one."

Wiley spoke up then. "Your prisoner bought all that stuff out there on that packhorse and didn't pay the first penny for it, and I can't stand the loss of all that."

"I was just comin' to that," Will lied, for he hadn't thought about that, either. He was beginning to wish he had just shot Tarbow when he started out the door, then got on Buster and ridden away. He walked to the door and looked at the packhorse, then he looked back at the hulking outlaw still lying silent on the floor. He decided he would likely need the extra supplies. "Have you got the bill for all that?"

"Right here on the counter," Wiley answered. He picked it up and handed it to Will.

"Mr. Tarbow will be glad to pay you what he owes," Will said. He walked out the door and went directly to the chestnut sorrel at the rail. He searched through the saddlebags until he found a huge roll of money and counted out the amount owed Wiley. *It's a Texas bank's money,* he thought, *but what the hell?* Back inside he went, and handed the money to Wiley. "There you go, paid in full. Now I'll go swap those horses." He handed Tarbow's .44 to Seth. "I don't think he's goin' anywhere, but if he tries to, shoot him."

"I sure will," Seth said, taking the pistol eagerly.

Will climbed on the chestnut and rode it down to the stable, where he pulled the saddle off and put it on a blue roan that reminded him a lot of the one that had killed his old boss, Jim Hightower. This one seemed not to possess the evil streak, however. Before returning for his prisoner, he went in the room beyond the tack room and rolled John Carver's body out from under the bed. He picked it up and laid it on the bed, just so the deceased would have a little more dignity when his friends came to take care of him.

By the time he returned to the store, Tarbow had managed to come to his senses and was growling at Seth and Wiley as he strained against the ropes that held him, trying to break free, even though he knew he couldn't. Seth appeared to enjoy the miscreant's frustration, remembering the bullying suffered at his expense. "Strain a little harder," Seth goaded him. 'Cause the deputy said I could shoot your sorry ass if you broke loose."

"All right," Will said when he walked in the door. "I reckon I'd best get started." He ignored the scathing gaze aimed squarely at him from the man on the floor as he talked to Seth and Wiley. "You men oughta go down to the stable and take care of your friend. Might be better if your wife doesn't see the body. Tarbow messed him up pretty good." They both nodded their understanding. He turned his attention to the prisoner then. "I'm gonna untie your ankles and get you up on your feet, so you can walk to your horse. I'll make it as easy on you as you'll let me." Tarbow didn't say anything, but continued to glare with dark intensity at the man responsible for the death of his brother and three of his gang. His nose was broken and bloody, his thick, black beard streaked with blood, his eye patch skewed to one side so that part of his empty socket could be seen. This was the first time he had really seen the relentless deputy up close, and he was trying to gauge the mettle of his enemy. He could not help but note the apparent ease with which Will pulled him to his feet. But he was sure he would win the battle of wills before it was over. He had cowed every man who had ever ridden with him, and he had ridden with the cruelest of outlaws. He felt smug in the knowledge that it was a long way to Fort Smith. Somewhere over that rough country he would get his chance.

Finally he spoke as he walked out to the horses at gunpoint with only his hands tied. "That's a mighty long ride. I ain't sure I wanna go." He figured he might as well test the deputy's steel right from the start.

"Well, I ain't lookin' forward to the trip with you, either," Will said. "Grab the saddle horn and step up on that horse."

"I need my hands untied," Tarbow said.

"Like hell you do. Step up in that stirrup."

"Why don't you put me up there?" Tarbow challenged.

Once again, Will wished he had just shot him. So it looked like Tarbow was gambling on winning a battle of wills, thinking that somewhere along the line he could frustrate the deputy into making a mistake. Will gave him a patient look. "Like you said, it's a long way from here to Fort Smith. It'd be a sight easier on you, and quicker, too, if you were to ride that horse. But hell, if you'd rather walk, that's fine with me." He tied the fifteen-foot lead rope he had attached to Tarbow's bound wrists to the saddle horn of the blue roan. Then he tied the roan to the second packhorse, forming a string of the four horses, with Tarbow walking at the rear. "I reckon we can get started now," Will announced.

Grinning smugly through the whole complicated procedure, Tarbow declared, "I still ain't walkin'. If you're arrestin' me, you gotta transport me in a jail wagon. I ain't walkin'.'"

"I'm surprised you know that, Tarbow, and that's exactly what I'm gonna do. But my wagon is settin' over in the Arbuckle Mountains, where you shot the team of horses that pulled it. So we're gonna have to go get the wagon, either ridin' or walkin', your choice, but it's a pretty good walk from here, a good fifty miles."

"I ain't walkin'," Tarbow insisted.

"We'll see," Will said, then directed a question at Seth. "How far is the river from here?"

"Six miles," Seth said. "Follow that trail beside the stable. It'll take you straight north, across the river and on up into Injun Territory. You'll be back in Oklahoma Territory then."

"Much obliged," Will said, and stepped up into the saddle. He looked back at Tarbow then and said, "We'll get started now." He nudged Buster with his heels and his string of horses got under way, one by one as the slack was lost between each horse, until the rope became taut between the roan and the stubborn prisoner. With his feet planted defiantly, Tarbow pulled against the rope, but was forced to stagger forward, overpowered by the horses. Passing the stable, Will nudged Buster to a faster pace that pressed Tarbow to the limit of his ability to keep up, and soon he was running to keep from falling. Being a stout man with a huge upper body, but short legs, Tarbow was not built for running. He soon came to the point past his limit to remain on his feet, and went stumbling to the ground, flat on his belly. Will pressed Buster to lope, dragging the foolish protester up the rough trail toward the Red River. It didn't take much of this treatment before he heard cries of surrender from his resistant prisoner. Feeling no compassion for the cold-blooded murderer, Will continued dragging him for another hundred yards to make sure Tarbow never forgot it. By the time he got the bruised and bleeding outlaw settled in the saddle, Tarbow had learned that it was painful to challenge the somber deputy.

Behind them, Wiley, Winona, and Seth watched in silent amazement until the deputy and his prisoner were out of sight. Wiley broke the silence then. "If that don't beat all . . ."

"That sure as shootin' oughta take some of the meanness out of him," Seth commented. "I've heared of saddle-breakin' a horse, but that's the first time I've ever seen anybody saddle-break a man." He walked out to the center of the street, still staring after them.

With Seth out of earshot, Wiley looked at his wife and grinned. "We sure made the biggest sale of merchandise we'll ever see again anytime soon. I'll go put the money back in the cash drawer." He handed her the bundle of money they had removed from under the mattress. "I was thinking that we had better put this money in the safe under the porch with the rest of the money, but now I don't know. Maybe we'd best put it back under the mattress, in case we have another robbery sometime."

"You might be right," she said. "You and Seth better go down to the stable now to see about poor John. I guess the least we can do for him is to give him a decent burial."

"What's gonna happen to his stable?" Wiley wondered, then the thought struck him. "Seth, why don't you take it over? It'll go hand in hand with your business."

Seth paused to consider the suggestion. "I reckon I could run the stable. Tell you the truth, I've been thinkin' about movin' on, 'cause I wasn't makin' a livin' with my smithin'. But with both of 'em, I might be able to make it."

"Good," Winona said. "We don't need to lose anyone else, or we're never really going to be a town."

CHAPTER 10

Will did not spare the horses, or the bruised and
battered body of Max Tarbow. It was fully fifty miles
to the valley in the foothills of the Arbuckle Mountains, and he intended to make the trip in one day.
With one stop halfway to rest the horses, he hoped to
reach the ravine where the wagon was parked before
dark, even with the late start. He soon found out,
however, that he was not going to be able to cover
that distance in one day. His chain was as strong as its
weakest link, and the two horses picked up at John
Carver's stable turned out to be that weakest link.
They proved not to be as stout as Will's buckskin or
his packhorse, showing signs of tiring after a distance
he estimated at a little short of twenty miles. He was
disappointed that he would not reach the mountains
until the next day, because he knew it would be much
easier to transport Tarbow chained in the wagon.
And he couldn't be sure that the wagon would still
be there, even though he figured the odds were slim
that anyone else would happen along to find it. In
the meantime, Tarbow was content to rock along in

the saddle after his treatment at the end of a rope. Will figured it would take a few days for him to recover from the beating he took.

After stopping in the middle of the day to rest the horses and feed his prisoner, Will pushed on to make camp by a tiny stream about ten miles short of the ravine in the foothills where Charlie Tate had parked the wagon. After he told Tarbow to step down, he led him to a tree and sat him down with his back against the trunk. With a long length of rope he wrapped a couple of turns around his chest, binding him up tight against the tree. He tied the loose ends to a limb about six feet from the ground. With Tarbow unable to move away from the trunk, he could not get up to untie the rope from the tree limb, leaving Will free to take care of the horses and get a fire started to cook something to eat.

Helpless to do anything but sit quietly and watch the deputy marshal make camp, Tarbow said nothing until Will brought him a metal plate with a generous portion of sowbelly and pan biscuits, and a cup of coffee. "This ain't much to eat," Tarbow complained, breaking his long silence.

"No, it ain't," Will agreed. "I ain't much of a cook, but it's the same grub I'm eatin', so it won't do you much good to bellyache about it."

"You need to untie my hands, so I can eat," Tarbow said.

"No, that's where you're wrong," Will replied. "You just do it like this." He slapped his wrists together and reached down as if picking up an imaginary cup with both hands and bringing it up to his mouth. "See, it's easy. Now go ahead and eat. If my wagon's still where I left it, and the chains are still in it, you'll be able to get your hands free some of the time. If the wagon ain't there, I expect you'll be ridin' all the way across Indian Territory with your hands tied."

"You son of a bitch," Tarbow spat. "It's a damn lucky thing for you that you got a chance to coldcock me when I wasn't lookin', or you'd be visitin' with that other deputy down in hell right now."

"We might as well get one thing straight right now," Will said. "Your life ain't worth any more to me than the life of that gnat I just smacked, and I'd end it without stoppin' to think about it. I'm sure those bank tellers you and your gang killed were most likely decent people, and you deserve to hang for that. I frankly don't give a damn about them, but you murdered two good men that I do care about, and I'm inclined to cut your throat like you did to that feller back at the stable. The only chance you've got to live a little bit longer is to behave yourself, 'cause you'd be a helluva lot less trouble to take back layin' over the saddle."

Tarbow realized that the somber deputy meant what he said, and it gave him pause to rethink his situation. He was counting on a careless moment somewhere between here and Fort Smith that would give him an opportunity to overpower his captor. So he was not encouraged by Will's inclination to end his life immediately. "You talk big," he blustered, "but you're bound by law to take me in for trial."

Will favored him with a dispassionate frown. "I don't hold myself bound by much at all," he said. "I killed your men, and I killed that knobby-headed brother of yours, so anytime you think you've got a

chance and wanna try me, then, hell, give it a shot."
That ended the discussion for the rest of the evening.

When it was time to turn in for the night, Tarbow
complained again. "I can't sleep settin' up against
a tree."

"You wanna lie down to sleep?" Will asked.

"Sure, I wanna lay down. I told you I can't sleep
settin' up."

"All right," Will said. "I'll let you lie down." He
looked around him to find two trees close enough together for his purposes. Deciding on two willows
about twelve feet apart, he took a length of rope and
looped it through Tarbow's wrists again. Then, holding the free ends, he untied the ropes binding him
to the tree and directed him toward the willow trees,
his Colt .44 in his hand. Tarbow, on his feet and held
only by the double length of rope, hesitated, wondering if this was an opportunity to act. Will guessed
what was going through the doleful outlaw's mind.
He cocked the hammer back on his Colt and cautioned softly, but deadly, "Remember what I told
you before." Tarbow decided this was not his opportunity.

Will tied the ends of the rope attached to Tarbow's
hands to one of the willows, then told him to sit
down. When Tarbow complied, Will grabbed him by
his boots and quickly yanked him to a prone position. "What the hell . . . ?" Tarbow yelped. Before he
knew what he had in mind, Will coiled another
length of rope round and round his ankles and tied
it off. Then he tied the other end to the second
willow. When he was finished, Tarbow found himself
stretched out between the two trees, flat on the

ground, and helplessly restricted. In an effort not to be totally inhumane, Will adjusted his ropes with enough slack for Tarbow to be able to bring his bound hands down to his chest, but not far enough to reach the knot tying his ankles together.

"That oughta do you just fine," Will said. Then he took a blanket and draped it over him.

"What if I gotta take a leak durin' the night?" Tarbow asked.

"Then I reckon you'll just have to hold it till mornin'," Will said. "If you can't, I reckon your trousers will dry out tomorrow."

Early the next morning, Will got his prisoner up and let him answer nature's call while he watched him with his Winchester 73 trained on him. Sore and complaining, Tarbow claimed that he couldn't breathe through his nose since it was flattened all over his face. Will was not sympathetic, already regretting his decision to take Tarbow back to Fort Smith. He told himself that he had to do it, however, after giving it more thought. He wasn't sure that Marshal Stone would accept his story about the tragic mission that had accounted for Fletcher Pride's death, as well as that of Charlie Tate. If nothing else, Max Tarbow was evidence that he had engaged the Tarbow gang. There was the considerable amount of the bank's money that he was bringing with him, but Tarbow himself was the proof that the gang had been stopped. So he resigned himself to the task. He no longer had Pride as a trainer for his job, but he figured common sense should go a long way toward getting it done. He made a decision that morning that, if he was retained as a deputy marshal after he got back, he was going to do the job his way. And one thing he planned to change—he would work alone. This experience had left him with no desire to have to worry about anyone but himself—no posseman, no cook, and no wagon. Pride had explained the necessity of using a wagon when the assignment was to travel to Fort Sill, Fort Reno, or Anadarko to pick up prisoners. Will could understand that requirement, due to the long distances to transport the prisoners. They would have to be fed and guarded, so it was going to be difficult to refuse the posseman and the cook on those occasions. But for the most part, he preferred to work alone.

When he got Tarbow in the saddle, he started out to find the ravine again. Since it was only a ride of less than ten miles, he planned to eat breakfast after they got to the wagon. Since they were approaching the ravine from a direction a little more west than the trail on which they had left, it took slightly more time to locate the valley he searched for. Tarbow was much more familiar with the country, so he could have steered him on the proper trail, but he was not of a nature to help his jailer. Even if he had been, Will was not inclined to believe any directions that Tarbow might have offered. He knew he would eventually find it, and he did, when finally he came upon familiar landmarks. "Took you long enough to find this valley," Tarbow scoffed. "I thought we was gonna starve to death before you found out where the hell we were." Will didn't bother to reply; he was just glad to see the wagon still there. He went straight to it to see if the long, heavy chain was still there, as well as the leg irons and shackles. They were, so he was satisfied that his prisoner would make the rest of the journey to Fort Smith a great deal more securely.

Watching Will as he looked in a tool compartment in the wagon for the keys for the leg irons, Tarbow realized how being in irons was going to reduce his chances of breaking free. "Hey," he yelled. "You ain't gonna put them things on me, are you?" Will didn't bother to answer, so Tarbow yelled again. "Hey! Ain't no need for them damn irons. I ain't gonna try nothin' funny."

Busy picking through the metal box that contained several different-sized keys and locks, Will ignored him until finally finding the combination he searched for. "Quit your bellyachin'," he said. "You'll ride a lot more comfortable once you don't have your hands tied all day." The long chain was designed to secure as many as ten prisoners, with heavy rings attached every few feet. Will passed Tarbow's leg iron chain through one of the rings and locked it with a padlock. He locked the end of the heavy chain around the rear axle of the wagon. Satisfied that Tarbow wasn't going anywhere now without pulling the wagon with him, he untied his hands. "There you go," he said as he let the chain drop in the wagon bed. "Now, as soon as we have a little breakfast, we'll get started to Fort Smith."

With Tarbow securely chained, Will took care of the horses before he made any motions toward cooking breakfast. Still to be determined was which two horses to hitch up to the wagon. He wondered if the two he had picked up from the late John Carver had been introduced to the traces of a wagon. He decided that he would try them as a team first, so he put Tarbow's saddle and the packs in the wagon.

After a breakfast of the same fare they had eaten the night before, Will put Tarbow in the wagon and secured the end of the long chain under the rear, so that it prevented his prisoner from moving about in the wagon and also made it impossible for him to use the free end of the chain as a weapon. With the horses tied on lead ropes behind, Will climbed up in the seat and drove the wagon out of the ravine. It would take at least three days to reach Atoka Station at the wagon's pace and at least a week from there to Fort Smith, if everything went well. It was not a trip he looked forward to. He was much more comfortable in the saddle.

Lem Stark turned, startled when he heard the creaking of the hinges on his front door, for he had not heard a horse approaching his store. In the dim light of the early evening, the visitor was not recognizable until he stepped out of the shadow into the light provided by the lantern on the counter near the door. Lem recoiled at first, surprised by the unexpected guest. Tall and rangy, dressed all in black, from his flat-crowned hat to his polished leather boots, he wore two Colt .44's, handles forward. He said not a word as he stood gazing at the old man, but his razor-thin smile under a waxed black mustache conveyed the sinister confidence of a heartless killer.

Still frozen by the sudden appearance of the phantomlike personification of uncut evil, Lem was speechless for a moment while he recovered from his surprise. "Eli," he softly murmured, as a prideful smile spread slowly across his face.

"Pa," Eli Stark returned. "I heard about Jeb. I came as quick as I could get here. The word I got was that he got shot by a deputy marshal. Was it that son of a bitch Fletcher Pride?"

"I knew you'd come back soon as you found out," Lem said. "I'da sent word, but I didn't have no idea where you was. I don't know if it was Pride that shot him or not. There was a new deputy with Pride, name of Will Tanner. Coulda been him. The two of 'em came by here lookin' for Max Tarbow and his gang. Jeb rode up to the Arbuckles to warn Max they was lookin' for him. It was just plain bad luck that Jeb stayed up there at that cabin by the waterfall. One of my whiskey runners, Sam Deer Killer, brought Jeb's body back home. He said he musta got there not too long after it all happened—said there musta been a helluva shoot-out up and down that mountain. He found Jeb and some other feller's body up at the cabin. Down at the foot of the mountain, there was a wagon and more dead men. There was one grave he found, but there was two other bodies. Sam dug up part of that grave, just to see who was in it. There was two bodies buried in it. One of 'em was Fletcher Pride. Sam recognized him for sure. So that's one mean son of a bitch we don't have to worry about no more. Sam didn't know who the other feller was—an older feller, likely the wagon driver—but it must notta been the other deputy 'cause he was a younger feller."

Eli paused for a moment to consider what he had just heard. Then he asked, "What about Tarbow? I know that bastard. Did the deputy get him?"

"Sam couldn't say," Lem said. "Maybe he got away, but if he did, that deputy mighta got on his trail. He said there was one of them jail wagons up there. He looked it over, but he didn't wanna be caught with it, so he let it be, figurin' the deputy might be comin' back to get it, if he is still alive. So he decided to put the grave back the way he found it, too." He shook his head slowly while he pictured that. "I'd like to be there when he came back to get it. I'd damn sure pay him in full for killin' my son."

"That's what I came home for," Eli said. "Somebody's got to pay for killin' Jeb, and I'm gonna see to it. If that deputy—what did you say his name was?"

"Will Tanner," Lem said.

"Will Tanner," Eli repeated. "I ain't gonna forget that name. If he ain't dead already, he's gonna be dead pretty damn quick. Nobody kills a Stark and lives to tell about it."

"Whaddaya gonna do?" Lem asked.

"I'm thinkin' about what Sam told you about that wagon he found up there. I think he's right— somebody's most likely gonna come after it. So I figure the best thing for me to do is to get up there to that cabin and find that wagon. Then I'll just see who comes to get it, and I think I'd best be quick about it."

"You've got the right idea, son," Lem said. "But it's late in the day now, and you just got here. You need you somethin' to eat, and rest your horse. You might as well stay here tonight and head out in the mornin'. You can be up in the hills below that cabin this time tomorrow. Sam said the wagon was in a ravine near where that stream runs down the mountain. You know I'd go with you, don't you? But, hell, ain't no use in me tryin' to fool nobody. I can't ride no more."

"I know that, Pa," Eli replied. "Don't you worry about that none. I'm the one to put that son of a bitch in the grave. You know you can count on me." In truth, Eli didn't want to be hampered by the old man. He always hunted alone, and on this hunt, he wanted the full satisfaction of the killing all to himself. His younger brother had almost worshipped him, and he was determined to avenge his killing. That's what big brothers did.

"Come on, son, let's go in the house and I'll get Minnie to fix you somethin' to eat," Lem said.

Eli grunted indifferently. "Is that skinny squaw still here? I thought she'da run off by now."

"By Ned, she tried it once about three months ago," Lem scoffed. "I caught her two miles up the river, tryin' to get to Switchback Creek. I cut me a stout limb off a laurel bush and I whupped her till she couldn't stand up. She ain't tried to run off no more." He laughed as he recalled the incident.

Eli laughed with him. "I swear, you sure got a way with women." He followed Lem to the kitchen, where Minnie Three Toes was cleaning up the supper dishes. As Lem had, she jumped, startled when she turned to see Eli behind Lem. "Minnie," Lem said, "Eli's home and he needs somethin' to eat."

"I fix," the frightened Chickasaw woman replied at once. She had always had a fear of Lem's eldest, every bit as much as she had for his father. He held a deep contempt for anyone of Indian birth. There were some biscuits and two slices of ham left over from supper, so Minnie put them on a plate and placed it on the table. She poured the last of the coffee from the supper pot into a cup and set it down beside the plate, then stepped back away from the table.

"I am kinda hungry," Eli said. He pulled a biscuit apart and stuck a slice of ham in it, took a big bite, and washed it down with a gulp of coffee. "Damn!" he swore, almost choking on it. "Make me some fresh coffee," he ordered the timid Indian woman. "This stuff tastes like horse liniment. When'd you make it, yesterday?" He looked at Lem then. "I swear, Pa, I think you're lettin' this squaw get lazy on you."

His son's vocal abuse and downright disrespect for Minnie only amused Lem, causing him to chuckle in response. Eli's cruel nature was something that Lem had always taken great pride in. "It ain't that old," he said, still chuckling. "Minnie made it fresh this mornin'. Maybe the pot got pushed closer to the fire while she was cookin'." As a rule, the big gray metal pot was pulled over to the edge of the stove to stay warm after it had boiled. "I poured the last cup outta the pot. I musta set it back down over the belly of the stove. Minnie'll make you some more."

Accustomed to the verbal abuse whenever Eli came

home, the Indian woman was already at the pump, rinsing out the coffeepot. Choosing never to speak directly to Lem's belligerent son if she could avoid it, Minnie asked Lem, "I cook? He want more?"

Lem turned to Eli. "You gonna want somethin' else to eat?"

"Nah," Eli said. "Couple of ham biscuits and some decent coffee'll do."

When the fresh coffee was ready, Lem and his lone remaining son sat at the table and talked while Minnie cleaned up around them. So as to make sure Eli could identify Will Tanner, Lem tried to describe him as accurately as he could remember. "He's a good-sized man," Lem said, trying to recall the clothes Will wore. "Warn't nothin' special about him—looked pretty much like any cowhand, I reckon. Rides a buckskin horse. I do recollect that."

The next morning, Eli was off to the Arbuckle Mountains soon after sunup. Lem wished him good hunting. "I remember, now that I think about it, that deputy didn't wear no mustache or beard, and he had kinda sandy-colored hair. It'd make a fine-lookin' scalp."

Eli smiled at that. "I expect it might. I'll bring it back for you." Like the clothes he wore, his horse was black. He stepped up into the saddle, gave it a kick of his heels, and set out to find Will Tanner.

Late in the afternoon Eli arrived at the scene of the shoot-out that Sam Deer Killer had described. Looking around the clearing where the stream cut through the little valley, he saw the remains of two bodies, at least what the buzzards had left of them, as well as the bones of two horses. He grunted indifferently and said, "Looks like they had a real party." But there was no wagon, even though there were tracks that plainly showed him where it had been parked and which way it had gone when it had left the ravine. "Damn," he swore, for he had hoped to find the wagon still there, thinking to wait in ambush for someone to come for it. Examining the tracks closely, he estimated that it had been no more than a couple of days since the wagon left. He figured that, as slow as a wagon traveled, he could catch up with it in one or two days. At least, he could have if he did not have to rest his horse. He cursed the horse as if it were to blame for delaying him. Since there was no choice for him, other than to camp there and start tracking the wagon in the morning, he rode up the stream a good distance to escape a smell of rotten flesh that still lingered in the ravine.

Morning broke clear and cooler, and he started out as soon as it was light enough to make out the wagon tracks. He soon decided that there were two horses trailing along behind the wagon, and after following for a short while, when the tracks headed straight west, he figured they were heading to Atoka. Maybe, he thought, if he was lucky, he could catch him before he reached that station. He had a much better chance of killing this deputy if that was possible, and he had come to think that it was most likely the deputy who had come back to get the wagon. If he got to Atoka, it might complicate things. Jim Little Eagle, Indian policeman for the Union Agency, worked out of Atoka, and he was often deputized to work with a U.S. Deputy Marshal. Eli had no knowledge of Will Tanner, but he recalled some close run-ins he had experienced with Jim Little Eagle when he was a Choctaw Lighthorseman. He preferred not to have to deal with him and the deputy together.

CHAPTER 11

Keeping a steady course due west, Will's plan was
to pick up the trail he and Pride had traveled from
Fort Smith, once he reached Atoka. There was nothing on his mind now but the job of transporting Max
Tarbow to stand trial in Judge Parker's court. As best
he could estimate, he had traveled a good forty miles
after the second full day since leaving the little ravine
where his journey had started. His team of horses was
showing signs of weariness since resting them at
noon, but he decided to push them a little farther in
hopes of finding a stream. The two horses had performed satisfactorily teamed together, causing him
to suspect it wasn't the first time they had been
hitched to a wagon. He had a long way to go before
reaching Fort Smith and he had no intention of
overworking them. But he also wanted to avoid the
inconvenience of having to make a dry camp with no
water to drink or cook with. Because of this, he was
glad to see a line of trees about a mile ahead that
surely indicated the presence of water.

Luck was with him. When he reached the trees, he

found that they bordered a fair-sized stream, as he had suspected, and it had an adequate flow of water, in spite of the dry conditions of the last few weeks. He was sure then that he had reached Clear Boggy Creek, and if that was the case, he could be only about another day's drive from reaching Muddy Boggy Creek and Jim Little Eagle's place. He planned to stop at Jim's home to inform him of Fletcher Pride's death and let him know that Max Tarbow's gang was no longer a threat. He figured that it was information that Jim needed to know.

Preferring a potential campsite he saw on the other side, he crossed over the creek and drove the wagon under a large cottonwood, where he parked it for the night. He glanced briefly at his prisoner, sitting sullen against the side of the wagon as he un-hitched the team and turned them out with the other two horses to graze on the creek bank after drinking from the creek. Already accustomed to the defiant leering of his ominous captive, he was somewhat surprised when Tarbow broke a silence that had lasted since their last stop to rest the horses. "What are you aimin' to do with all that money you got from me?" he asked.

"Huh," Will snorted, amused by the question. "Turn it over to the court."

"You'd be a damn fool if you do," Tarbow said.

"Maybe so," Will replied, seeing no use for further discussion.

Tarbow wasn't ready to drop the subject. "I don't know if you've took the time to count how much of that money's left. A man could go a long way with that much money—about ten years of a lawman's pay—maybe more 'n that. How much they pay you, anyway?" Will didn't bother to reply as he proceeded to gather wood for a fire, leaving Tarbow to ramble on. "I'll tell you somethin' else to think about," he said, raising his voice so Will could still hear him as he walked away from the wagon in search of dead limbs. "If you was smart enough to hook up with me, we could make a helluva lot more money than you're holdin' right now. I know some banks that are settin' there just waitin' for somebody to walk in and take the money. No rangers, no sheriffs, nobody to keep you from robbin' 'em. You oughta think about that, Tanner, 'stead of wastin' your life away doin' the government's work for nothin' and endin' up with worn-out boots and dust in your saddlebags."

Will walked back near the wagon to dump an armload of limbs on the ground. Then he turned to face Tarbow. "That's a right interestin' argument, Tarbow, but look where it's landed you. Now, if you're wantin' to eat any supper, you'd best shut up now, 'cause I can't cook when my ears are hurtin'. And I was plannin' on cookin' us up some beans to go with that sowbelly tonight." Visibly irritated by the deputy's apparent honesty, Tarbow said nothing more. Will figured he had attempted to entice him with promises of riches, and now he would return to his original plan, looking for an opportunity to overpower him.

As he had the night before, Will unlocked one end of the chain while leaving the end around the rear axle locked, allowing Tarbow the freedom to get out of the wagon, even though his foot was still shackled to the chain. Will then built his fire just far enough from the wagon to permit Tarbow to reach one side of it before reaching the limit of the chain. He was careful to unload the packs with all the weapons and ammunition he had collected well out of the chain's reach.

Already sick of the chore of cooking, he thought back on his earlier decision not to travel with a cook. *It would be damn nice to have one now,* he thought. *Should have shot the son of a bitch.* He shrugged and went to the wagon for the bucket of water under the seat, where the dried beans had been soaking since morning.

The night passed peacefully with Tarbow returning to the sullen state he had affected before his unsuccessful pitch to Will to cross over to the other side of the law. After securing his prisoner in the wagon and hitching up, he started out again, heading for Muddy Boggy Creek with no thought of any further threat other than when Max Tarbow might attempt to escape. Jim Little Eagle's cabin came into view a little before noon. Will recognized the short, stocky Indian policeman working with a hoe in a little garden patch next to the cabin. Jim saw him at about the same time and stood watching them approach. When he recognized Will on the wagon seat, he started walking toward the front of the cabin to meet them. He said nothing until Will pulled his team to a stop. With a brief nod of greeting, Jim took a hard look at the man chained in the back of the wagon before turning back to address Will. "That don't look too good," he said, fearing the worst.

"It ain't," Will replied, and climbed down from the wagon.

"Looks like you and Pride caught up with those men you were looking for," Jim said, waiting patiently for the story.

"You're lookin' at everything that's left," Will said, then went on to tell Jim all the events that had happened to bring him to this point.

The stoic Choctaw policeman listened with no show of emotion, nodding only occasionally while Will told him about the several confrontations that had happened on the ill-fated assignment. When he had finished, Jim nodded toward Tarbow, staring defiantly at him from the wagon. "That's Tarbow?" he asked. Will said that it was. "You gonna take him back to Fort Smith?"

"That's what I'm figurin' on," Will answered.

Still showing no emotion, Jim walked around to the rear of the wagon and looked at the chain and the method Will had used to secure the prisoner. He nodded his approval, then asked, "The others, all dead?"

"Yep," Will answered. "Me and him, we're all that's left of the whole damn mission."

"It's a long way to Fort Smith," Jim said. "You want me to go with you?"

"No, that ain't why I stopped by," Will said. "I just wanted to let you know what happened to Pride— that and the fact you don't need to be on the lookout for the Tarbow gang no more."

"That's right," the sullen Tarbow suddenly blurted. "We don't need no damn Injun taggin' along. You stay home and hoe your garden."

Still with no change in his stone-cold expression, Jim turned to Will and offered, "You want me to cut his tongue out, so he don't make noise no more?"

"Lemme think about it," Will said with a smile. Judging by the indifferent expression on the Indian's face, he wasn't sure if he was serious or not. "I think I'll move on down the creek a ways to rest the horses and cook something to eat. Then I expect I'll pick up the trail we rode when we came from Fort Smith." He had an idea that he would be welcome to rest and water his horses there at Jim's cabin, and maybe an offer from Jim's wife to cook for them. But he didn't think it the right thing to do. Maybe after he had worked with the Choctaw policeman a little more, he might be on a friendlier basis, similar to that Jim had shared with Pride. "So I reckon I'll see you sometime," he said, and climbed back up on the wagon seat.

Jim stepped up close beside the seat and said, "Fletcher Pride was the best lawman I ever knew. I'm sorry he's gone." He stepped back away from the wagon.

"I am, too," Will said. "It's gonna be mighty hard to follow in his footsteps." He could appreciate the simple statement of mourning from the stoic Indian, knowing that it came from a deep respect for the larger-than-life lawman.

Eli Stark guided his horse over toward a low ridge, dismounted, and went on foot the rest of the way up the short incline to the top. He had ridden the big Morgan gelding hard in an effort to catch up with the man who killed his brother. Now, finally, he caught his first sighting of the wagon ahead of him. It had pulled up in front of a small log cabin by the creek ahead, and the man sitting in the wagon seat had to be Deputy Marshal Will Tanner. He was too far away to take a shot with the Henry rifle he carried in his saddle scabbard, and he wanted to be close enough to guarantee a sure hit. So he could only watch as a man came from beside the cabin to meet the deputy. "Damn," he cursed under his breath, for the land between him and the cabin was mostly rolling prairie with few trees. Desperate for some way to get closer to his target without being seen, he looked toward the creek ahead of him. It looked like the banks of the creek might be high enough to hide a man running at a crouch behind them. *That oughta work*, he decided, and hurried back to get his rifle.

He had no way of knowing how long Tanner would stop at the cabin, so he wasted no time in running across an open swale between the hill and the edge of the creek. He dropped below the bank and, running hunched over, he trotted along the creek, intent on getting to a small stand of cottonwood trees where the creek took a sharp turn to the north. That should just put him in fair range of his rifle. When he reached the bend in the creek, he found that this would have to be the spot, for to go farther would place the cabin between him and the two men talking by the wagon. Being careful to stay in the cover of the few trees beside the creek, he crawled up on the bank and moved up to kneel beside a large tree trunk. From his position beside the tree, he had a clear shot at Tanner as well as the man in the back of the wagon.

Hesitating for a moment, he trained the Henry on the prisoner. *Well I'll be damned*, he thought, *Max Tarbow. That deputy caught him.* The discovery made it even more satisfying to kill Tanner. He couldn't help grinning when he thought about the wild ride Tarbow was going to experience when he started shooting and those horses bolted—because, even though he couldn't tell from this distance, he was sure Tarbow was chained to the wagon. Suddenly the grin froze on his face when another thought struck him. If Tanner had Tarbow, then more than likely he had recovered a big part of the money Tarbow and his gang had stolen. His mind began to race with the prospects of suddenly becoming a very wealthy man. In fact, there was no reason to share the money with Tarbow after he killed Tanner. *Hell, I'll kill Tarbow, too*, he thought. *I never had any use for that one-eyed big-mouth, anyway.* What had started out as a purely vengeful assassination had turned into a possible windfall of bank money. It occurred to him that his brother Jeb's death might have been a lucky thing, after all. He felt no guilt in thinking such a thought as he returned his concentration to the job at hand.

He swept his front sight back around to center on Tanner's back. *Now, you murdering son of a bitch*, he thought, but at that moment, the other man stepped into the picture, and Eli hesitated, just then recognizing him. *Jim Little Eagle*, the thought struck him, the man who had driven him out of the Nations. He quickly brought his rifle to bear on the stocky Indian policeman, but still he hesitated, thinking that if he killed Little Eagle, he would chance missing Tanner. Another thought struck him. *If I kill that Indian bastard, I'll have the whole Indian Police Union on my tail again.* He had only dared to return to the Choctaw Nation after a year because he thought they might have given up on him by now. He would not have risked it now except for his determination to avenge his brother. He lowered his rifle and questioned the risk he might take if he wasn't successful in killing both men. He would become the hunted instead of the hunter; he preferred the latter role.

Much to his frustration, his hesitation cost him to miss the opportunity to take a shot at either target, for Tanner drove the wagon out of the yard at that moment. Frustrated at having been thwarted in what he had first thought to be a perfect opportunity, he backed away from the tree in anger. He hurried back to retrieve his horse at the foot of the ridge, telling himself he would have a better chance later on, after Tanner had left Atoka Station and was all alone in the wilds between there and Fort Smith. "I ain't in no hurry," he counseled himself. "I've got a week to get the shot I want. Maybe I'll play and mouse with him for a while." The thought amused him. There was no sense in taking chances where there were possibly witnesses to tell the marshals who did the shooting, anyway. "If I had my choice," he boasted to the dark Morgan he rode, "I'd meet him face-to-face." Feeling better about the hesitation he had experienced, he turned the Morgan's head in a more southerly direction, with the intention of circling around to pick up Tanner's trail after he cleared Atoka.

* * *

Will drove the wagon another mile and a half before finding the spot he sought to rest his horses, a wide stretch of grassy prairie on both sides of a tree-less stretch of creek. He parked the wagon on the bank of the creek and began what was already a routine for him. As he went through the motions, he thought about Fletcher Pride, and wondered how the man had been able to tolerate it all the years he was in the service. Now that the dirty work was done, and the prisoner captured, his job was no more than a cook and nursemaid until he could turn Tarbow over to the court. He turned to meet Tarbow's eyes, and the grizzlylike villain's smug gaze seemed to infer that he knew what Will was thinking. "I gotta take a leak," he said, grinning.

Will unlocked the length of chain that limited Tarbow's movement in the wagon so he could climb down and move as far from the wagon as the remaining chain would permit. While his prisoner was taking advantage of his limited freedom, Will un-hitched the horses and took them down to the water. After they had been watered, he let them graze on the short-grass meadow that ran down to the creek. He wasn't sure of the two horses pulling the wagon and his packhorse, so he hobbled them. As far as Buster, he wasn't worried about him because he knew he wouldn't wander. After tending the horses, he found enough dead branches around the berry bushes on the bank to build a small fire to cook some meat and boil some coffee for him and his prisoner. When it was ready, he set a plate down on Tarbow's side of the fire. "Eat," he said. "This is all you'll get till dark."

"You're gonna starve me to death," Tarbow complained, looking at the salt pork on his plate. "They ain't gonna have to hang me. You don't give a man enough to eat to stay alive." Will didn't bother to respond to his grumbling, which tended to irritate him more. "Ain't there somethin' in the rule book that says you gotta feed a prisoner three meals a day? You ain't feedin' me but two times a day."

"I'm thinkin' 'bout feedin' you just once a day," Will said, "if you don't stop carpin' about everything. If you wanted to be treated like a gentleman, you shoulda took up a different line of work." He drained his coffee cup and went to get the horses, planning to make ten more miles before making camp.

It was approaching sundown when they came to a narrow stream making its way through a gulch dividing a low ridge running along a line of tree-covered hills. Will felt the horses were good for another couple of miles, but with the rapidly fading light, he decided he'd best not gamble on finding another stream before darkness caught them. So he pulled the wagon over close to one side of the gulch and started the routine of making camp once again.

For a change, Tarbow had little to say about the way he was being treated, his only complaint being the fact that Will had misjudged the length of the chain, preventing him from getting close enough to the fire. He ate the food Will prepared with no complaints, however. Will couldn't help wondering if maybe the gruff outlaw had finally accepted the fact that he was going to jail, and then to trial. *Whatever the reason,* he thought, *it's a hell of a lot easier on my ears.* While he appreciated the silence, he was astonished a moment later when Tarbow came out with a confession of guilt.

"I reckon I have done some mighty bad things to a lot of people," he blurted. "Some of 'em deserved it, some of 'em didn't. So I reckon it's right that I pay for what I done, and I don't hold it against you for just doin' your job. I mean it. I don't hold nothin' against you."

Will was almost stunned. His first reaction was suspicion. He found it difficult to believe the man was truly remorseful. This was a man who had shot Fletcher Pride in the back of the head and hung him from a tree to warn other lawmen. Will was sure he was up to something. "Well, I reckon that's something you'll have to work out between yourself and God—or the devil, whichever one you see first."

"I don't blame you for thinkin' I'm lyin'," Tarbow said. "It was just somethin' that needed sayin'. Maybe at least it was worth another cup of that coffee before I turn in."

"Well, yeah, sure," Will said, still unable to believe what was coming out of the mouth of the notorious murderer. "Set your cup down—you know how."

Tarbow was accustomed to the procedure the deputy had established to give him coffee or his plate of food. With the chain permitting him to get only so far from the wagon, his food was always placed on the ground just close enough to the end of the chain for him to reach out and pick it up. Will had seen no sense in taking any chances with the brute. Tarbow dutifully reached out and set his cup on the ground, so Will picked up the pot, leaned over, and started to fill it. Before he could straighten up, he was thrown off balance when Tarbow suddenly grabbed his arm and yanked him up against his massive chest. Caught completely by surprise, Will dropped the coffeepot, and fought to free himself, but Tarbow's huge hands were already locked around his neck. Will's only option was to pound away at the brute's midsection, but just as suddenly as he had attacked, Tarbow relaxed his stranglehold, and a split second later, Will heard the shot. An instant after that, he heard the second shot, and Tarbow's body sagged and slid to the ground.

It seemed longer, but only seconds passed as Will dived for his rifle on the other side of the fire and rolled out of the circle of firelight. With no time to figure the why of it, his concern now was to seek cover until he could determine where the rifle fire was coming from. So he crawled a few feet farther to a narrow gully carved in the side of the gulch. One look back at Tarbow told him that his prisoner was done for. The huge body lay still, where it had fallen. There were no more shots after the two that killed Tarbow, so Will had no idea if they had been attacked by one man or many. Their purpose was also a mystery. Maybe they were after the horses and whatever was in the wagon. If it was a planned assassination, then he had to assume that he had been the real target, and Tarbow had just been unfortunate to get in the way. He realized then that if Tarbow had not grabbed him, he would have been directly in the line of fire. It was his impression, although he could not be sure, that the shots had struck Tarbow at a flat trajectory. Consequently, he was led to guess that his assailants did not fire from the ridges on either side of him. So he concentrated his search on the mouth of the gulch, scanning back and forth across the dark void to pick up the muzzle flashes if more shots were fired.

Long minutes passed and still there were no more shots. Pinned down there in the dark, he could only wait until daylight unless he tried to go on the offensive and see if he could find his attackers. His safest option was probably to just stay put and wait them out, but he had never been one to sit and patiently wait for something to happen. He told himself to remain where he was for a few minutes longer to see if his assailants might try to move in closer to his camp. After several minutes ticked slowly by, he said to hell with it and crawled up the back of the gully to the top, then he crawled over the side onto the ridge. Making his way through the trees that covered the ridge, he moved as quickly as he dared while being cautious in case he met someone with the same idea that he had.

From his new position on the side of the slope, he could look back on his camp below him. There was still no sign of anyone advancing on the faint circle of firelight, so he continued on along the ridge until he reached a point that he estimated to be a little outside the decent range of a rifle. Then he made his way down through the trees to the bottom of the slope, where he dropped to one knee and paused to look around him. It was a good deal easier to see now that he was outside the dark gulch, but he saw no sign of anyone. He started to move in closer to his

camp when he was suddenly stopped by the sound of
a horse's hooves off to his left. He whirled at once,
cocking his rifle as he did, but saw no one. The sound
of the hoofbeats, fading away in the darkness, told
him that his assailant was only one, and he had evidently decided to break off the attack.

Standing there in the dark, Will tried to make
sense of the attack, and why the gunman had broken
off and retreated. The sight of a full moon just then
shining through the trees on top of the ridge behind
him might have had something to do with it. Maybe
the shooter feared he would be more easily seen
when the moon rose from behind the ridge. "Maybe,"
Will allowed. "But it looks like he's gone for now." He
turned after another look down the valley and walked
back to his camp.

"Well, I reckon you cheated the hangman's rope
after all," Will mused aloud as he stood looking down
at Tarbow's body. "Maybe I oughta thank you for
savin' my life." He shook his head, amazed now by
what had just taken place. "You damn near fell in the
fire." He grabbed the big man's boots and dragged
him back from the edge of the campfire. "I reckon
you might be lookin' at a helluva lot bigger fire right
about now, though." A puzzling thought occurred to
him then. "How the hell did you get that close to the
fire, anyway?" Curious now, he picked up the chain
to take a closer look. When he reached down to take
hold of it, he saw no difference. A few feet back, however, he saw a short stick jammed in one of the links.
Curious as to how it had managed to get there, he
examined the chain more closely and discovered another stick a couple of feet farther down. It struck

him then that an equal length of the chain could be doubled over, effectively making the chain two feet shorter. Tarbow had held it in place by jamming the two pieces of a stick between the links. And he probably did it while he was answering nature's call. *That's how he was able to grab me when I started to pour him some coffee*, Will thought. *The chain was two feet longer than I thought.* He had taken no notice of the doubled-up section of chain lying behind Tarbow in the darkness. He was reminded then of something Fletcher Pride had once told him. *In this business, you can think you're being careful when you're transporting felons, but it'll most likely be some little mistake that'll do you in.* "Well, Fletcher," Will said, "I reckon I just found that out." He pictured the good-natured grizzly nodding and chuckling in response.

Damn! Eli swore to himself as he whipped his horse for more speed. *That big one-eyed fool had to jump in the way.* He had the deputy marshal in his sights, and Tarbow had picked the exact moment he squeezed the trigger to lunge at the lawman. As quick as he could crank another cartridge in the chamber, he had fired again, hoping to hit Tanner, but hit Tarbow again. Now Tanner knew he was being stalked and it was bound to make killing him a whole lot harder. The thought of trying to work in closer to get another shot at him had entered Eli's mind, but the rising full moon caused him to reconsider. There was no sense in finding out if the deputy was a good shot the hard way. It was still a long way to Fort Smith. He would pick his spot more carefully next time.

* * *

As a precaution, Will pulled his horses in and tied them between the wagon and the side of the gulch. He had an idea that the shooter might not be back that night, but he didn't want to take any chances. He made his bed away from the campfire as a further precaution and kept his rifle by his side.

The night passed without incident, and the next morning he saddled Buster and made a little scout around the mouth of the gulch to make sure he was alone. After that, he looked for the spot he had gotten to the night before when he heard the shooter leave. Tracks he found verified what he had already surmised—this assassin was working alone. It was easy to see where he had tied his horse and where he had fired from. Two spent cartridges by a mound of dirt told him from where the man had actually fired. Will turned and sighted toward his wagon to see the target as the shooter had. He shouldn't have missed, if Tarbow hadn't made his move.

Back at the wagon, he stood looking at Tarbow's body for a few minutes, trying to decide what he should do. Somewhere out there a man with a rifle was evidently planning on killing him. For what reason, Will still didn't know. His inclination at this point was to leave the wagon and start tracking him, but he had to decide what to do about Tarbow. He had been determined to take the outlaw back to Fort Smith, no matter what. That's what he and Pride had been charged to do. It seemed especially important since Pride had been killed. There was also the matter of the large quantity of money he was carrying. He would feel a lot better after he turned that over to the court.

But now Tarbow had to go and get himself shot. If he hauled his body back in that wagon, it might take him six days to do it, and that corpse would get mighty ripe by that time. On the other hand, if he left the wagon and headed for Fort Smith on horseback, he could make it in three days, and probably less. It was a difficult decision to make. He had a fresh trail to follow if he set out to track the gunman right away. However, he was hampered by the fact that he had not a clue who the gunman was or why he attempted to shoot him. There was always the possibility that the man had just happened upon him and thought it an opportunity to steal four horses and whatever was in the wagon. The problem he had to consider was, if he went after him and lost his trail, he would have wasted valuable time that would have been spent packing Tarbow's body to Fort Smith. *I'll probably never see that shooter again*, he thought finally. *I'd best get started before Tarbow gets really ripe.*

He put Tarbow's saddle on the blue roan the outlaw had ridden and loaded his body across it, along with some firearms and ammunition he had collected. The other horses that had pulled the wagon were again loaded with packs. He stepped up into the saddle and took one last look around him to remember where he had left the wagon. He was thinking that maybe, when he reached Fort Smith, someone could telegraph Atoka Station to tell Jim Little Eagle where it was. Glad to be rid of it then, he turned the buckskin to the northeast and headed for Fort Smith. He was leading his string of three horses, one of which carried a grotesquely awkward load across the saddle. Since it had been almost nine hours since Tarbow's death, his body was already stiff. Wrapped in a canvas sheet, it had given Will a devilish chore to secure it on the horse. The trail he set out on was a well-traveled one, and was the very track on which he, Pride, and Charlie Tate had traveled to Atoka. Unknown to Will, his choice of trails was of particular interest to the man watching him from a ridge a mile away.

Eli was satisfied to see that the deputy seemed intent upon following the Jack Fork Mountain trail. He knew that trail well. There were any number of places along it to wait in ambush. It would not be easy, however, because Tanner had left the wagon and was pushing his horses to maintain a fast pace. Eli could see that he was going to have to ride hard to keep up with him.

CHAPTER 12

Will had made good time during the morning, holding the horses to a steady pace for what he estimated to be about twenty-five miles. It was time to let them rest, so he was glad when he came to a small creek south of the Jack Fork Mountains. He was hoping to make fifty miles that first day, but it would depend on the condition of his packhorses after the morning segment. He already knew that Buster was up to it, and the roan seemed to be just fine. Of course, everything depended on the packhorses. If they didn't hold up, he'd have to stop sooner than he wanted to.

Following the creek for fifty yards or so, he came to what he considered a good spot to rest the horses. There was a small grassy clearing in the cottonwoods that lined both banks of the creek that would provide grass for grazing. The south bank formed a chest-high bluff where the creek took a sharp bend to the north. He decided that to be the best place to build a fire to cook something for himself, since the bluff would provide good cover in the event he might suddenly need it. Although he had tried to constantly keep a sharp eye on the trail ahead of him, there had been nothing to arouse his suspicions. And the farther he had ridden without any sign of trouble, the more he suspected the attack of the night before was a random act by a would-be horse thief—and he most likely had not known whom he was shooting at. That made more sense, anyway, for he hadn't been a deputy long enough to have made any enemies besides Max Tarbow's gang. And they were all dead. Still, it was always a good idea to keep a sharp eye for trouble of any sort. There were a great many outlaws of all kinds hiding out in Indian Territory. It had not stuck in his mind that one of the men killed on this mission had been Lem Stark's son Jeb.

He took the saddle off his horse and unloaded the packhorses. Since Tarbow had gone into full rigor mortis, his body was stiff as a pine log, and because of his size, was just about as heavy. Will led the horse over to a tree, untied the body, and let it slide off. Holding it upright, he leaned it up against the tree. That way, when it was time to load it up again, he could simply let the body fall across his shoulder, making it much easier to shift it from his shoulder to the horse's back. It wasn't a big thing, but it did eliminate having to lift the dead weight up from the ground. As he pulled the saddle off, he was about to compliment himself for being innovative when he was startled by the first shot.

A chunk of bark flew by his face as the rifle slug buried in the trunk and the heavy report of a Henry rifle sang out across the creek. With no time for thinking, Will dived to the ground as a second and third shot snapped sharply as they passed overhead. "Damn!" Will exclaimed in anger. "That son of a bitch ain't gonna give up!" He rolled over until he got the tree between him and where he thought the shots were coming from. Then he scurried backward on his hands and knees while the rifle shots continued to snap and whine all about him. The problem facing him now was that his rifle was still in his saddle sling, and the saddle was on the ground about fifteen feet from him in the clearing. He was pretty sure the shooter was firing blindly now, just hoping to get lucky, for Will knew he couldn't see him because of the tree. *But as soon as I make a run for my rifle, he'll see me*, he thought.

Then, as suddenly as it had started, the shooting stopped. *Empty magazine?* Will wondered. How many shots had been fired? He had been too busy trying to keep from getting killed to think about counting the shots. The silence was suddenly deafening. He hesitated for only a couple of seconds more before he made a dash for his rifle, hoping he could cover the distance to his saddle and back before his assailant could reload his rifle. He made it to his saddle and was almost back under cover before a bullet kicked dirt up between his feet. "The bastard didn't load the whole magazine," he complained, as if there were rules to the deadly game.

Armed with his rifle now, and with a good idea where the shots were coming from, Will dropped over the lip of the creek and made his way to the bend in the creek where the bank was higher. As soon as he settled in against the sandy bank, he brought his Winchester to bear on a small cluster of trees atop a low rise about one hundred and fifty yards away. Sighting on one side of the cluster, he squeezed off the first shot, then walked the Winchester across the width of it, a few feet at a time, until the magazine was empty. Then he reloaded and reversed the volley, starting from the other side, intending to make it too hot for his adversary to stay in the trees.

Dismayed by the hailstorm of return fire he had incited, Eli Stark hugged the ground behind a scrub oak while the series of rifle slugs snapped the leaves over his head. In his excitement to kill Will while he was in the open, unloading his horses, he had hurried his shot, and consequently missed. In frustration then, he tried to fire as fast as he could, thinking one of his shots would find the target. Now he was getting the same volley from the deputy, and he immediately regretted choosing the clump of smallish scrub oaks for his cover. He was reluctant to continue firing at the creek bank for fear that Will might pinpoint his position in the oaks and concentrate his fire on that spot. His decision to retreat was made for him when a bullet clipped a large limb directly over his head and dropped it across his back. Bitter with the taste of his second defeat in his attempt to avenge his brother and grab the bank money, he dragged himself backward to the edge of the trees and ran down the rise to his horse.

From the protection of the creek bank, Will fired four shots in a circular pattern, centering on what appeared to be the thickest part of the clump, then waited for the sniper's response. Several minutes passed with no further return fire, causing Will to wonder if one of the shots had found the target. He was not of a mind to climb up on the bank, however, in case it was a ploy to lure him out in the open. Half a minute later, he saw a rider gallop up from the swale behind the rise, then disappear again into the hills behind it. Fully half a mile away by that time, Will could not get a close enough look at the man's face to remember it again. All he could tell was that he appeared to be dressed all in black, including his hat, and the horse he rode was black as well. "That son of a bitch!" Will blurted, afraid he was going to get away again. Holding his rifle in one hand, he ran to the horses. With no time to saddle him, he jumped on Buster's back and gave him his heels. Galloping up from the creek, the big buckskin responded faithfully, even though already tired from a hard ride that morning.

As he swept past the knoll from which the sniper had fired, Will tried to make sense of his adversary's second attempt to kill him. If it were the horses he was out to steal, why didn't he just try to slip in during the night and drive them off—and leave him on foot with no means to give pursuit? This thief was intent upon killing him. There had to be a reason, and he had to wonder if the gunman somehow knew that he was carrying a large amount of stolen money. These thoughts only added to his consternation, so he returned his focus to the job at hand. If he caught the son of a bitch, maybe his questions would be answered.

Totally absorbed in his burning desire to catch his would-be assassin, and lost in the steady rhythm of Buster's thundering hoofbeats on the hard ground, he forgot that the big buckskin was already in need of rest. Not until the faithful horse broke stride for just a moment did Will realize his negligence and rein him back to lope, and then to walk. "I'm sorry, boy," he apologized, realizing that he was asking the horse for more than the animal was capable of giving. And knowing his horse as well as he did, he had no doubt that Buster would have run himself to death. He had no alternative other than to dismount and give up the chase. As he walked back to his camp, he couldn't help wondering if he was going to be constantly assaulted every step of the way to Fort Smith, or at least until one of them managed to shoot the other.

Lying in ambush at the top of a low hill, Eli Stark waited for the hated lawman to ride up out of the swale he had just raced across. Unknown by the deputy, Eli had been faced with the same problem that caused him to break off the chase. Eli's horse was weary, too, having been ridden just as hard as Will's horses in an effort to keep up with them. The big Morgan had finally faltered while climbing the low hill where Eli now lay in wait. When he had retreated from his position in the scrub oaks, he had not planned to wait for Will to catch up with him. But the condition of his horse had made that decision for him. When he thought about it, it was the perfect setup to achieve his goal, so he was genuinely disappointed when Will suddenly broke off his pursuit. Apparently the deputy was planning to continue on the common wagon trail to Fort Smith, so Eli decided to try to parallel the trail and make another attempt when Will stopped for the night.

Will was pretty much of the same thinking as his adversary, and his patience was rapidly running out. He was feeling akin to a target in a shooting gallery, and sooner or later he was going to get hit. This jasper who was after him was going to keep up with him and keep picking places to dry-gulch him. He had an almost overwhelming desire to forget everything else and hunt the shooter down. That thought caused him to take a look at the awkward canvas bundle leaning against the tree. "If it wasn't for your sorry ass," he blurted, "I wouldn't have to hurry." He was still determined to deliver Tarbow's corpse to Fort Smith before it began to rot, but he was convinced that, if he stayed on his present course, the gunman would be waiting to take another shot. The only choice he saw was to leave the common trail and try to lose the gunman, so when his horses were rested again, he struck out farther north toward the Sans Bois Mountains. He couldn't be sure if his assassin was watching him, but he figured he'd find out soon enough.

He started out on a course across a rolling terrain where there were no trails of any kind, his string of horses behind him. A question that came to him then concerned the grotesque canvas bundle lying across one of the horses. He wasn't sure how long a body remained in that awkward stiff state, but he knew that it wasn't forever. And he guessed that when it lost the stiffness, that would be the time it would become putrid. Changing directions now was going to add a little time to his journey, but he hoped not enough to make much difference in the condition of the evidence he was trying so hard to deliver.

As the afternoon advanced, he began to believe that he had, in fact, lost his stalker, at least temporarily. He was riding across a wide valley that permitted him to see a fairly long distance on either side of him, and all afternoon he had spotted no one. Now, as the sun began to settle down on the horizon behind him, he looked for a place to camp that might offer some cover. So he turned his horse toward the low foothills that approached the Sans Bois Mountains. With a little luck, he might find a stream coming down from the mountains, hopefully before riding much farther, because his horses were needing rest. He had pushed them hard again, but the terrain had not been rough on them.

A couple of miles farther on brought him in sight of a double line of small trees and bushes, which indicated a stream coming down out of the hills. When he reached it, he decided to follow it back up into the hills a little way in search of a good place to camp. It didn't take long before he found what looked to be the place he was hoping for. The stream led him to the mouth of a ravine leading up a low foothill about half a mile from the base of the closest mountain. There was plenty of grass for the horses at the mouth and protection provided by the trees on the steep sides of the ravine.

It was his feeling that his stalker had not been within eyesight of him all afternoon, because he had not sighted anyone trailing him ever since he changed directions. He hoped that the shooter was searching for him along the common road, and if that was so, he'd have to be mighty lucky to find him in this ravine. Looking toward the back part of the ravine, he could see that it ran quite a long way before it closed to a point. In fact, he couldn't actually see the end of it.

He unloaded his horses, stood Tarbow up against another tree, then left the horses to graze by the mouth of the ravine while he gathered kindling to start a fire. By the time the sun disappeared behind the hills, Will had coffee ready and sowbelly strips cooking over the fire. He had the means to make pan bread, but lacked the initiative to bother with it, especially since there was a killer roaming around hoping to get a clear shot at him. As darkness started to settle into the hills, he went out and brought the horses into the narrow part of the ravine behind his campfire. He was about to return to the fire to have another cup of coffee when Buster whinnied, and his ears flickered nervously. One of the other horses answered with a whinny also. Will became immediately alert; he had always paid attention to the buckskin's awareness of other creatures. Most of the time it was the appearance of another horse, or a coyote or wolf skulking about, and nothing to cause Will concern. But under the circumstances of the day just passed, he was not prone to take chances. So instead of returning to the campfire, he quickly drew his rifle from his saddle scabbard and climbed up the side of the ravine to seek a position over his camp.

In a few moments, he saw a figure in the dark

mouth of the ravine approaching cautiously. This was a departure from his stalker's usual routine of sniping from a distance. Will raised the Winchester up against his shoulder and laid the front sight on the shadowy form and waited for his visitor to make the next move. To Will's surprise, his visitor did not advance any farther. Instead, he suddenly called out, "Hello, the camp!"

Not inclined to believe the man was merely an out-of-work cowhand riding the grub line and seeing an opportunity for some coffee and maybe a little food, Will did not respond. For one thing, the man was on foot, so Will carefully made his way down the side of the ravine until he was directly behind the man, who was now straining to look into the camp, even to the point of standing on his tiptoes in an effort to get a better look. "There's a Winchester rifle aimed right between your shoulder blades," Will announced matter-of-factly. "Make one move and it'll be your last."

"Whoa!" the man yelped and jumped, almost stumbling. "Don't shoot! I was just lookin' for a cup of that coffee I smelled from back yonder. I didn't mean to cause you no trouble. Just take it easy with that rifle, and I'll be on my way."

"Do what I tell you and you won't get hurt," Will said, having already determined that it was not the man dressed in black he had seen riding away after the ambush. "Let's take a walk over by that fire, so I can take a look at you."

"Yes, sir," his visitor immediately replied, "whatever

you say. I ain't out to cause you no trouble." He went at once to stand by the fire, so Will could see him.

"Where the hell did you come from?" Will asked, since there was no sign of a horse or wagon. A short man with a face full of curly white whiskers, he wore no weapon on his hip and carried no rifle.

"Back yonder," the man said, pointing toward the top of the ravine. "I got me a domicile on the back-side of this hill, and I was just wantin' to see who was makin' a camp right on my front doorstep. My name's Perley Gates. I've been outta coffee for over a month and I've got a powerful cravin' for some. I've been watchin' you make camp and when you fired up that coffeepot, I swear, I had to come on down. I ain't sure if you're one of them outlaws that hole up in that cave up there in the mountains or not. But I ain't got nothin' worth stealin', so I figured it was worth a try. Are you an outlaw on the run? 'Cause if you are, and you're lookin' for that cave, I can tell you how to get there. It ain't but about three miles yonder way." He pointed toward the top of the ravine again.

"I'm a U.S. Deputy Marshal," Will said, and pulled his vest aside far enough to show his badge. Perley's reaction was a serious nod. Will couldn't resist asking, "Perley Gates—is that your real name?"

"Yes, sir, Marshal, Mama Gates gave me the name of Perley, all right. It sounds like that one in the Bible, just spelled different."

Will could see no threat in the elflike man, so he could see no harm in sharing some coffee with him. "All right, Perley, pour yourself a cup of coffee." He picked up his coffee cup, emptied it, and tossed it to Perley.

Perley wasted no time filling the cup. He backed a foot or two away from the fire and sipped the hot black liquid noisily. "Ahh," he moaned. "I swear, that's mighty fine coffee." He sipped some more, then asked, "Mind if I set?"

"No, go ahead and set," Will said, and Perley crossed his feet and sat down Indian style. "You want something to eat?" Will asked. He figured the strange little man was a wandering beggar and most likely had not eaten in a while.

"Thank you kindly, but I've done et," Perley replied. "If I'da knowed you was a lawman, and not one of them outlaws, I'da brung you a slab off of a deer haunch I kilt this mornin'. I reckon I can still bring you some, if you want it." He nursed a little more coffee out of the hot tin cup, then asked, "What are you doin' in these parts, Marshal, chasin' somebody?"

"Tell you the truth, Perley, right now I'm bein' chased," Will said.

"Come again?" Perley replied.

"I said I'm bein' chased," Will repeated.

"By who?"

"That's the problem," Will said. "I don't know who. All I know is he's wearin' all black clothes and rides a black horse."

"Eli Stark," Perley blurted at once.

"Who?" Will asked, immediately interested.

"Eli Stark don't wear nothin' but black outfits," Perley said. "They match his black heart—meaner man ain't never been born."

Eli Stark, Will repeated to himself, *Lem Stark's eldest son*. Pride had asked the old man where Eli was, and Lem said he was long gone from this territory. Everything started to make sense now. Eli was out for vengeance because he thought Will killed his brother. Perley might be right—his stalker could be Eli Stark. The irony of it was that Will didn't kill Jeb Stark. One of Tarbow's men killed him in a duel. Will shot the man who killed Jeb. *He ought to be trying to thank me for killing his brother's killer*, he thought, *instead of taking potshots at me*. Pride had told him that Eli was long gone from Indian Territory. He wondered how Eli had gotten the news that his brother was dead. Maybe, he thought, news travels fast among outlaws, like it does with Indians. More likely Eli had been back in the Nations for quite a while. Turning his attention back to Perley, he asked, "When was the last time you saw Eli Stark?"

Perley shrugged. "I don't know. Two or three months ago, I reckon. I try not to see him if I can help it. Last time, if I recollect, was when I was huntin' about two miles west of here. I was pretty close to a trail that leads up to that cave in the rocks, and I saw Eli on that black Morgan he rides, comin' down that trail. He didn't see me, so I stayed hid till he passed on by. He ain't never give me no real trouble, but it don't pay to hang around him on account of his hair-trigger temper." He shook his head thoughtfully, then asked, "What's he chasin' after you for—just 'cause you're a lawman?"

"He thinks I shot his brother," Will answered.

"Jeb?" Perley responded. "I ain't heard that Jeb

was dead. I never saw him before, but I've heared tell of him. Did you shoot him?"

"No, but I would have if I'd had to," Will replied frankly. "It was one of the men he was ridin' with that shot him. What is this cave you keep talkin' about?"

Perley hesitated before answering, thinking that maybe he had already said too much about the secret hideout for the few outlaws that knew of its location. "You ain't gonna tell nobody I told you about it, are you? 'Cause, like I said, Eli and some of them others ain't bothered me none, but if some of 'em was to find out I told a lawman about it, they might do a little more than just bother me a little." After Will assured him that he wouldn't tell, Perley continued. "I stumbled across that cave fifteen years ago. Solid rock all around it. I was chasin' a doe I'd shot a little farther down the mountain, and she led me up to this openin' to a cave in the stone side of the mountain, and she ran in the mouth of it. I figured I had her trapped in there. That cave ran a good forty feet back into the mountain, and when I got to the end of it, she was gone. Come to find out, there was a back door to it, and she slipped out of it."

"And you say it's a hideout for outlaws?" Will pressed.

"Like I said, there ain't many people that know about it," Perley said. "After the war, a few army deserters hid out there, but after that a few outlaws on the run found it, and they've been usin' it ever since. It's hard to beat for a hideout, hard to find and easy to defend, and there's a spring of fresh water runnin' right through it. If you ain't wantin' to defend it, there's a hidden door out the back. It's even got a natural stone corral at the bottom of the cliff to keep your horses safe."

"You think Eli Stark is hidin' out there now?" Will asked.

"I don't know for sure. I ain't been up to the cave in quite a spell, but I wouldn't be a bit surprised if he ain't."

Will paused while he thought about the possibility that Eli had been hiding out in the mountains above Perley's camp. It wasn't likely that he was up there now, since he had been trailing him ever since he had left Atoka. He glanced at the awkward bundle leaning against a pine tree and reminded himself of his priorities at the present time. Pride had told him that there were arrest warrants out for Eli from both Kansas and Missouri for murder and robbery. He would do well to scout this outlaw's cave out, but only after he was successful in delivering Max Tarbow and the stolen money to Fort Smith. Eli would have to wait, he decided. Complete this job first, then think about Eli. There was a strong possibility that Eli was going to pick up his trail again. There was no doubt that he knew he was heading to Fort Smith. But if he did manage to get there without getting shot, he was damn sure going to return to look for Eli, whether Marshal Stone kept him on as a deputy or not. And he still considered the possibility he might not because of the heavy loss of lives suffered on his first official assignment. Perley could lead him to that cave Eli had been using as a hideout.

Perley had not missed Will's pensive glance at the large canvas bundle leaning against the pine. He drained his coffee and asked, "You mind if I have another cup of that coffee?" Will said that he didn't, to help himself if there was any left in the pot, so Perley emptied it. "Much obliged," he said, and set the empty pot away from the coals. "Ain't none of my business, but what's in that big bundle standin' up against that tree?"

"A gentleman named Max Tarbow," Will said. "And I figure I've got about a day and a half to two days to get him to the undertaker at Fort Smith before he starts to spoil."

"My stars . . ." Perley gasped. "What did he do?"

"A helluva lot," Will replied, "and all of it bad. For one thing, one of his men killed Jeb Stark, and that's why Eli's doggin' my trail. He thinks I did it."

"Max Tarbow." Perley pronounced the name slowly. "I ain't never heared of him. How long's he been dead?"

"Since about this time last night," Will said. "I was takin' him in for trial, but your friend Eli took a shot at me and hit Tarbow instead. And now I'm tryin' to get him to Fort Smith while he's still in some kinda shape to identify him."

"Eli ain't no friend of mine," Perley quickly corrected. "Eli ain't got no friends." He got up and walked up next to the body. "He was a big feller, warn't he? Why don't you just bury him, instead of haulin' him all the way to Fort Smith? Hell, I'll help you dig a hole." Will explained that he wanted the marshal, and anybody else that needed to verify it, to get a look at the corpse before it started to putrefy. He didn't confess that he was a new deputy marshal, this was his first experience transporting a corpse, and he wasn't sure they'd take his word that he had arrested Max Tarbow if he buried his body. So he wasn't taking any chances on their doubting it.

Intrigued by the challenge of transporting the corpse in time now, Perley scratched his whiskers as he contemplated the problem. "And you say he's been dead since last night this time?" Will nodded. "That's twenty-four hours, ain't it?" Perley went on. "How long you figure it's gonna take you to ride from here to Fort Smith?"

"I'm hopin' a day and a half," Will answered, "providin' I can stay ahead of Eli Stark."

"That'd put him dead two and a half days," Perley said. "That's cuttin' it pretty close. I killed a deer one time a year or two ago and didn't get back to butcher it till two days later. I remember that meat had already started to turn. I ate it, anyway. I had a god-awful bellyache and the gallopin' shits for a whole day after that. But the meat didn't taste bad atall, kinda sweet, as a matter of fact. Now that I recollect, though, I had tried to drink a whole gallon jug of moonshine corn whiskey I'd got hold of. It mighta had somethin' to do with my sick belly. Come to think of it, it was the reason I didn't get back to butcher that deer for two days." He shook his head and chuckled just thinking about it. "I don't know, son . . ." He paused. "What is your name, Marshal?"

"Will Tanner."

"Pleased to meet you. I don't know, Will," he went on. "Like I said, you might be cuttin' it pretty close. If it was winter, wouldn't be no problem, but it ain't cold enough to keep meat from turnin'." He changed the subject abruptly. "Speakin' of meat, how 'bout that deer meat I offered? You want some?"

Will couldn't help grinning, almost forgetting the hazardous circumstances he found himself in. He was fascinated by the little man's unbridled rambling. It occurred to him that Perley seldom ran into another human being to talk to, so he probably wasn't aware that he was rattling on so. "I'm thinkin' you live alone," Will said.

"I reckon I do," Perley replied. "How'd you figure that?"

"Just a lucky guess," Will answered.

"I lived with a Choctaw woman for the better part of three years," Perley said. "She was a fine cook, ugly as homemade sin, but I reckon that's the only reason she moved in with me in the first place. It's been a little over a year now since she run off with a Chickasaw buck. He wasn't no more particular than I was, I reckon, and he was a lot younger 'n me, so she took off. I expect I'da gone after her if she was a little better-lookin'. I miss her cookin', though." He paused for a moment, obviously recalling the woman, then he asked, "How 'bout you? You got a wife at home somewhere?"

"Nope," Will answered at once. "No wife." For no reason he could explain, his thoughts went immediately to the last image he had of Sophie Bennett and her proper suitor. *The young law clerk, what was his name—Garth something?* She'd probably be fairly amused to think he had thoughts of her. He silently chided himself for cluttering his mind with meaningless thoughts when he had considerably more to concern himself with. "I appreciate the offer of some deer meat," he said, returning to Perley's question. "But I've got plenty of supplies in those packs, includin' a couple of sacks of coffee beans. How 'bout I leave you one of 'em?"

"Why, I surely would thank you for that," Perley replied. "I ain't got nothin' to trade for it right now, except some of that deer meat."

"You don't need to trade for it," Will said. "I've got some extra, and you can owe me a favor sometime. That'll be a fair trade." He was thinking that he would call on him to lead him to the outlaws' cave he had talked about.

"I can do you one small favor right away, if you're still set on gettin' that carcass to Fort Smith in a day and a half—might cut a little time offa your trip," Perley said, capturing Will's interest right away. "I expect you're thinkin' 'bout cuttin' back to the wagon road to Fort Smith when you leave here in the mornin'."

"I thought I would," Will said, "after I get past the Sans Bois. I only cut up through here to try to lose that jasper tailin' me."

"That's what I figured," Perley said. "I know an old Injun trail that the Choctaws used to ride between their villages. It ain't got so many turns and bends as the wagon road, and the wagon road takes a wide swing to the south 'cause it has to find a place to ford the river. It'll save you a little time. And maybe ol' Eli's waitin' for you to show up on the wagon road somewhere down the line."

"That sounds good to me," Will said. He was thinking that it might have been a real stroke of luck to run into Perley Gates. "I'm plannin' on bein' in the saddle before sunup in the mornin'. I'm not gonna eat breakfast till I have to stop to rest the horses."

"That's all right," Perley said. "I'll be back here before sunup to lead you through the hills to strike the Choctaw trail. It might be a little hard for you to find it in the dark. It don't look like much more 'n a game trail till you get outta the trees in these hills. That's 'cause that's what it is, a game trail." He got up then to rinse Will's coffee cup in the stream. Handing it back to him, he said, "I expect I'd best get along now. I'll be back to get you in the mornin'." Will went to his packs to find the sack of coffee beans he had offered. When he gave them to Perley, he thanked the simple little man for his help.

"No trouble atall," Perley replied.

CHAPTER 13

Just as he had promised, Perley showed up riding a mule before dawn while Will was still loading his horses. When it came time to load Tarbow's body on the horse, Perley offered to help, but Will said he had a loading procedure that worked out fine. "But it would help if you'd hold that horse steady while I load him. Sometimes he gets a little skittish."

"I reckon so," Perley replied with a chuckle. He took the blue roan's bridle in hand and watched as Will tilted the bizarre package away from the tree and onto his shoulder. "I swear," he exclaimed. "That feller's a load, ain't he? How long's he gonna stay stiff like that?"

"I don't know," Will grunted as he dropped the corpse across the saddle and quickly looped a rope around the end of it. "But it sure makes it a hard load to tie on." He passed the other end of the rope over to Perley when he reached for it. "He'll bend a little bit when I draw down on this rope, but he don't want to."

When he was ready to go, Perley got on his mule

and led the procession straight up the ravine toward
the top. Will wondered if he knew where he was
going, because the ravine appeared to end at a solid
rock wall. He had walked halfway up it when he
drove his horses in behind his camp the night
before. When he had seen the rock wall, he felt assured that no one would be able to sneak into his
camp from above him. Now he was beginning to
wonder if he should have walked all the way up to the
wall. A few minutes later, he chided himself for being
careless, because when Perley reached the rock face,
he turned his mule sharply to the right and followed
a narrow path down the side of the hill. Will realized
then that this must have been the way Perley came
into his camp the night before. Not willing to risk
getting shot, he must have made his way down
through the trees on the side of the ravine, so he
could approach the camp from the mouth. He had
been on foot, so his camp should not be too far away.
That question was answered a few minutes later
when the little man called back over his shoulder
when they reached a small meadow at the bottom of
the hill. "This here's my domicile. If you warn't in
such a hurry, I'd invite you in." Will looked all
around him for a few seconds before he spotted a
rough log cabin backed up against the foot of another hill on the other side of the meadow. On one
side of the cabin, a partially enclosed shed was attached, no doubt for Perley's mule. A thought occurred to Will that it seemed highly unlikely Perley
could have smelled his campfire, much less the
coffee, deep down in this valley.

Perley continued to lead him along a narrow

valley that wound snakelike through a series of hills until finally arriving on an open prairie, where he pulled his mule to a stop and waited for Will to pull up beside him. "I reckon I'll let you go on from here." He pointed to a low ridge, barely visible in the predawn light, about five or six miles in the distance. "If you'll just put your nose on that ridge yonder and follow it, you oughta strike that Choctaw trail on the other side of the ridge. It'll run right along the foot of it. Stay on that trail and it'll lead you to a wide creek. That's gonna be about twenty miles from here. Just follow the creek and it'll take you to the Poteau River. You'll still see the old Choctaw trail running along that creek. When you strike the Poteau, you won't be but about twenty-five or thirty miles from Fort Smith."

Will reached over and offered his hand. "Much obliged, Perley, I 'preciate your help. I'm plannin' to come back this way before long. Maybe I'll bring you another sack of coffee beans."

"That'd be mighty fine," Perley said. "You take care of yourself, young feller. Keep a sharp eye."

"You do the same," Will said, and gave Buster a little nudge with his heels.

Perley reined his mule back when it started to follow the string of horses, then he sat there for a long while watching the young lawman's progress, his three horses trailing along behind him—one of them carrying the odd bundle. "Nice young feller," he commented to his mule when the horses started to fade in the darkness. "I hope he lasts longer than a lot of those deputy marshals riding Indian Territory." He turned the mule then to return to his cabin as he thought of making himself a fresh pot of coffee.

Riding across a rolling prairie that gradually took shape as the sun finally made an appearance on the eastern horizon, Will approached the ridge that he had set his course on. Directly ahead of him, there was a narrow gap that looked to be a good place to cross over to the other side. When he entered the gap, he stopped and dismounted, left the horses there, and went on foot to the top of the ridge to have a look around him. Checking his back trail first, he looked back as far as he could see. There was no one in sight. Looking ahead of him into the sun, the results were the same—no one in sight. He felt reasonably sure that his stalker had not been able to determine his route, so he returned to his horses and continued on through the gap to the creek.

Upon reaching the creek, which was as easily identified as Perley had predicted, he pushed his horses on for another five miles or so before looking for a place to rest them. He picked a spot where there was a meadow about fifty yards wide with cottonwood trees on both sides. It suited him just fine. He unloaded the horses in the trees, then turned them out to drink and graze while he built his fire where he could watch them from the protection of the trees. When he was satisfied that his horses were ready to go again, he loaded up and continued following the trail beside the creek, planning to camp for the night when he reached the Poteau.

With still no sign of Eli Stark, he pushed on until

sunset, when he reached the Poteau River. Although there had been no threat for the entire distance between the Sans Bois Mountains and the river he now approached, he saw no reason to relax his vigilance, so he selected his campsite accordingly. Having come this far, he was more determined than ever to finish the task he had started. There appeared to be a trading post at the confluence of the creek and the river, but he chose to skirt it, preferring not to let his presence be known. As long as he was still in the Nations, he trusted very few people. It was best not to let people know he was hauling a corpse into Fort Smith. So he led his string of horses along the river for another mile or so before going into camp in the trees on the bank.

When he began to unload his horses, he was surprised to discover the ropes tying Tarbow on the horse had gone slack, and the body was now hanging relaxed. He at once thought of putrefaction. How much time did he have before Mr. Tarbow was going to make his presence offensive to the nose? So far, there was no offensive odor, but he had half a day's ride to Fort Smith, and the horses needed rest after a long day's work.

The night passed peacefully enough, a fact he attributed to the short distance it was to Fort Smith. It made sense that Eli might not be bold enough to risk an attack on a deputy marshal this close to the marshal's headquarters. Now, with only half a day's ride left, and still no offensive odors from his traveling companion, he loaded his horses and prepared to complete his journey. With one foot in the stirrup, he was suddenly spun around when the .44 slug slammed into his shoulder. Down he went with the toe of his boot still caught in the stirrup. The sound of the rifle shot startled his horse, causing the buckskin to jump to the side, dragging Will several feet before his boot came free of the stirrup. He heard the scream of the packhorse when it was hit by a couple of slugs from the barrage of shots that followed.

With no time to think, Will reacted instantly, rolling over the edge of a four-foot bluff that bordered the river. He drew his Colt .44 and lay flat on his back on the sandy river bank. His left shoulder, numb after the bullet's impact, was now throbbing painfully, and there was nothing he could do to stop the bleeding, or even to know how bad it was. From his position on his back, he could not see above the low bluff to determine where the shooter was, and he scolded himself for having gotten so careless. Eli had evidently finally gotten onto his trail, and must have ridden through the night to overtake him. With a trail hard to see at night, he must have gambled on the probability that he would strike the Poteau somewhere close to the trading post at the confluence of the creek and the river.

Well, I can't just lie here on my back and wait for him to come finish it, he thought. But before he could roll over on his side, he heard the horse's hooves on the bluff above him. A moment later he looked up at the smirking face of Eli Stark. The vengeance-seeking assassin leered down at him from the saddle of the dark Morgan gelding. Hesitating a moment to gloat was Eli's mistake, for Will's pistol was already cocked and in hand. Lying on his back, he was not that accurate with his pistol. His first shot grazed Eli's neck, but the second struck him just below his collarbone. Eli jerked violently on the Morgan's reins in an attempt to escape the deadly fire from under the bluff.

It was clear now that the advantage had changed sides, so Will ignored his wounded shoulder and scrambled to his feet to send two more shots after the retreating gunman. The range was already too great for Will's pistol, so he missed with both shots, but it was enough to convince Eli that he should best save his bacon. The amount of bleeding he was suffering from his wounded shoulder, plus the stinging gash across the side of his neck made him fear he was badly wounded. His thoughts in this moment of panic were that it was critical that he get his wounds doctored, and that meant to ride to his father's place in Tishomingo.

Will stood watching the dark assassin galloping away along the riverbank until he was sure he showed no sign of circling back. Then he turned to look at the horse lying mortally wounded behind his buckskin, the lead rope holding the horse's head up as Buster stepped back and forth nervously. "That son of a bitch," he muttered under his breath to see the horse suffering. He had reason enough to go after Eli Stark already. This was just one more. He reloaded his Colt and walked over to calm Buster down. Then he stroked the dying horse's face for a few moments before holding the .44 up close to its head and pulling the trigger, causing the other horses to start.

After calming them down, he untied the lead rope from the back of his saddle and redistributed the load among the two remaining horses, with some of it tied to the saddle bearing Tarbow's body. Only then did he pause to assess the damage to his shoulder. There was a good deal of bleeding that had soaked his left shirtsleeve, but not enough to overly concern him. He figured to heal rapidly, and then his priority was to go after Eli Stark, whether in an official capacity or on his own.

It was a little past noon when Will walked his horses down the street that fronted the courthouse, glad to complete his journey and anxious to rid himself of his unpleasant cargo. Upstairs, Marshal Dan Stone stood at his office window, looking down at the street, his curiosity having been aroused by the sight of a single rider leading two horses with what looked like a body draped across the saddle of one of them. As the rider drew closer, Stone took a harder look. "Look at this," he said, calling Ed Pine over to the window. "That's my new deputy, isn't it?"

Ed, who had been in Stone's office the day Will was signed on as a deputy, took a look and replied, "Yep, that's him, but I don't see Pride nowhere."

The two lawmen leaped to the same conclusion when they saw the body draped across the saddle on the blue roan. Stone was the first to say it. "Fletcher Pride," he said in utter shock, thinking the body was that of the big deputy. "This is something I hoped I'd never see."

"I never believed it would ever happen," Ed Pine

lamented. "Just never believed it." They both hurried out the door and headed for the stairs. Outside, they were in time to stand waiting when Will pulled the horses to a stop before the steps, realizing only then that Will was wounded.

"Damn, boy," Stone blurted, "you need a doctor."

"I'll be all right," Will said. "It can wait till after I get rid of him."

"Pride?" Stone responded curtly, thinking the young deputy's tone a little brusque, considering the respect he thought Fletcher Pride deserved.

"Fletcher Pride's dead," Will said. "Shot in the back of the head by that son of a bitch lyin' across that saddle. I buried Pride and Charlie Tate at the foot of a hill in the Arbuckle Mountains."

"Damn," Stone responded soberly. "Who is that?" He walked over to take a look at the corpse.

"Max Tarbow," Will said, "the outlaw you sent Pride and me after."

"What about the rest of the gang?" Stone asked. "Are they still on the run?"

"No, sir, they're all dead," Will said. "Max's brother, Billy, and the three fellers ridin' with 'em. I never learned their names."

"All five of the gang dead?" Ed Pine felt compelled to ask. "None of 'em wanted to surrender?"

"Nope. Tarbow didn't want to surrender, either, but I had him under arrest, and I was bringin' him back in the wagon. I didn't kill him. He was shot by Eli Stark when Eli took a shot at me and hit Tarbow instead."

"Eli Stark?" Stone exchanged a look of astonishment

with Ed, then asked Will, "You're saying he was shot by Eli Stark?" Will nodded.

"Who shot you?" Stone asked.

"Eli Stark," Will replied.

Stone went on. "Eli Stark has been wanted for murder and robbery in Kansas and Missouri, and you're telling me he's back in Indian Territory?" Will nodded again. "You're gonna have to explain the whole thing to me," Stone went on. "Start at the beginning and take me through what happened step by step."

Will did as Stone requested, telling him everything that had occurred. When he had finished, he told him why he had returned with the corpse of Max Tarbow. "I wasn't sure you'd believe me, so I brought Tarbow back to show you." He nodded toward the horses. "I brought back most of the weapons they had, and three saddlebags full of money they stole from those banks they hit in Texas."

"Is that a fact?" Stone asked. "How much is it?"

"I don't rightly know. I didn't count it."

"But you say you captured Tarbow in Texas?"

"It wasn't very far in Texas," Will replied, wondering if he was going to be in trouble for that, since Texas was officially out of his jurisdiction.

Stone and Ed Pine both grinned at his response. "Well, let's have a look at him," Stone said, and pulled the canvas away from the corpse. "Whoa!" he exclaimed, and stepped back. "He's already starting to get a little overripe." But still curious to see the notorious outlaw, he lifted the canvas again long enough to see the face, which at that stage the skin had turned green. "I reckon that's him, all right," he said, "just like they said, with the eye patch and the pirate's beard." He dropped the corner of canvas he was holding. "But I'll tell you what you need to do. Take it to the undertaker right now." He paused to ask, "You know where that is?"

Will said he did. "Mr. Kittridge, right? The same feller that took care of those fellers Pride and I shot in the Mornin' Glory Saloon."

"Right," Stone said. "Then go have Doc Peters take care of that wound before you bleed to death. After he fixes you up, go on home and get some rest. Come back here in the morning and we'll review the whole thing. Okay?"

"I'm thinkin' I need to go back in the Nations to find Eli Stark," Will said. "I know I put one bullet in him, but I didn't stop him."

"We'll talk about that in the morning, too," Stone said. "Go on and get that shoulder taken care of."

Will took the saddlebags that held the stolen money off the horses and handed them to Stone, then he stepped up in the saddle and rode off to deliver the body. Stone and Ed stood to watch him as he rode away. "That's damn sorry news about Fletcher Pride," Ed said. "They just don't make 'em like Pride no more."

"You're right about that," Stone said, still watching the rider disappearing down the street. "But damned if I don't think we've got a helluva replacement."

CHAPTER 14

Sophie Bennett paused in her sweeping of the front steps to take another look at the man walking toward her from the direction of Vern Tuttle's stables, his saddlebags over his right shoulder and his rifle in his hand. Although knowing him for only a brief time, she easily recognized his long stride, and she frowned, concerned, to see his left arm in a sling. She stood, awaiting him, her broom in hand, and when he had approached within earshot, she greeted him cheerfully. "Well, I see you're back in town, Mr. Tanner. Looks like you've had a little mishap."

"Yes, ma'am," he replied, "a little." As before, he stumbled for words in her presence. "My name's Will. Please don't call me Mr. Tanner."

"All right, Will," she said, favoring him with a friendly smile. "Where's Fletcher?"

"Fletcher's dead, miss, shot down by a murderin' outlaw, and I'm really sorry to have to bring you that news."

"Oh my Lord," Sophie gasped. "Fletcher dead?" It was almost too terrible to believe. "He always came back home." She thought at once of her mother and her fondness for the gruff-looking lawman who was just a big teddy bear when he was at home in the boardinghouse. "Mother will be so sad to hear he's gone." Even as she said it, she knew just how hard it would hit her mother. Thinking then of Will's obviously wounded arm, she asked, "But you're hurt, too. Is it serious?"

"No, ma'am," Will answered. "It's a gunshot wound. Doc Peters dug the bullet out about an hour ago, said for me to give it a chance to heal some before I try to use it."

Ruth Bennett came out on the front porch, curious to see whom Sophie was talking to. "Well, Mr. Tanner," she greeted him in the same cheerful voice her daughter had used. "We're glad to see you back." She didn't ask, but glanced up the street as if looking to see if he was alone.

"Mama," Sophie said, "Fletcher was killed."

It was too sudden for Ruth to hide her shock. Although she tried not to show the impact the horrible news had upon her, she was not successful in controlling the grief in her eyes. She grasped the porch corner post to steady herself while she tried to recover her composure. "That is tragic news," she finally managed. "He will be sorely missed. We were all quite fond of Fletcher. He was with us so long, he was almost like family."

Will leaned his rifle against the front steps to free his hand. "I brought you something I thought you might wanna have." He reached into his pocket and pulled out a metal object wrapped in a cloth. "This is Fletcher's deputy marshal badge. I think he'd feel pleased if I gave it to you to remember him by. I think he thought you were a special lady." Pride had never talked to him about Ruth, so he was not really sure if he had any real affection for her or not. But he was of the opinion that it wouldn't hurt to let Ruth think that he did, and judging by her facial expression, he figured he had done the right thing.

"Why, thank you, Will," Ruth said, obviously deeply touched. "It was a nice thing for you to do. I'll take good care of it." She started to ask him about the arm he was favoring in a sling, but suddenly became emotional. "I'd best see how supper is coming along," she said hurriedly, and spun on her heel to go back inside.

In was an unusually quiet supper table that night at Ruth Bennett's boardinghouse. Fletcher Pride had normally been missing from the table on more nights than he was present, due to the nature of his job. But on this night, his absence loomed larger than ever before and was felt by everyone at the table. After supper, Sophie inquired again about Will's wound and offered to help him care for it. "I 'preciate it," Will said, "but Doc Peters said to leave the bandage on and change it tomorrow if I thought it needed changin'."

"All right," Sophie said. "We'll take a look at it tomorrow and clean it up if it's needed."

A little while after Will had gone to his room, there was a knock on his door. He answered it to find Ruth standing there holding a couple of towels. "I didn't know if you needed extra towels or not," she said, "but I brought them in case you did." He thanked her and took the towels from her, but she remained in the doorway. "Mind if I come in for a minute?" she asked. "I won't keep you but a minute." He had a fair idea of why she wanted to come in, so he stood back and held the door for her. Inside, she hesitated before coming out with it. "I am so sorry to hear about Fletcher's death, and I was wondering if you would tell me how it happened."

"Yes, ma'am," he said. "There's not much to tell you." He didn't see any reason to re-create the scene he'd found with Pride's body hanging from a tree, a warning sign written on his long underwear, and his forehead shattered by the fatal bullet as it had exited from his skull. "We split up while we were lookin' for Max Tarbow and his four men. I reckon somehow they got behind Fletcher, and they shot him in the back. That was the only way they coulda got him was to sneak up on him. At least that's the way I figure it. Like I said, I was on the other side of the mountain. It was unlucky, but like Pride told me, *Everybody's got a number, and ain't no use worryin' 'bout when your number gets called.* I reckon his number was up."

She stood there for a long moment after he finished, trying to settle the incident of his death in her mind, before she spoke. "Thank you, Will," she said. "I was just wondering, that's all. He was a special man, and he will be missed by everyone who knew him." She turned to leave, then paused. "I'm sorry that you were wounded," she said, almost as an afterthought. "Did you catch the outlaws?"

"Yes, ma'am, they're all dead."

"Good," she said, and walked away.

* * *

Before reporting to Dan Stone, Will went down to the telegraph office to send a wire to Jim Little Eagle, telling him where he had left the wagon he had to leave behind. With that done, he walked back to the courthouse.

"Come on in, Will," Dan Stone said when Will rapped on the doorjamb of Stone's open door. "How's that wound—Doc say you're gonna live?"

"He said to wear this sling for a few days, but I'm thinkin' 'bout maybe takin' it off tonight. I don't want my arm to get too stiff." He was not too sure what Stone thought about the way his initial assignment played out. None of the five outlaws they were sent to arrest were alive to stand trial, and Stone's best deputy was killed in the process. Will wasn't sure how much Stone held him responsible and whether or not he still had a job.

"I reckon you know how your shoulder feels," Stone said. "But make sure you don't rush it." Then he asked Will to again give him a detailed accounting of the attempted arrest and the actions that led to the killings. Will took him step by step from the stop at Lem Stark's place in Tishomingo, to the final shoot-out with Eli Stark on the Poteau River. "Sorry piece of business," Stone commented when Will was finished. "The lives of those five murderers wasn't worth the loss of Fletcher Pride."

"Yes, sir," Will said. "I agree with you on that." He watched Stone's expressions intensely as the marshal seemed to be concentrating on the loss. Finally, Will had to ask, "Have I still got a job?"

Stone looked at him in surprise. "Hell, yes. Why would you think you didn't?"

"Well, I wasn't sure," Will started. "I mean, the way the whole thing ended up. I thought you mighta thought there was more I could do to save Pride."

"Was there?"

"No."

"I believe you," Stone said. "You did a helluva lot more than most men could have. You've still got a job, all right, and you've got some awful big shoes to fill, now that Pride's gone under."

"I wanna make a request, then," Will said, greatly relieved. "Eli Stark is a wanted man. I wanna go after him."

"You do, do ya," Stone replied, smiling. "I'm not surprised. All right, you can go after him, but you need to wait till you're all healed up. There's no sense in going after a killer like Stark with just one good arm."

"I heal pretty fast," Will claimed. "I oughta be ready to ride in a day or so."

Stone shook his head, impressed by his newest deputy's impatience to venture into harm's way again. "There's some things we've got to go over. I don't know how much Pride told you about the fee system. You already know about the six cents a mile you get paid for going to make an arrest, and the ten cents a mile for bringing a prisoner back. I'm gonna have to work on your payment, though, to see if we can fix it so we both get paid for all that work you did." Since under the fee system, a deputy wasn't paid anything if the suspect was killed, he was thinking he might have to be a little creative in his report.

Otherwise, they were both out some money, because Stone took 25 percent of a deputy's reimbursement for fees charged. As far as Will was concerned, he didn't care about the money he lost because none of the outlaws were brought back for trial. He still had a little money, and he was going after Eli Stark for personal reasons. If Eli wanted to surrender, he would have to honor that, but he didn't expect him to be so inclined.

The rest of the morning was spent on some rudimentary training for the new deputy, which didn't take as long as Will had expected. "You go on back and take care of that shoulder," Stone said when they were finished. "Stop by sometime tomorrow and we'll see how you're doing." He got up from his desk and extended his hand. "Welcome back," he said. Then as an afterthought, he asked, "You didn't happen to bring Pride's badge back, did you?"

"No, I didn't," Will said, then hesitated. "I thought it would be the right thing to bury it with him." He figured it wasn't really a lie, because he said he *thought* it would be right. He didn't say that he did bury it.

"You're right," Stone said. "That was the right thing to do."

"Am I too late to get something to eat?" Will asked when he walked in the parlor and saw Sophie coming from the dining room.

"No, you're just not early enough to get a head start," she joked. "You'd better hurry on in, though, while everything's still hot." She stopped him then for just a moment when she noticed a little sign of blood on the edge of his bandage. "After you eat, you'd better let me take a look at that wound." He started to protest, but she shushed him, and ordered, "Go eat. When you've finished, we'll go to the washroom and put a fresh bandage on it."

He laughed and said, "Yes, Miss Bennett, whatever you say."

Will sat down at the table beside Leonard Dickens, one of the residents whose name he knew. Leonard had not been to breakfast that morning, or supper the night before. So he was curious when he saw Will's arm in a sling. "I heard you were back," he said. "Looks like you got winged."

"Part of the job, I reckon," Will replied, not really wishing to discuss it, since he had already explained to everyone else that it was a gunshot wound.

"Did you give the other fellow as good as you got?" Leonard pressed.

"You could say that, I reckon," Will said.

Ruth, recognizing Will's reluctance to talk about something that was hardly suitable table talk, came to his rescue. "I expect Mr. Tanner would rather eat than talk, Mr. Dickens. He's been away from good family fixings for a while."

"I expect you're right, ma'am," Will said with a smile of appreciation.

When he had finished eating, he was met by Sophie in the parlor. She was holding his other shirt. "You're not forgetting about your bandage, are you?" She held the shirt up for him to see where she had sewn a patch over the bullet hole in the shoulder. "I took the liberty of patching that hole for you."

Surprised, he said, "You didn't have to go to that trouble. I coulda just worn it like it was." He reached out to take it.

"That's what I figured," she said, and held it away from him. "It needs to be washed. I'll throw it in the wash, but I don't know if I can get all the bloodstains out or not. Now, let's get that shoulder taken care of." She pointed toward the back door and the porch that led to the washroom.

"Do you take care of all your boarders like this?" he couldn't resist asking.

"No, just the ones who need help really bad," she answered in playful sarcasm, and pointed toward the door again. He did as he was ordered.

A witness to the exchange between the two young people, Ruth Bennett said nothing, but the forwardness of her daughter was enough to concern her. No one more than she knew the folly of becoming overly fond of a lawman in this ruthless territory. For her daughter's sake, she hoped it was no more than a harmless flirtation. Will Tanner seemed like a nice, well-mannered young man, but as he had quoted Fletcher, *Everybody has a number,* and it was certain that deputies that worked in the Nations had smaller numbers than anyone else. Also of concern to her was the matter of income. Fletcher had told her that deputy marshals seldom earned over five hundred dollars a year, and she could not help comparing that to the income of someone like Garth Pearson, who would one day be an attorney. *And Garth would be home for supper every night,* she told herself.

Sophie followed Will into the washroom, holding his patched shirt as well as a clean cloth she planned to cut up for bandages. Directing him toward a chair near the stove, she placed his soiled shirt on a table by the door to be worked on later. Then she got a bucket of water from the pump and placed it on the stove to warm. While the water heated, she untied the sling and carefully pulled it off, then watched as he gingerly straightened his arm, testing the pain and mobility. "Not too bad," he claimed, although grimacing with the discomfort.

"Let's see if we can get that shirt off," Sophie said, and started unbuttoning it.

"Wait," Will said. "I can do it." She stepped back and watched impatiently while he unbuttoned his shirt down to his belt. "Now, if you can take my sleeve and pull it off my shoulder, you oughta be able to get to the wound."

Sophie laughed at his shyness, and after the shirt was pulled out of the way, she untied the bandages and inspected Dr. Peters's work. "It looks all right, I think—a little red, but not too bad. Maybe you're right about healing fast, but it's gonna take some time yet. Your shirt might have gotten damaged worse than you did." She moved his arm a little to the side and he flinched. "Still a little painful to move your arm, though. You're gonna have to give it a few more days. I'll clean off some of the dried blood and put a fresh bandage on it." She took the bucket off the stove and cleaned around the wound, applied a fresh bandage, and retied his arm in the sling. When she was finished, she gave him a playful pat on top of his head and said, "Next!"

"How much I owe you, Doc?" he joked as he finished buttoning his shirt.

"Nothing for the doctoring," she returned, "but a hundred dollars for stitching the shirt." She laughed and added, "The washing's free."

"You did that like you've treated a lot of bullet wounds," he said. "Have you done this before?"

"Nope," she said. "You're the first."

"Well, then I thank you very much."

Sophie changed his bandages two more times with Will insisting he didn't need her medical expertise anymore. He discarded the sling on the second day, but Sophie promptly put it back on that night, along with a stern scolding. While she ran her fingers lightly over his bare shoulder above the wound, she was prompted to ask a question. "Why do you always tense up every time I touch you? I'm not going to hurt you."

He could not tell her that it had nothing to do with a concern for pain. It was a sensation he experienced whenever he felt her touch. "I don't know," he said, laughing. "You've just got a mean look in your eye, I reckon."

"I beg your pardon," Sophie replied, pretending to be insulted. "You'll know it when I get a mean look in my eye." She affected her most stern expression and put her face eye to eye with his, so close he could smell the soap on her cheeks.

It was at this awkward moment that her mother walked in the washroom. Alarmed by what she thought she saw, Ruth just stood there for a moment, speechless. Unconcerned, Sophie backed away from Will and said, "All right. I'll check your wound tomorrow. Don't get it dirty."

Finding her voice then, Ruth said, "I was going to ask if you would like me to help with the bandages."

"Nope," Sophie answered nonchalantly as she breezed by her.

During the next couple of days, when Will had little to do, he came to be quite friendly with Ruth Bennett's attractive daughter, much to her mother's continued concern. She was encouraged somewhat, however, when Sophie allowed Garth Pearson to call on her on one of those nights. Ruth took the opportunity to invite Garth to have supper with them the following night. She suspected it was not coincidence that Will decided to have supper at the Morning Glory that night, explaining that he hadn't had a drink in quite some time. "Don't you do anything to aggravate that shoulder," Sophie said to him as he went out the door.

"I won't," Will replied. "I'll use my good arm to raise the glass," he joked.

"Why don't you eat supper here before you go drinking alcohol?" she asked.

"You're havin' company for supper," he replied. "I'll just let him take my place, so it won't be too crowded at the table."

"Well, look who's back," Gus Johnson announced when Will walked in the Morning Glory. "I was wonderin' if we was ever gonna see you again." He affected a quick frown on his face and said, "That was awful sorry news about Pride. It ain't the same without him around here."

"I reckon not," Will said. "Pride left a big hole when he left."

"What'll you have?" Gus asked.

"I think I'll have a drink of your good whiskey, and I'll drink a toast to Fletcher Pride. Then I think I'll take supper, if Mammy's still cookin' that cowboy stew."

"She sure is," Gus said. "Mammy's cowboy stew is the best because . . ."

". . . she uses real cowboys instead of beef," Will finished for him. "I know."

"Right," Gus said with a chuckle. "I'll drink to Pride with you, and it's on the house."

Overhearing, Lucy Tyler got up from a corner table and walked over to the bar to join them. "I think I'll take a shot of that in honor of Pride."

After they all drank to Fletcher Pride's memory, Will took a seat at one of the tables. Lucy sat down with him and stayed to talk to him until a couple of cowboys came in. She asked Will if he needed anything more than supper. When he said he didn't, she smiled and left to join the two strangers. In a minute or two, Mammy came from the kitchen with his supper. She gave him a brief nod of hello, then said, "Glad to see you again," which surprised him. The stew was up to standard, but not quite as good as Ruth's cooking. The thought made him wonder if Sophie was as good a cook as her mother. Then he asked himself why he even cared.

Each day, Will tested his arm, knowing that Eli was

wounded and racing to heal as well, and he intended to win that race. It was his thinking that Eli would most likely have gone to his father's place in Tishomingo to get help. But it was also possible that he wouldn't stay there long, and if so, he would need a place to hide out. That brought to mind the cave in the Sans Bois Mountains. He could only guess how badly Eli wanted to avenge his brother's death. He might be inclined to give up on hunting Will down and flee the territory again, now that his return was sure to be known by the law. In view of this, Will made sure that everything was ready to ride as soon as he felt he had most of the movement in his shoulder back. He made sure that Buster was well fed and rested. And he sold the blue and the packhorse to Vern Tuttle. The day came when he tested his shoulder and decided he had better than 75 percent movement. On that day, he told Dan Stone that he was heading for Tishomingo the next morning, and he notified Ruth at supper that night. He was astonished to find himself confronted by an apparently irritated young lady in the parlor right after supper.

"Why didn't you tell me you were planning to leave again in the morning?" Sophie demanded.

Surprised by her attitude, he replied, "I did tell you, just now at supper."

"You're more like Fletcher Pride every day," she remarked curtly. "Can't wait to go out and get yourself shot at." She spun on her heel and returned to the kitchen, leaving him mystified. She was hard put to explain her attitude, even to herself, and she was reluctant to admit that it had to do with Garth Pearson's proposal of marriage the night before. She had begged for a little time to think about her answer. She wasn't sure why, but she knew she needed time to decide if being Garth's wife was what she really wanted to be. *And she knew that damn rugged, untamed mountain lion was causing her hesitation—and he didn't even know it.*

When morning came, Will felt even stronger in his shoulder. As he and Pride had done on that morning of their fatal assignment, he waited to have breakfast there at the house before starting out. When he walked out the front door, carrying his saddlebags and rifle, both Ruth and Sophie walked out on the porch to bid him a safe journey. "You take care of yourself, Will Tanner," Ruth said.

"Don't worry, I always come back," Will said, causing her to wince. Fletcher had always said that very thing.

"Don't come back here with any more holes in you," Sophie called after him, her mood improved from that of the night before. "My rates have gone up."

He laughed. "I'll keep that in mind." He walked up the road a few yards before turning to look at Sophie again. "I will be back," he stated emphatically. Then he continued on to the stable to get his horses. As usual, he would ride Buster and take his pack-horse. When Stone had asked, he told him that he didn't want a wagon, a cook, or a posseman. He worked better alone. To Stone, it appeared that Will was going after Stark with the sole intention of killing him, so he reminded him that his assignment was to arrest Eli and bring him back for trial. Will had assured him that he understood, and he would bring him back alive if at all possible. "I still don't want to fool with a wagon. When I catch Eli Stark, I'll bring him back on that big Morgan he rides.

"That damn-fool horse doctor don't know what he's doin'," Eli complained. "My shoulder's still red and all swole up. We shouldn'ta gone to him in the first place."

"Lemme see," Lem said, and bent over his son to examine the wound in his shoulder. "Yeah, it don't look too good, but Jack Pike's the only doctor within twenty miles of here. The only other 'un is that Choctaw medicine man over at Switchback Creek, but he ain't no real doctor."

"He's likely a sight better 'n the fool that done this," Eli said, looking at the swollen area around his wound. "Help me saddle my horse. I'm gonna ride over there tonight and get him to take a look at it."

"Are you crazy?" Lem blurted. "That's gettin' too damn close to Jim Little Eagle's headquarters. What if he finds out you're back in these parts?"

"What if he does?" Eli fired back. "He can't do nothin' about it."

"He can damn sure tell the marshal," Lem insisted.

"He ain't gonna find out. I've gotta get this damn wound healed up if I'm gonna find that son of a bitch that shot Jeb, and that's for sure."

"You shoulda kilt that deputy when you had him on his back," Lem grumbled. "He killed your brother."

"It wasn't as simple as that, Pa. I told you, he had me where I couldn't get a shot at him unless I stuck my head over that bank. Besides, I was already hit twice. I didn't have no choice but to get the hell away from there. There was a bunch of folks at a store about a half mile away and they heard the shootin'. I had to get outta there." He reached up to touch the bandage on his neck and grimaced as if it was extremely painful. It didn't draw any sympathy from Lem.

"If you hadn't missed with your first shot, you wouldn't be in the fix you're in right now," Lem said.

"I didn't miss, Pa. I hit him, and if he hadn'ta fell back against that horse, I'da finished him off."

Lem stood over him, a look of disgust on his face. "All right, dammit, let's go see that Injun doctor and see if he can do anything for you." The pride he had always felt for his eldest son was beginning to weaken somewhat, a result of Eli's apparent inability to kill this one deputy.

"I don't need you to go with me," Eli said.

"You know where his shack is?" Lem asked curtly.

"No, sir," Eli admitted sheepishly.

"Then I reckon you need me to go with you, don't you?"

"I reckon," Eli said. He got up from the chair and started for the door, hating the way he had cowered before his father, something he would never do before any other man. He couldn't understand the dominance his father held over him. It had been that way with both Jeb and him ever since they were boys. He

decided the only way to break Lem's hold on him
was to kill him. And when his shoulder was well, he
decided that was what he might be tempted to do.
But first he wanted to kill that deputy, Will Tanner, so
he could tell his father that he did.

The old Choctaw medicine man opened the door
of his shack and held a lantern up to see who was
coming to see him at this late hour. "Who is there?"
he called out when two men on horses pulled up
before him.

"Are you the one they call Walkin' Crow?" Lem
asked as he stepped down.

"Yes, I am Walking Crow. Why do you come to me?"

"Step down, son," Lem said. "Walkin' Crow, we
came to see if you've got the big medicine you claim
you got."

"What is it you want my help with?" Walking Crow
asked.

"Show him, boy," Lem said.

Eli walked up before the old man and showed him
his shoulder. "I got me a gunshot wound," he said.
"And it won't heal up proper. You got somethin' that'll
fix it?"

"I don't know," Walking Crow said. "Come inside
in the light, and I will see if I can help."

They followed the old man inside. He placed the
lamp on the table and started removing the bandages from Eli's shoulder. When he could see the
wound, he examined it closely before giving his diagnosis. "It is plain to see why it troubles you. The
wound is festering. It looks like someone dug the

bullet out, but must have used a dirty knife. I can take the swelling out, so it will feel better, but I'll have to lance it to do it. Then I can put some medicine on it to make it heal."

"Well, go ahead and do it," Lem said. "We're in a hurry."

Having no desire to offend them, since he knew who they were, and their reputation, Walking Crow prepared to work on his patient. After he sterilized his knife in the fireplace, he said, "This may be a little painful until I can release the pus."

"Go ahead," Eli scoffed, "I don't mind no pain." Lem watched for a while before deciding to go outside and wait with the horses. They were awfully close to a few other Choctaw houses, and it would not be good for anyone to find out they were there.

Inside the shack, Walking Crow completed the lancing of the swollen area around the rough incision the self-taught veterinarian had made, and applied some salve that he said would heal the infection. He gave Eli some of the salve in a jar to apply daily until it was gone. "You know who I am?" Eli asked when he took the jar.

"You are the son of Lem Stark, who has the store in Tishomingo," Walking Crow answered.

"That's right, and you don't need to be tellin' nobody we was here," Eli said.

"As you wish," the old man said.

Outside, Lem turned to meet his son when Eli came out the door. "Everything all right? Did you pay the old man?"

"Yep, he got paid. He ain't gonna tell nobody we was here."

"I hope he ain't," Lem said, "but I don't trust these damn Injuns when it comes to us white folks."

"You ain't got no reason to worry 'bout that," Eli said confidently, "unless he can talk with his throat cut."

Lem exploded. "You damn fool! You cut his throat? What'd you go and do a damn-fool trick like that for? You've just drawed the Injun police into it, for sure."

Startled by his father's violent reaction, for he expected Lem's approval for taking care of Walking Crow, Eli stammered in reply. "He knew who we was, Pa. I couldn't take no chance on him spillin' his guts to the police. Ain't nobody gonna know we was even here."

"Looks like I coulda had at least one son with a thimble's worth of sense," Lem fumed. "What's done is done, I reckon. Let's get outta here before some of these other folks see us."

They rode out of the tiny cluster of shacks and cabins without noticing the lone man who stopped on his way across his backyard when he saw them leave Walking Crow's home. Still clutching his armload of firewood, he walked around to the front to see them disappear down the dark trail leading to the wagon road. Leon Coyote Killer was not certain, because of the darkness, but one of the riders reminded him of the outlaw who dressed in black and rode the black horse. Eli Stark was his name, and he was a very bad man. Leon wondered what business a man like Stark had with Walking Crow.

* * *

Old Walking Crow's body lay on the floor of his shack for over two days before anyone thought to check on him. It was not unusual for the old medicine man to drop out of sight from time to time, and the few people who lived near him were not overly concerned until Mary Raintree went to see him, seeking a poultice for her backaches. Mary knocked on his door, but there was no answer. She looked at the small corral behind his house, and Walking Crow's old paint pony was there, so she went back to knock on the door again. With still no response, she rapped harder—hard enough, in fact, that the door opened ajar, far enough for her to see the medicine man's body on the floor.

Mary ran down the path that linked the cluster of houses, screaming for help. Her screams soon brought everyone outside, including Leon Coyote Killer, who went at once to Walking Crow's shack. He found the old man lying on the floor with a pool of dried blood beneath his head. While some of the others gathered at the scene of the ghastly murder, Leon saddled his horse and rode to Atoka to fetch Jim Little Eagle.

"He's been lying here for a couple of days," Jim said when he investigated the scene. The condition of the corpse quite obviously proved that. "Who can tell me anything?"

"I can," Leon spoke up immediately. "Two nights ago, late, I was in the backyard chopping wood, and I saw two riders coming from Walking Crow's house."

"Did you recognize them?" Jim asked.

"No, it was too dark to see their faces," Leon said. "But one of them looked kinda like that Stark fellow, the one who always rode the black horse and wore black clothes."

"Eli Stark?" Jim asked.

"Maybe," Leon hedged. "Like I said, it was dark, but that's who it looked like."

Jim paused only a moment to consider what Leon said. He had recently received a telegram from the marshal's office in Fort Smith to alert him that there was an encounter with Eli Stark and the new deputy marshal near the Poteau River. Deputy Marshal Will Tanner was on his way to Atoka Station and would be contacting him. "It didn't take him long to get back to his murdering ways," Jim muttered to himself. "But why did he kill Walking Crow? The old man could not have done him harm." There was little doubt in his mind that Eli Stark was the guilty party.

Some of the neighborhood women gathered to prepare Walking Crow's body for burial. Satisfied that the old man was being taken care of, Jim Little Eagle decided to ride down to Tishomingo right away. The problem was that Stark's place was forty miles away, a good day's ride from here, and it was never good to show up somewhere on a tired horse. In light of that, he decided to go halfway that afternoon and call on Lem Stark the following day. He briefly considered waiting for the deputy marshal before taking action, but the wire from Fort Smith said only that Tanner was on his way—but not when he had left. And Jim figured that they had already lost a great deal of time. Eli Stark might have left the territory by then.

Walking Crow was held in high esteem in the small village of Choctaws. Jim owed it to the old man to work as fast as he could to catch his murderer. So he returned to his cabin to pack some supplies and tell his wife, Mary, that he would be gone for maybe a few days.

CHAPTER 15

"See what that damn dog is barkin' at," Lem Stark grumbled.

Minnie Three Toes placed a plate of corn cakes on the table between the two men, then went to the door. Peering out at the front yard, she recognized the rider at once. "Jim Little Eagle," she announced indifferently.

Her warning caused an immediate response from the men. "Damn!" Lem cursed. "I shoulda knowed that damn Injun would show up here." He turned to Eli, who was already strapping his gun belt on, and said, "Go out the back door and hide in the shed. I'll get rid of the nosy son of a bitch."

"Maybe I oughta be the one to meet him at the door," Eli snarled.

"Go out the back door, like I told you," Lem barked. "If you weren't so quick to kill somebody, he wouldn't be showin' up at my place. Now, git!" He waited until Eli went out the back before warning Minnie to stay out of sight. Then he took one more gulp of coffee before leaving the kitchen to meet Little Eagle in the store.

"Well, Jim Little Eagle," Lem said when the Choctaw policeman walked in the door. "What brings you out this way? Kinda long ride from Muddy Boggy Creek, ain't it?"

Jim didn't answer right away. He took a moment to look around the large room to make sure there was no one behind either of the two long counters. When he replied, it was in his typical emotionless tone. "I heard your son Eli was back in this territory."

"Eli?" Lem exclaimed in fake surprise. "Why, who told you a thing like that? Eli's long gone from these parts. I ain't got no idea where that boy is. Montana Territory, like as not."

"Is that so?" Jim replied. "There's somebody up in Switchback Creek who said he saw Eli and another fellow over that way the other night. I don't suppose that other fellow was you, was it?"

"Switchback Creek?" Lem responded. "What would I be doin' up there? I don't know that I've ever been there before. And like I said, Eli ain't nowhere near these parts. What makes you come askin', anyway? You think I've been sellin' whiskey to some of them bucks over that way? 'Cause I ain't."

"It's a little more serious than selling whiskey," Jim said. "Two men rode into that community and murdered the old medicine man, Walking Crow."

Lem gasped in fake shock. "Well, now, that is poor news for a fact. I'm right sorry to hear that."

"I figured you might be," Jim said. "I don't reckon

you'd mind if I look around the place, just to do my duty. There might be somebody hiding around here without you knowing it. We've got a murdering dog running loose, and I wanna make sure he ain't any threat to you and your woman."

Lem tried to affect a smile, but could not prevent favoring the Indian policeman with a smirk, knowing they were both playing a game of bluff. "Now, Jim," he said, "you're kinda oversteppin' your authority, ain't you? You Injun police ain't really got no authority when it comes to dealin' with white folks."

"I'm working with a U.S. Deputy Marshal on this," Jim said. "So I reckon I'm not overstepping my authority. I was just gonna look around a little, figured you wouldn't mind, since Eli ain't hiding out here."

"That's right," Lem said, more than a little irritated at this point. "Eli ain't nowhere near this place, and I don't know nothin' about that business with the old medicine man. I just don't like anybody snoopin' around my place for any reason."

"All right, Stark, if that's the way you feel about it, I'll take your word for it. I'll be on my way, then. I'll just tell the deputy that I made sure Eli wasn't here." He had found what he came to find. He was fairly sure Eli was there, the black Morgan in the corral was the first clue. He was also sure that, if he forced his way into the house behind the store, he would most likely walk right into the muzzle of a rifle. "Good day to you, then," he said. "If you see any strangers that don't look right, get in touch with me. All right?"

More at ease, now, Lem fashioned a friendly smile. "I sure will—always ready to stand up for them that's keepin' the peace." He walked outside with Jim and watched while he got on his horse, and remained there until the policeman disappeared down the river road. When he returned to the kitchen, he opened the door to find Eli sitting at the table, his arm steadied on the table with his .44 aimed at the door. "You can put that away," Lem scolded. "I thought I told you to go hide in the shed."

"I thought it'd be better to cut him down if he walked in that door and be done with him," Eli replied.

"You thought?" Lem exclaimed. "If you could think, we wouldn'ta had that Injun here in the first place. I talked him outta searching the place for you, but I ain't so sure he won't be back with a marshal and a posse. So I expect you'd best not be here when he does."

"Hell, Pa," Eli said, "he ain't gonna be comin' back here. I heard him say he'd take your word for it." He wasn't anxious to go back to his hideout up in the Sans Bois Mountains and leave Minnie Three Toes's cooking. He moved his arm up and down as if testing the range of motion. "My shoulder's gettin' dang nigh back to normal already. I'd like to stay here till it gets all the way back. That old Injun musta knew his stuff."

Impatient with his son's lack of common sense, Lem said, "It don't pay to take a chance on that Choctaw lawman. He's a lot smarter than you think. You just do like I tell you. I don't want a bunch of lawmen around here, shootin' up the place."

"All right," Eli said, knowing there was little to gain in arguing. "I'll head out in the mornin'."

"You get your possibles together and head out now.

You've still got about four hours of daylight. And don't ride out the river road, in case that Injun's waitin' around to see if he flushed you out."

"Damn, Pa," Eli protested, but said no more, knowing it was useless. He looked at the sullen Chickasaw woman, standing silently witnessing the discussion between her husband and his son. Eli had seldom had a kind word for the long-suffering woman, looking upon her as no more than a servant. He looked to her now for sympathy, hoping she would persuade his father to let him stay, at least long enough to cook something for him to take with him. She only looked at him with a tired smile, then turned away. *Damn Injun*, he thought. There was no sympathy from that quarter. He got his things together, packed his saddlebags, and saddled his horse.

"Cross over the river and ride up the other side toward the hills," Lem said. "No use takin' a chance on that Injun waitin' around to take a shot atcha."

"I know, you done told me once," Eli replied, annoyed. "I'll head to the Sans Bois, to that hideout up in the cave. I'll lay up there for a spell, till I'm sure this wound is healed proper. Then when things die down a little, I'm aimin' to get on that deputy's tail."

"Good," Lem said. "That's somethin' that needs gettin' took care of."

That's what I thought, Jim Little Eagle said to himself when he saw the rider come up out of the river. The Choctaw policeman had positioned himself to watch the back of the house, suspecting that the outlaw would most likely make a run for it, and he didn't think he would leave by the road. The big Morgan broke into a lope after it climbed up on the bank and started up the river. Jim led his horse out of the trees on the low rise beyond the river, stepped up into the saddle, and guided his horse along the other side of the rise. He planned to angle across the foot of the hill to cut Eli off.

Still chafing over his father's abusive dismissal of him, Eli held the Morgan to a steady lope as he approached a low hill that ran parallel to the slow-moving creek. So absorbed in his anger at having been sent to hide out in the mountains again, he did not realize the threat until he rode past the trees at the base of the hill. Startled, he pulled up short when he found himself facing Jim Little Eagle's rifle aimed directly at him. He started to reach for his .44, but Jim warned him, "One move and I'll cut you down."

Eli thought better of it and put his hands in the air. "You got no reason to point that rifle at me," he snarled. "I ain't no Injun."

"You're under arrest for the murder of Walking Crow," Jim said. "You can go peacefully, or over the saddle of your horse. I don't care which. It's up to you."

"I don't know no Walkin' Crow," Eli replied. "I didn't murder nobody."

"Is that right?" Jim asked. "How'd you get that bandage on your shoulder?"

"None of your business, Injun," Eli spat. "Now get outta my way. I've got places to go to." He started to nudge his horse, but stopped again when Jim brought his rifle up to his shoulder and prepared to shoot.

"Damn it!" Eli blurted. "Hold on!" He put his hands up again and said, "You're makin' a mistake. I don't know nothin' 'bout no murder."

"The judge in Fort Smith will decide that," Jim said, and pulled his horse up beside Eli's. "Now, take those pistols out, real slow, with just two fingers, and hand them to me handle first."

"All right," Eli spat back at him, "but my left arm is still hurt some." He made a big show of pulling the pistols one at a time, using only his right hand. When the weapon cleared his holster, he leaned forward as if about to drop it. Too late to react, Jim was caught reaching for the pistol at the moment when Eli suddenly drew the other one. The Choctaw policeman had no time to fire his rifle before Eli put a bullet in his chest. Jim dropped the rifle and slid off his horse to land hard on the ground. Eli didn't wait to see if he was dead or not. He kicked his horse hard and galloped away.

Retracing the journey he had made with Max Tarbow's body, Will left the creek he had been following and headed due west toward the Sans Bois Mountains. Ahead of him, he could see the line of hills where he had parted with Perley Gates, and he kept Buster pointed straight for a gap in the middle of them, certain that it was the pass Perley had led him through. Once he reached it, he backtracked along the narrow game trail that had led them to the gap. If he remembered correctly, the trail would lead him to Perley's camp.

Busy skinning a deer, Perley paused abruptly when he heard his mule whinny. The mule, though ornery, was as good as a watchdog whenever something or someone approached his camp. Always cautious, Perley put his skinning knife down and reached for the Henry rifle propped against the tree the deer's carcass was hanging from. He didn't get many visitors, and he wasn't anxious to receive any now, since he had learned that Eli Stark was back in the territory. In a few minutes' time, he spotted a rider leading a packhorse through the trees that circled the clearing at the base of the hill where his cabin stood. When the rider cleared the trees, Perley relaxed and set his rifle back against the tree again, for he recognized the man riding the buckskin horse. "Well, I'll be . . ." he started, then called out, "Will, I didn't expect to see you back here so soon."

"Hello, Perley," Will returned. "That's a fine-lookin' doe you've got hangin' up there."

"Shot it this mornin'," Perley said. "Step down and we'll cook up some of it." He waited for Will to step down before continuing. "Did you get that body to Fort Smith before it started to stink?"

"Just barely," Will replied. "The undertaker wasn't very happy about it."

"Well, now that I see you back here, I reckon I don't have to ask if you were able to give ol' Eli the slip."

"That ain't exactly the way it went," Will said. Then he went on to tell Perley about the encounter at the Poteau River. "So he winged me and I winged him," Will concluded. "And he hightailed it."

"So now you're chasin' him, instead of the other way around," Perley said. "And I reckon you're wantin' me to lead you to that cave up in the mountains."

"That's a fact," Will said. "I figure he's most likely gonna be at that cave, or at his father's place in Tishomingo. So this is the first place I'm gonna look." Perley nodded solemnly. "All I want from you is to take me to it, or if you'd rather, tell me how to find it. Will you do that?"

"Why, sure," Perley replied, "I'll take you to it, but I hope to hell Eli ain't up there. I'd just as soon have him a long way from here." He hesitated and gave his deer carcass a glance. "Are you wantin' to start out right now?"

"No," Will said. "My horses are tired, so I expect it's best to wait till mornin'."

"Right," Perley said, relieved. "I need to get this meat cured. I waited too long to get started on it as it is."

"You go on with your butcherin'," Will said. "I'll take care of my horses." He started to lead his horses to the stream in front of Perley's cabin and looked back to say, "By the way, I brought you some more coffee." The grin on Perley's face told him that he appreciated it.

The next morning, Will saddled Buster, Perley saddled his mule, and they set out for the outlaw cave up in the mountains. Will soon realized how skilled Perley was as a tracker. They stopped several times for him to take a closer look at the tracks they found on the game trails leading up into an area of looming boulders with hundreds of hidden crevices. He pointed out the more recent tracks that told him there had been a horse on the trail within the last two days. Perley insisted that tracks coming down from the rocks above them were fresher than the others, which caused him to speculate that whoever had been up to the cave was no longer there. Will considered himself a fair tracker, so he was not entirely convinced that Perley was accurate in his speculation. "I just don't believe ol' Eli is up there now," Perley maintained. "Look at this track on the edge of this stream—big ol' hoofprint, horse the size of that Morgan he rides. And they was made yesterday or the day before. They're all headin' down the mountain, and ain't no new tracks goin' back up." He looked at Will as if unable to understand his uncertainty. "He was up there, but he ain't up there now."

"Maybe you're right," Will allowed, "but I want to get a look at that cave, anyway, in case I have to come lookin' for him back here again when he is up there. It's best to know what I'm walkin' into, if that does happen. So let's go on up and find this cave." To himself, he thought, *Nobody's that damn good at reading a trail.*

When they neared the mountain where the cave was located high up on a rocky cliff, they decided to proceed on foot in case someone was watching the trail. So they dismounted and left their horses on a low rise covered with oak and hickory trees. Watching the boulders and crevices above them, they approached the natural stone corral at the foot of the cliff. There were no horses in it, but there was sign that a horse had been there recently. After Perley examined the droppings, he said his original speculations were correct, Eli was gone. "I reckon you're right," Will conceded, "but I wanna take a look at that cave."

They climbed up the cliff and Will found that Perley had not exaggerated in his description of the cave. It was formed of solid rock, ran back a good forty feet into the mountain, and had a back door to escape if necessary. There was plenty of evidence that someone, presumably Eli, had been there, and Will was ready to admit that Perley was as good a tracker as he claimed. Eli Stark had gone. The question was where to, and Will figured Tishomingo was the most likely place.

They descended the trail back to Perley's camp, where Will had left his packhorse. He thanked Perley for his help and the supply of smoked venison he gave him, and prepared to set out at once for Tishomingo, planning to enlist the help of Jim Little Eagle to look for Eli Stark. It was at least seventy-five miles to Jim's cabin on Muddy Boggy Creek, and most of the morning had been used up by the climb up to the cave. So he figured to look for a place to camp for the night somewhere south of the Jack Fork Mountains. Even from there, he would have a full day's ride to reach Jim Little Eagle's place. Perley wished him "good hunting" and stood watching him ride off toward the valley. A thought crossed his mind that it might be the last time he would ever see the young, sandy-haired deputy marshal. They didn't come any meaner than Eli Stark. "That'd be a downright shame, too," he muttered. "Seems like a right nice feller." He turned to find his mule staring at him. "Never can tell, though. He's got a way about him."

It was almost dark when Will came to a stream southwest of the Jack Fork Mountains and decided he'd pushed his horses far enough for the day. After he had taken care of them, he set about building a fire to boil some coffee and cook some of the venison Perley had given him. While he ate the roasted meat, he thought about the task that lay before him and the likelihood that Eli was still in the territory. He didn't know how badly Eli was hurt. Things had happened too fast to be sure. He knew he had wounded him, but he thought it was in the shoulder, so it could be bad, or no worse than his own wound. Stone had telegraphed Jim Little Eagle that Will was on his way to join him. He hoped Jim would have done a little scouting and might have discovered if Eli had returned to his father's place on the Blue River.

There was plenty of time to think before climbing into his blankets for the night. As he sat there drinking the last of the coffee he had made, thoughts of Fletcher Pride came to him. He still felt somewhat responsible for Pride's death, even though his logical mind told him there was no way he could be. He had killed to avenge Pride's death, but he had been cheated out of the satisfaction of seeing Max Tarbow hang for the murder. Eli Stark had cheated him out of that satisfaction, so Will had a natural desire to extract his vengeance from Eli. He found himself hoping Eli would resist capture. Then another thought came to him, one he had troubled over before. Did he have the patience and compassion to be a good deputy marshal? Without consciously thinking about it, he worked his arm up and down, testing the stiffness. It was a question that he had no answer for.

Starting early the next morning, he intended to camp that night at Jim Little Eagle's cabin on Muddy Boggy Creek with one stop halfway to rest his horses. After leaving the rolling hills that led into the Jack Fork Mountains, he angled his course to intercept the common wagon road to Atoka to make it easier for the horses. The buckskin seemed in a mood to travel, so Will let him set the pace. As a result, they made good time, and before sunset, he arrived at Jim's cabin to find a small group of people gathered there. A fire had been built outside the cabin and there were a couple of women cooking something in pots. If it was a celebration of some kind, it was not a joyous one, for the people standing around were not making much noise. Several men standing near the cabin turned to meet him as he rode up in the yard. Two older men walked out ahead of the others, and judging by their grave faces, he wondered if he had ridden in on a funeral.

He stepped down to talk to the two elders. "I

apologize for disturbin' your meeting," Will said. "My name's Will Tanner. I'm a deputy marshal from Fort Smith, and I just need to talk to Jim Little Eagle."

"Jim Little Eagle has been seriously wounded," one of the old men said. "A young man from our village found him near the Blue River. He had been shot in the chest by a man he went to arrest."

Will was too shocked to speak for a moment. He knew, without having to be told, that the shooter was Eli Stark. If he was found near the Blue River, then it meant that Jim had gone to Lem Stark's store to arrest Eli. *He should have waited for me*, Will thought. "I'm awful sorry to hear this terrible news. How bad is he hurt? Can I see him?"

Hearing the conversation outside the house, Mary Light Walker walked out to greet him. "Jim will want to see you," she said. "Please come in."

Will followed her inside to find Jim Little Eagle lying in bed, his chest bandaged heavily. Evidently there had been massive blood loss, for he looked pale and drained of strength. He opened his eyes halfway and gave Will a weak nod. "How ya doin', partner?" Will asked. "You gonna make it?"

"I'll make it," he vowed weakly. "I'll not let that son of a bitch put me in the ground." He shook his head slowly. "I made a big mistake. I got careless." He went on to tell Will how Eli had gotten the jump on him.

"Hell, he winged me, too," Will said, trying to console him. "But we'll get him. I'm on my way to find him now. You just rest up and get on your feet again."

They didn't talk long, since it appeared to Will that it was tiring Jim out. So when Mary came back in with a look of concern on her face, Will decided it best that he took his leave. "You get well," he said. "I'm lookin' forward to workin' with you." He said good-bye to Mary and stepped up into the saddle, planning to use what daylight was left to shorten the distance between him and Tishomingo before he made his camp that night.

CHAPTER 16

"What the hell is he doin' back here?" Lem demanded when he looked out the door of his store and saw the big Morgan heading for the corral behind the house. He had heard about Jim Little Eagle and knew Eli was the one who shot him because it happened so close to his store. He rushed out to head Eli off and repeated the question when he caught his son at the corral gate.

"I need some doctorin'," Eli replied, "and there ain't no place else to go. I reckon I musta tore somethin' loose in my shoulder when I shot that Injun policeman. It's been bleedin' ever since."

"I shoulda figured you'd do somethin' stupid like that," Lem fumed. "But damn it, if you had to shoot the son of a bitch, why the hell didn't you at least make sure he was dead—then hide the body somewhere? I swear, it don't seem right. I had two sons and all the brains went into Jeb's head and you didn't get a lick of sense." He paused to take a breath. "And there ain't no doctor here, you oughta know that.

You killed the Injun doctor. Ain't nobody left but the horse doctor, and he messed that wound up the first time."

"Maybe Minnie can doctor it," Eli said. "All them Injun women know about makin' medicine outta roots and leaves and stuff."

Exasperated by his son's total lack of common sense, Lem was tempted to shoot him, himself, to keep the law from coming down on him. He used to take great pride in Eli, but lately it seemed like Eli just made one stupid move after another, and each mistake gave the law reason to focus on his little store. Eli's latest blunder was the wounding of the Choctaw policeman, Jim Little Eagle. Lem supposed Eli had no choice, since Jim was trying to arrest him. But instead of making sure he was dead, Eli left him alive, right on the bluffs close to the store, where somebody was bound to find him. "Minnie don't know nothin' 'bout makin' medicine," Lem said. "You shoulda stayed up there in the mountains and let it heal. All you're gonna do by comin' home is lead the marshal right to my doorstep."

Eli thought about that for a moment, then said, "Well, ain't that what we're wantin'? I chased him all the way to the Poteau. Now maybe he'll come to us, and when he does, I'll settle with him for killin' Jeb."

Lem had to think a moment then. He was still tormented by the need for vengeance for the killing of his youngest son, and he was convinced that Will Tanner was the man who shot Jeb. As appealing as the thought of shooting the deputy marshal down at his front door was, Lem had to listen to his common sense. If Tanner was shot, trying to make an arrest at the store, that would bring a whole posse of marshals down on him. "Use that little brain of yours," Lem finally said. "I don't want you anywhere around here if that marshal shows up."

"Why, Pa?" Eli exclaimed. "I winged him before. I'm gonna finish it if he shows up here lookin' for me. And I guarantee, this time, won't nobody find the body."

"Listen, you dang fool," Lem lashed out, his patience exhausted. "Do you think when you shoot that lawman, that that'll be the end of it—that there won't be no more showin' up on my front step? I don't want you here. That marshal needs killin', and it's your responsibility to do it, but not on my doorstep. So don't even unsaddle your horse—you've got to put some distance between you and my store."

"But my shoulder ain't healin' like it oughta," Eli protested, childlike.

Lem relented briefly. "I'll tell Minnie to look at it and see if there's anythin' she can do for it. But she ain't gonna take long. Maybe we can give you some food to take with you. Then you get back up to that hideout in the Sans Bois. That's the best place to wait for Tanner to show up, and he most likely will. And when he does, dammit, kill him."

Finally seeing the sense in what his father was telling him, Eli abandoned the idea of lying around Lem's house while Minnie Three Toes waited on him. His father was right about one thing, a man could keep a posse at bay from that stone cave on top of the mountain. Leaving the saddle on his horse, he followed Lem to the house, where his father told Minnie to tend to Eli's shoulder.

Alarmed to see the evil son's return, the mistreated Indian woman did as she was ordered. Lem seemed to always treat her even more roughly whenever Eli was there. Perhaps it was to demonstrate his dominance over her, as if she were a problematic horse or dog. If she was lucky, and responded quickly to his orders, maybe she would get by with nothing more than verbal abuse. With that in mind, she removed the crude bandage that Eli had stuffed over the wound and cleaned it as best she could. "I put clean bandage on wound," she said. "I don't know more to do. Maybe you go see Walking Crow. He give you medicine." She was surprised when they both laughed.

"Yeah, that'd be the thing to do," Lem said, chuckling. "Go see ol' Walking Crow and see what kinda medicine he's got." He had not told Minnie that the old Choctaw medicine man had met with a violent death. When she continued to seem confused by his remark, he decided to inform her. "Ol' Walkin' Crow's dead." He grinned at her, amused by her look of horrible surprise.

"Walking Crow is dead?" she asked.

"That's a fact," Lem said. "Got his throat cut, is what I heard." She looked at once toward Eli, who was grinning in response to his father's remarks, and knew who killed him. It was disturbing news, for the old medicine man was held in high respect among his people. A wave of hopeless disgust swept over her entire body for the blatant disregard for human life.

As for Lem, his angry reaction when Eli first boasted of Walking Crow's murder was now forgotten. "Get busy and get some grub for Eli. He's got to get on his way before dark," Lem said.

Relieved to learn that Eli was not going to stay, she gathered some food for him to take with him, hoping to hurry him on his way. Still grumbling about his wound and the pain it was causing him, Eli nevertheless climbed back into the saddle and walked the Morgan back toward the river trace. Peeking from the kitchen door, Minnie watched Lem as he stood by the corner of the corral after seeing his son off. When he turned to come back to the house, she went quickly to the stove to make sure the coffee was still hot. He would want it as soon as he came through the door. And to avoid a beating, she would have it waiting for him.

There had been very few customers coming to the store over the last couple of days. This, on top of all the recent trouble with Jeb and Eli, was enough to keep Lem in a foul mood. Even the usual Loafer Indians who came to buy illegal whiskey had not been in to trade for the firewater that made them crazy. Minnie knew the reason they had not come was because word had gotten around that Eli was back. In Lem's twisted brain, however, he somehow convinced himself that it was because this lawman, Will Tanner, was out to kill all his customers. Once again, a thought came to her that she had entertained often over the summer months, and that was to escape from this hell she was forced to endure. If she was going to make another attempt to run away, she was going to have to do it soon. Summer was rapidly drawing to a close now. Bad weather was not far away, and she did not want to repeat the mistake that led to an almost crippling beating once before. She had foolishly run down the river during a snow-storm. Lem had drunk himself into an unconscious stupor, so she ran, thinking the snow would continue falling and cover her tracks. To her horror, however, the storm abated when she was no more than two miles from the store, failing to cover her footprints. Shuddering with the memory of it, she uncon-sciously reached up to feel the long scar beside her ear, a constant reminder of the folly in running from the cruel man obsessed with owning her. She had made up her mind, however, that if he caught her again and beat her to death, as he had promised, it would ultimately be a fate preferable to continuing to live as his slave. She turned from the stove to gaze at him, seated at the kitchen table, drinking his coffee. *Soon*, she told herself, *soon*. The next time he drank himself to sleep, she was determined to make her break for freedom.

It was close to midday when Will reined Buster to a halt on the low bluffs above the Blue River. From where he sat, he could see the store and the attached house slightly below the level of the bluffs. He could see the barn and corral from there, as well as a wagon shed, a smokehouse, and an outhouse. There were three horses in the corral, but no dark Morgan. That was disappointing, but he couldn't rule out the possibility that Eli's horse was somewhere else, somewhere out of sight, maybe inside the barn. With thoughts of someone drawing a bead on him with a rifle, which he remembered as Eli's style, he decided to ride on down quickly before he was spotted.

Cursing a barrel of molasses that was reluctant to be moved from under the counter, Lem Stark was not aware of the rider pulling up to the hitching post outside his store. He continued to struggle with the stubborn barrel, jammed in behind two barrels of lard, until in exasperation, he stood up to call for Minnie Three Toes. Startled to discover the formidable figure of the deputy marshal standing in front of the counter, Lem staggered back a step before recovering from the shock. He quickly fumbled for words to cover his surprise. "I didn't hear you come in, Tanner. What are you doin' out this way again? I done told you I don't know where Eli is, if that's what you come to ask me."

"Is that a fact?" Will replied. "Then you won't mind me takin' a look around the place, will you?"

"And look for what?" Lem demanded. "Somebody else to kill? Ain't nobody else to shoot, but me and my woman. You done killed my boy Jeb, and he didn't break no laws."

Will glanced toward the door to the house to see the frightened Chickasaw woman peeking into the store, having heard Lem talking to someone. He was not sure what part she played in Lem's family, so he did not dismiss her as harmless. Responding to Lem's question, he said, "Your son was killed because he was ridin' with Max Tarbow. He was killed by one of Tarbow's men when he drew down on him in a gunfight."

"Well, ain't that interestin'?" Lem replied sarcastically. Course there warn't nobody left standin' to talk about it, was there?"

"No, there wasn't," Will said. "And that included Deputy Fletcher Pride and Charlie Tate."

"Damn you," Lem spat. "You shot my boy, just as sure as you shot all the rest of those men up there. And now you come here, lookin' to shoot Eli."

"I came here lookin' to arrest Eli," Will said. "Whether he gets shot or not depends on him. I'm tired of jawin' with you, so I'm gonna take a look around that barn now." He started toward the door. When he did, Minnie disappeared from the door to the house, causing him to cock his Winchester, in case she was up to something. Wary of getting shot in the back, he kept an eye on Lem as he went outside and walked toward the barn, ready to react to whatever he found. It was a bold move he was making, and maybe a foolish one, walking alone into what had the ideal makings of a trap. But he was determined to know if Eli was here, or hiding close by.

He quickly brought his rifle up when the kitchen door suddenly opened and the Indian woman reappeared. Instead of a weapon, however, she carried a small tub with a washboard in it, which she promptly placed on the ground and began washing some cloth items that looked like towels. He was distracted for a moment by her odd behavior and would have looked away had she not pulled some short strips of cloth up to inspect. He noticed then that the strips looked to have bloodstains on them, and he glanced up to lock eyes with her. She responded with one slight nod, and he realized that she was telling him that Eli was there, or that he had recently been there. He acknowledged her signal with a nod as well, aware that Lem had followed him out the door, but unaware of the .44 pistol he had stuck in his belt. Will failed to interpret her heavy frown as a signal that Lem was armed. He continued to the barn to cautiously push the door open, and went inside.

Behind the deputy, Lem rested his hand on the handle of his pistol as he quietly stepped up to the barn door. His mind was racing with conflicting thoughts, stirred by his overpowering hatred for the tenacious lawman. Now he was presented with an opportunity to extract the vengeance he so desperately craved, with no one to witness the execution. All evidence of the killing, the body and his horse, would have to be disposed of far away from his store. There must be no possible connection to him, for he was barely tolerated by the law in Fort Smith as it was. He thought of Minnie then. She would have to be silenced as well. There was no use in taking a chance.

The question now was did he have the nerve to do it? His blood seemed to be draining from his brain as he quietly stepped inside the barn to find the deputy kneeling before one of the stalls, examining the tracks on the dirt floor, his back toward him. It was now or never, he thought as he drew the .44 from his belt. He almost panicked when the front sight of the weapon caught momentarily on his belt, fearing that Will would turn to discover him at any moment. When the pistol came free, he hurriedly aimed it at the unsuspecting deputy's back, but still he hesitated. He could not miss. The range was point-blank. His hand trembled as he held his arm straight out before him, the front sight aimed at a point squarely in the center of Will's back. *Do it*, he told himself.

The stillness of the small barn was suddenly shattered by the explosion of the shot. Will rolled over on his back, his rifle set to fire, startled to see Lem suddenly drop to his knees, a ragged hole blown in his side. He remained on his knees for only a few seconds, his eyes staring in horror, before he slowly keeled over to lie dead. Totally confused until he saw the solemn Indian woman standing by the barn door, holding the double-barreled shotgun loosely in her hands, Will only then realized what had happened. His first thought was to reprimand himself for having been so careless. He had not thought Lem possessed the nerve to take action. The next thought was one of amazement that the woman had killed her husband to save him. He got to his feet then and went to her. She obediently handed him the shotgun and continued staring at the corpse lying on the floor of the barn. "You just saved my life," he said simply, stating the obvious.

"He is very bad man," she replied. "He was gonna shoot you. I shoot him."

The faraway expression in the weary woman's eyes told him a great deal more than the simple explanation she had offered. "He was a very bad man," he repeated. "I think maybe he treated you pretty bad. Is that right?" She nodded and unconsciously felt the scar beside her ear. "Well, I reckon you're free now," he said.

She responded with a single word: "Eli."

"Are you afraid of Eli?" She nodded again. "Is he hidin' near here somewhere?"

"Eli leave yesterday," she said. "He go to mountains, to cave they talk about. He wants to kill you."

"Well, I'm already aware of that," he said, thinking of the ride to Fort Smith with Max Tarbow's body. "What about you? Are you stayin' here, or do you have some place to go? Where are your people?"

"I don't know. When the white men stole me, my village was on the Wichita River in the Chickasaw Nation. They brought me here, four days on horses, and sold me to Lem. I try to run away, but he caught me and say he will kill me if I try again. I think now maybe I go to Choctaw village on Switchback Creek. Maybe they will take me in."

He paused for a minute to think the situation over. He felt sorry for the woman, left alone as she was, even though it was better than being owned by the likes of Lem Stark. She was certainly too old to entertain thoughts of marriage, if anyone would even want her after her time with Lem. But she was right—the Choctaws would most likely accept her. He wanted to help her, and the perfect solution suddenly occurred to him. "You're a rich woman now. Since Stark's dead, you've got a store full of goods that all belong to you." He saw her eyes brighten at that. It had clearly never occurred to her. "I'll bet ol' Lem's got some money hid around here, too," Will said. "You don't have to go to that Choctaw village lookin' for charity. You can pay your way. I'll take you there. We'll load that wagon in the shed back there with everything it'll hold. Everything belongs to you. What we can't get in the wagon we'll hide it away somewhere and come back to get it."

It was almost more than the sullen woman could grasp. After having been bullied and abused by the white man and his evil sons for so long, it was difficult for her to believe that she should have such good fortune. "You are a good man, Will Tanner. I will share this with you."

"Oh no, ma'am," Will said. "This all belongs to you. I just wanna see you settled proper in a new village. If you wanna share with the Choctaws, that would go a long way toward welcomin' you to live with 'em. You don't owe me anything." Reconsidering then, he said, "Maybe some of those .44 cartridges Lem has on the shelf—and some coffee beans. That's all I ever need—coffee and cartridges." She smiled at him then. It was the first time she could remember having smiled for any reason. "Speakin' of coffee, I ain't had any today," he said. "And I could use some right now. If you'll fix us some, I'll drag that ugly carcass off back of the barn and dig a hole for it. All right?"

"All right," she answered with a happy smile, spun on her heel, and hurried toward the house, a woman set free from a life of hell.

He hesitated long enough to watch her hurry to the kitchen door, thinking that his offer to help was going to delay his pursuit of Eli. But Eli was only a day ahead of him, according to what Minnie had told him. In all likelihood, he would still be holed up in that cave for a long while. There was time to help

Minnie move her wealth to Switchback Creek, and right at the moment, that seemed the more important.

It was close to dark by the time Will and Minnie had loaded Lem's wagon with as much as it would hold, and too late to start out for Switchback Creek. Even with the wagon piled high with supplies, it was still far short of the possessions to be transported to the Choctaw village. There were still some supplies left in the store, as well as a good stove and some furniture. To complete the move, several more trips with the wagon would be required, a fact that could not help but concern Will with his urgency to go after Eli. *We'll just have to wait and see how it turns out*, he thought as he addressed the two barrels of whiskey he found in a small storeroom in the back of the store. There were some quart jars on a shelf above the barrels, so Will, being a practical man, filled one of them with the illegal whiskey. *For medicinal purposes*, he told himself, and took the jar out to his packhorse. Then he pushed both barrels over to let the contents flow out to drain through the cracks of the storeroom floor. Minnie cooked and they stayed there overnight, with Will opting to sleep in the barn with his horses.

The next morning their short journey to the small gathering of houses on Switchback Creek brought them to a village of curious, but compassionate Choctaws, who graciously accepted the lone Chickasaw woman into their community. When Minnie expressed a desire to share much of the wealth she brought, the welcoming turned into a real celebration and a suggestion that she should move into Walking Crow's vacant cabin. Will's concerns were immediately lessened when Leon Coyote Killer volunteered to drive Minnie's wagon back with her to get the rest of her belongings. There was no longer any reason for him to remain; he could leave knowing that she had been well received, and there was nothing more he could do for her.

When she saw him step up into the saddle, preparing to ride out, Minnie hurried to stand at his stirrup. "I owe you much," she declared sincerely.

"Not as much as I owe you," he reminded her. "You saved my life in that barn when I got careless." He knew what she meant, however, and paused to gaze at the people of the small community gathered to make her feel welcome. "You earned all this. I think you'll be happy here."

She stepped back away from his horse. "You be careful, Will Tanner. Eli is a bad man."

"I will," he said, then turned Buster's head to the northeast and set out for the Sans Bois Mountains, some ninety miles away.

CHAPTER 17

With only about half of the day left before darkness set in, Will rode the twenty miles to Muddy Boggy Creek. He made his camp for the night about a mile below Jim Little Eagle's cabin. He planned to make the rest of the trip in two days, so as not to make it hard on his horses. He wanted them fresh when he got to Perley Gates's cabin. In the saddle early the next morning, he camped that night at the same campsite below the Jack Fork Mountains that he had used before, leaving him about thirty-five miles from Perley's cabin, and a fairly easy day's ride remaining. As he had anticipated, he made the trip well before dark.

"Howdy, Will!" Perley called out from a stand of pines on one side of the ravine that served as a pass into his camp. Then he emerged from the pines and descended to the bottom of the ravine.

"Perley," Will acknowledged in surprise, having not seen his elflike friend hidden in the trees until then. "What are you hidin' up there in the trees for?"

"Can't never be too careful," Perley said. "I spotted

you from the top of the ridge when you was a good piece off. I thought it looked like you, 'specially since you was ridin' that buckskin. But my eyes ain't as good as they used to be, so I decided to come on back here and wait to see if whoever it was came to my place. I'm tickled it was you, 'cause I chased a deer back up that mountain near the outlaws' cave the other day and that damn black Morgan was back in the corral."

It was the news that Will wanted to hear. "Well, that answers the first question I was fixin' to ask you. Is he still there?"

"Damned if I know," Perley replied. "I've been mighty careful not to go anywhere close to that cave ever since, but I heard a couple of rifle shots from over that way yesterday. I figured he musta shot a deer or somethin'." He looked at Will and shook his head. "I reckon you're fixin' to go after him."

"Yeah, I reckon so," Will said. "That's what I came here to do. I thought if you don't mind, I'd leave my packhorse here with you, so I don't have to fool with him."

"I don't reckon I have to tell you to be mighty careful," Perley said, a look of earnest concern upon his face. "That man's about as mean a snake as ever was, and he's holed up in a place that's damn near impossible to sneak up on. You saw that for yourself that day we climbed up there."

Will thought about Perley's speculation that Eli had probably killed a deer the day before. If true, it meant that Eli had no need to come out of the cave for quite a while. That was bad news, for he had counted on Eli's need for food as one opportunity to catch him out of his stronghold. Minnie Three Toes had told him that Eli only had food for a day or two when he left the store. Will realized that he was going to have to go up to that stone cave after Eli, and that might take some doing. He would have to think the problem over. In the meantime, he would take care of his horses.

While Will turned his horses out to graze with Perley's mule, Perley put some strips of smoked venison over a fire to roast. "Might as well eat some supper," he said. "You ain't fixin' to do nothin' till mornin', I expect."

"I s'pose not," Will said, still deep in thought about the best way to flush Eli out of his hole. He really needed someone to cover one entrance to that cave while he covered the other, but he hesitated to enlist Perley to help him. He didn't want to put the little man in harm's way. And it was blatantly obvious that Perley possessed a healthy fear of Eli. Finally a plan occurred to him that would expose Perley to very little danger. Deciding it worth a shot, Will asked, "How'd you like to be a deputy marshal for a little while?"

"Oh, I don't know, Will," Perley said hesitantly. "I ain't as young as I used to be, and even when I was, I never had no desire to get in a gunfight with a gunman like Eli Stark."

"What if you didn't have to get in the way of any shootin'—just leave that to me?" Will went on then to explain what he had in mind, and what part Perley would play.

Perley heard him out, thought it over for a

moment, then declared, "Hell, I reckon I could do that much."

"Fine," Will said. "Now, do you think you could help me find that cave in the dark?" Perley said he could. "Good. Then we might as well eat some supper and wait till it gets dark."

"I'll go the rest of the way by myself," Will whispered to Perley. He could see the natural stone corral in the darkness ahead, but it was too dark to tell if the black Morgan Eli rode was inside. He left Perley in the trees and made his way silently toward the corral, working his way cautiously around the rock walls until coming to an opening with two tree limbs across it for a gate. Only then did he see the dark horse standing in the opposite corner. The horse whinnied softly and walked over to the gate. Will dropped his hand on the handle of his Colt and peered up toward the mouth of the cave. But there was no response to the horse's whinny from up above him.

The Morgan eagerly accepted the handful of grain that Will offered while he stroked the horse's neck. Eli had left the bridle on, which Will appreciated, so when the horse finished the grains, Will removed the two tree limbs and led the Morgan out of the corral. He walked the horse slowly back toward the stand of trees where Perley waited, half expecting a rifle shot from the cave at any second. With that thought in mind, he made sure he kept the horse close behind him.

"I swear," Perley said softly, "he's a big ol' horse,

ain't he? I never got a chance to see him up close before."

"I expect so, compared to your mule," Will said. They walked the Morgan back down the mountain and turned it out with Will's horses and Perley's mule. As a precaution, Will hobbled the horse, in case it took a notion to return home. "Now, you might wanna get a couple hours' sleep. We've gotta be back up there at daylight."

There was never any real thought of going to sleep by either man, since it was so important to be in position when the sun came up. So when the first gray light began to penetrate the branches of the oak trees bordering Perley's cabin, they were already on their way back up the mountain, leading Eli's horse. Will decided they'd need the horse to carry the saddle and anything else Eli had up there. He explained to Perley that he had gone to the trouble to steal the horse the night before because of the danger of being caught in the act in the morning light.

They picked a spot for Perley behind a huge boulder where he could see the mouth of the cave while being well protected, and tied the Morgan in the woods behind him. Before leaving him, Will asked him, "You remember what you're supposed to say?" Perley repeated the words he had been instructed to say. "Good," Will said. "And if he comes down outta the mouth of that cave, you run like hell."

"You don't have to tell me that," Perley said. "My short little legs know to do that automatically." He had one question before Will left him. "I can't understand why you don't just stay here, yourself, and shoot the son of a bitch when he comes outta the mouth of that cave."

"Like I told you last night, I'm mighty tempted to do that, but I told Dan Stone I'd try to bring him back alive for trial. Besides, I like the idea of stretchin' his neck instead of givin' him a quick out with a bullet." He left then to hurry up behind the cave, where the back door was located.

The sun had lifted fairly high in the valley before the morning light was enough to shine in the mouth of the stone fortress where Eli slept. Rousing himself from his bedroll, he went to the spring that flowed through the cave to drink and relieve himself. That done, he decided to take a look at his horse before reviving his fire. "Gonna have to go cut some more firewood," he mumbled to himself as he went to the mouth of the cave.

"What the . . . ?" he exclaimed when he looked down at the corral to discover his horse missing. "How did that horse get outta . . . ?" he started again, but stopped when he saw on the ground the two limbs that served as a gate. Furious that someone had stolen his horse, he was startled in the next instant when he heard the command from below.

"Throw out your weapons and come on outta there. You're under arrest," Perley shouted in as official-like voice as he could effect. "This is Deputy Marshal Perley Gates," he added as an afterthought, then grinned as he admired the sound of it.

Staggered, Eli backed quickly away from the mouth of the cave, unable to think at once. Then it came to him—they had sent other marshals from Fort Smith to help Tanner! Already they had taken his horse—he was on foot! *Maybe they don't know about the back door,* he thought. *I've got to get out of here!* He snatched up his weapons and ran stumbling in his haste up the length of the long cave to the small passageway in the back. Once he was clear of the opening, he crawled up the side of the boulder that guarded it and dropped to the rocky path beyond. At the same instant, Will rose up from a crevice in the rocks, his Winchester leveled at the startled outlaw. "Drop the rifle," Will commanded.

Caught in a panic of confusion, Eli hesitated for a split second, trying to make up his mind before suddenly raising his rifle. Anticipating the move, Will fired before Eli could level his rifle. The shot caught Eli in his right thigh, causing him to spin in pain, almost dropping his weapon. "Drop it, or the next round goes in your gut," Will demanded as he cranked another cartridge in the chamber. Knowing he had no chance, Eli let his rifle drop to the ground and sat down heavily on a boulder, wincing in pain. Will moved quickly to pick up the discarded weapon, while keeping Eli covered with his rifle. Then he put the rifle to his shoulder and took dead aim at Eli's head. "All right," he said, "now unbuckle that gun belt and let it drop." Left with little choice, as he stared at the muzzle of the Winchester, Eli unbuckled his belt and dropped the two pistols on the ground. With the barrel of his rifle, Will motioned toward the narrow path he had climbed up. "Start walkin' down that path."

"I can't walk," Eli complained. "You shot me in the leg."

"You can walk," Will said. "'Cause if you can't, I reckon I'll have to execute you right here." He raised the rifle again.

"All right! All right!" Eli blurted. "I'll walk!" He grunted with the pain as he strained to get on his feet. Wincing and cursing with each step, he limped down the path that circled around behind the cave.

"Come on out, Perley," Will called out when they were back by the corral. Perley came out of the trees, leading Eli's horse.

"You!" Eli exclaimed. "You little rat. You ain't no deputy."

"The hell I ain't," Perley crowed. "I'm Deputy Perley Gates, at least, this mornin' I am. Ain't that right, Will?"

"That's a fact," Will said. He directed Eli to a rock to sit on. "I need to get his saddle and anything else that's useful outta the cave. You wanna climb up there and throw it down, or would you rather stay here and keep an eye on Eli?"

Perley didn't hesitate. "I'll go up and get the saddle."

Since it was still early in the morning, Will didn't waste much time when they got back to Perley's camp, preparing to start out for Fort Smith as soon as his horses were saddled and packed. Eli, with his wrists tied together, sat with his back against a tree, his face a sullen mask. "You've gotta get me to a doctor to treat this wound," he complained. "I can't ride all the way to Fort Smith with my leg bleedin' like this."

Will was not convinced Eli was hurt as bad as he purported. The slug had obviously struck the muscle of his leg and had not broken the bone. It was his opinion that, although in some pain, Eli should be able to walk on it. But he was willing to offer him some compassion. He asked Perley for something to bandage Eli's leg with, and Perley came up with a piece from a worn-out shirt. "Hold your hands straight up over your head, and I'll untie your hands," Will said to Eli.

"I can't," Eli claimed. "This wound you put in my shoulder is too tender to raise that arm."

"Then I reckon you'll just have to go without a bandage on that leg," Will said, suspecting his prisoner of trying to avoid holding his arms up over his head. In that awkward position, it would be difficult to make any sudden moves, if he was still inclined.

"All right," Eli said, "I'll try, but it's gonna hurt like hell." He scowled at Perley, who grinned at him, amused by his pitiful performance. Eli raised his hands straight up and held them there while Will untied them.

"There you go," Will said, and dropped the strip of cloth in Eli's lap. "You can tie that around your leg, then we'll get you in the saddle." He watched him closely while talking to Perley. "You've been a lotta help, Perley. I appreciate it. It made my job a lot easier, so I'm thinkin' I owe you something."

"Ah, you don't owe me nothin'," Perley said. "I done it for all that coffee you gave me."

"That ain't hardly enough," Will said. "You stuck your neck out pretty far. How would you feel about tradin' that mule of yours for a fine Morgan geldin'?"

"Whoa! Wait a minute," Eli exclaimed. "You can't do that. That's my horse."

"You ain't gonna need it where you're goin'," Will said, then turned back to Perley. "What about it, Perley? Have you got a special attachment to that mule you've been ridin'?"

"Hell, no," Perley replied at once. "Sam's a good mule, but that sounds like a dandy trade to me. I expect if he had any say about it, he'd be proud to tote Eli Stark to the gallows."

"Done then," Will said. "Go get him, and we'll throw the saddle on him." He glanced over at a seething Eli, tying a knot in the bandage. "When you're done with that, get on your feet."

Eli made a show of pulling himself to his feet with help from the trunk of the tree he had been sitting against. Standing hunched slightly over as if it pained him severely just to be on his feet, he watched while Perley led his mule up to them. "I was thinkin'," Perley said. "That's a fine-lookin' saddle that son of a bitch was settin' on. Any chance it goes with the horse?"

"Why, sure," Will replied. "That oughta be understood."

"Good," Perley said, grinning. "I thought that mighta been part of the deal, so I threw my old wore-out saddle on Sam. He's more used to that one, anyway."

When Will turned to take the reins of the mule

from Perley, Eli decided it was the opportunity he was waiting for. He suddenly pushed away from the tree trunk and lunged at the lawman. Anticipating such an attempt, Will dropped the reins, spun around, and met Eli's charge with a stiff right hand flush on Eli's nose. The result of the punch stopped Eli's head while his feet kept going, and dropped him flat on his back. While he lay there stunned for a few moments, Will retied his wrists.

"I figured that bastard was playin' possum," Perley remarked soberly. "I reckon you figured the same thing."

"Tell you the truth," Will said, "I was kinda hopin' he'd try something like that." He and Perley pulled the stunned outlaw to his feet and helped him up into the saddle.

With Eli sitting on Perley's mule, his hands bound and his feet tied under the mule's belly, in case he took a notion to jump off and take off running, Will said "So long" to Perley. "I hope I'll see you again, if you're in this part of the territory again," Perley said.

"I expect you might," Will replied, and shook his hand. "Thanks again for your help." He stepped up into the saddle and turned Buster to the east.

Perley stood watching him until he could no longer see him through the trees. *That was one hell of a right hand*, he thought.

Marshal Daniel Stone happened to be at the jail under the courtroom when a weary deputy rode slowly down the street, his packhorse behind, followed by a prisoner on a mule. "Well, I'll be . . ."

Stone started. "He did it—that son of a gun did it. He said he'd bring Eli Stark back for trial. I ain't ever seen Eli Stark before, but I'm bettin' that's him sittin' on that mule." He hurried out to meet Will at the hitching post. "Randolph, you've got a prisoner to lock up," he called back to jailer Sid Randolph. Randolph went back inside and called a couple of guards out to take possession of the prisoner.

"Is that him?" Stone asked when Will stepped down, "Stark?"

"Yep," Will replied. "That's him, and he's got a few nicks and scratches the doctor might wanna look at."

"Well, we'll certainly do our best to make him feel welcome," Stone said sarcastically. "Anybody wanted in three territories like Mr. Stark, here, deserves the best we can give him." His remarks were met by the snarling countenance of Eli, still intent upon displaying a show of defiance. After watching the guards as they untied Eli's ankles and pulled him off the mule, Stone turned his attention to Will. "You look like you're a little hard for wear, yourself. I reckon he didn't come that easy, did he? Why don't you go on home and get something to eat, and get a good night's sleep, and we'll go over your report in the morning. All right?"

"I 'preciate it," Will said. "I could use a good home-cooked meal right now." There was a reason he was eager to go home that was more compelling than his desire for a home-cooked meal, however. And she would most likely be helping her mother to prepare for supper about now. "I'll see you in the mornin'," he said to Stone, then hesitated long enough to watch the guards escort Eli through the door to the jail before climbing back on the buckskin. Suddenly feeling tired, now that he was done with the Tarbows and the Starks, he turned Buster and Perley's mule toward the stables.

Stone watched him for a few moments before following Randolph inside the jail. There was no physical resemblance between the two men, yet he couldn't help being reminded of a younger version of Fletcher Pride. Pride's death was a monumental loss, and Stone hoped like hell Will was going to stick. He needed men like him. Stone was also experienced enough to suspect that Will was going to be doing a lot of thinking in the next day or two. He had a decision to make, and it had to be much more difficult, considering the circumstances he had been forced to deal with on his first assignment. In the short time Will had worn the badge, he had been baptized in a bloodbath of killing that would discourage the average man. If he had to bet on it, however, Stone would wager that Will Tanner would be back in the morning.

It was only the second time she had witnessed it, but already it seemed like a familiar sight. She lingered at the window for a few moments to watch the easy stride of the rangy lawman as he walked from the stables, his saddlebags over his shoulder, the rifle in his hand, the weathered flat-crowned hat pulled low over his sandy hair. She could not deny a fascination, like the fascination for a tawny mountain lion, handsome although deadly—and too dangerous to attempt to tame. Sophie knew her mother had had concerns about her casual attitude with Will Tanner, and Sophie was well aware of the folly in becoming involved with a man who lived by the sword. She knew better than to let herself think of him in any regard beyond a casual friend. *Or do I?* she thought as she went to the front door.

"Well, welcome home," Sophie called out cheerfully through the screen door when Will reached the porch steps. "Did you catch the man you went after?"

"Yes, ma'am, I did," Will answered.

"Good. Then I suppose you'll be in town for a few days now," Sophie said. "At least, that's the way it usually was when Fletcher arrested an outlaw. He stayed in town until they had the trial."

"I reckon," Will said. He had not really been told as much by Stone, but that seemed logical, since he was the arresting officer.

She opened the screen door for him and stood aside to let him pass. "You want me to heat some water for you? It looks like you brought a good bit of Oklahoma back with you."

"Ah yes, ma'am," he said. "I reckon I could use a soakin' at that, but I can heat the water myself." He did feel downright grimy. There wasn't much opportunity to take a bath when you were traveling with a man like Eli Stark, even if you wanted one.

She started to close the door, but suddenly paused. "By the way," she said as casually as she could affect, even though she was anxious to see his reaction, "Garth Pearson asked me to marry him."

It was too sudden for him to hide his shock, although he recovered quickly enough to respond indifferently. "I reckon I'm not surprised." A long moment followed with no response from Sophie. So Will was prompted to ask, "What was your answer—if it ain't too nosy for me to ask?"

She shrugged nonchalantly. "Well, Garth is a wonderful man, and he's got a great future ahead of him—you know, working for Judge Parker and all. I certainly have to consider that. But I told him I couldn't give him an answer right away. I'll have to search my feelings and decide if it's the best thing for me—and him, too." She gave Will a big smile and closed the screen door behind him. "Anyway, everybody but you already knows, so I just thought I'd give you the news." She watched him closely, waiting for his response. He said nothing right away, but she had seen his shocked expression upon first hearing her announcement. It told her what she had suspected all along.

After a long moment, during which he labored with his emotions, he stumbled through his reply. "Well, like I said, I reckon I ain't surprised. He'd be a fool not to propose—I mean, any man would be." He had a sudden impulse to tell her that he was half owner of the J-Bar-J ranch in Texas, and he didn't expect to be a deputy marshal all his life. But somehow it didn't seem right to tell her at this moment when she was considering Garth's proposal. She had known Garth much longer than she had known him. In fact, when he thought about it, he realized that she hadn't known him long enough to determine what kind of man he really was. He had a feeling her mother had given her plenty of warning of the heartache that came with loving a lawman, one working in

Indian Territory, to boot. "Well," he finally blurted, thinking he had come awfully close to making a complete fool of himself. "I reckon I'd best get washed up now. I don't wanna be late for supper."

She watched him walk away. *You're certainly not making it easy on me,* she thought, *but things have a way of working out like they're supposed to.*

New York Times and *USA Today* Bestselling Authors
William W. Johnstone
And J. A. Johnstone

Smoke Jensen was a towering Western hero. Now his two freewheeling, long-lost nephews, Ace and Chance Jensen, are blazing a legendary trail of their own.

Riverboat gambling is a blast, until hotheaded Chance finds out just what he won in his final hand against a Missouri River gambler named Haggarty. Chance's "prize" is a beautiful Chinese slave girl named Ling. The twins want to set Ling free and keep their cash, but at Fort Benton, Ling gives them the slip, robbing them blind. When they hunt her down in Rimfire, Montana, she's with Haggarty, lining up their next mark.

WHAT WOULD SMOKE JENSEN DO?

Ace and Chance want payback. So does hard case Leo Belmont, who's come all the way from San Francisco with a grudge and a couple of kill-crazy hired guns. Belmont wants revenge, and Ace and Chance are in the way.

PROBABLY THIS.

Soon the boys are fighting alongside Ling and Haggarty. Because it doesn't matter now who's right and who's wrong—blazing guns and flying lead are laying down the law . . .

THOSE JENSEN BOYS!
RIMFIRE

**The exciting new series!
On sale now, wherever Pinnacle Books are sold.**

CHAPTER 1

"Let's take a ride on a riverboat, you said," Ace Jensen muttered to his brother as they backed away from the group of angry men stalking toward them across the deck. "It'll be fun, you said."

"Well, I didn't count on this," Chance Jensen replied. "How was I to know we'd wind up in such a mess of trouble?"

Ace glanced over at Chance as if amazed that his brother could ask such a stupid question. "When do we ever *not* wind up in trouble?"

"Yeah, you've got a point there," Chance agreed. "It seems to have a way of finding us."

Their backs hit the railing along the edge of the deck. Behind them, the giant wooden blades of the side-wheeler's paddles churned the muddy waters of the Missouri River.

They were on the right side of the riverboat—the starboard side, Ace thought, then chided himself for allowing such an irrelevant detail to intrude on his brain at such a moment—and so far out in the middle of the stream that jumping overboard and swimming for shore wasn't practical.

Besides, the brothers weren't in the habit of fleeing from trouble. If they started doing that, most likely they would never stop running.

The man who was slightly in the forefront of the group confronting them pointed a finger at Chance. "All right, kid, I'll have that watch back now."

"I'm not a kid," Chance snapped. "I'm a grown man. And so are you, so you shouldn't have bet the watch if you didn't want to take a chance on losing it."

The Jensen brothers were grown men, all right, but not by much. They were in their early twenties, and although they had knocked around the frontier all their lives, had faced all sorts of danger, and burned plenty of powder, there was still a certain . . . *innocence* . . . about them, for want of a better word. They still made their way through life with enthusiasm and an eagerness to embrace all the joy the world had to offer.

They were twins, although that wasn't instantly apparent. They were fraternal rather than identical. Ace was taller, broader through the shoulders, and had black hair instead of his brother's sandy brown. He preferred range clothes, wearing jeans, a buckskin shirt, and a battered old Stetson, while Chance was much more dapper in a brown tweed suit, vest, white shirt, a fancy cravat with an ivory stickpin, and a straw planter's hat.

Ace was armed with a Colt .45 Peacemaker with well-worn walnut grips that rode easily in a holster on his right hip. Chance didn't carry a visible gun, but he had a Smith & Wesson .38 caliber, double action

Second Model revolver in a shoulder holster under his left arm.

However, neither young man wanted to start a gunfight on the deck of the *Missouri Belle*. It was a tranquil summer night, and gunshots and spilled blood would just about ruin it.

The leader of the group confronting them was an expensively dressed, middle-aged man with a beefy, well-fed look about him. Still pointing that accusing finger at Chance, he went on. "Leland Stanford himself gave me that watch in appreciation for my help in getting the transcontinental railroad built. You know who Leland Stanford is, don't you? President of the Central Pacific Railroad?"

"We've heard of him," Ace said. "Rich fella out California way. Used to be governor out there, didn't he?"

"That's right. And he's a good friend of mine. I'm a stockholder in the Central Pacific, in fact."

"Then likely you can afford to buy yourself another watch," Chance said.

The man's already red face flushed even more as it twisted in a snarl. "You mouthy little pup. Hand it over, or we'll throw the two of you right off this boat."

"I won it fair and square, mister. Doc Monday always says the cards know more about our fate than we do."

"I don't know who in blazes Doc Monday is, but your fate is to take a beating and then a swim. Grab 'em, boys, but don't throw 'em overboard until I get my watch back!"

The other four men rushed Ace and Chance.

With their backs to the railing, they had nowhere to go.

Doc Monday, the gambler who had raised the Jensen brothers after their mother died in childbirth, had taught them many things, including the fact that it was usually a mistake to wait for trouble to come to you. Better to go out and meet it head on. In other words, the best defense was the proverbial good offense, so Ace and Chance met the charge with one of their own, going low to tackle the nearest two men around the knees.

The hired ruffians weren't expecting it, and the impact swept their legs out from under them. They fell under the feet of their onrushing companions, who stumbled and lost their balance, toppling onto the first two men, and suddenly there was a knot of flailing, punching, and kicking combatants on the deck.

The florid-faced hombre who had foolishly wagered his watch during a poker game in the riverboat's salon earlier hopped around agitatedly and shouted encouragement to his men.

Facing two to one odds, the brothers shouldn't have been able to put up much of a fight, but when it came to brawling, Ace and Chance could more than hold their own. Their fists lashed out and crashed against the jaws and into the bellies of their enemies. Ace got behind one of the men, looped an arm around his neck, and hauled him around just in time to receive a kick in the face that had been aimed at Ace's head, knocking the man senseless.

Ace let go of him and rolled out of the way of a dive from another attacker. He clubbed his hands and brought them down on the back of the man's neck. The man's face bounced off the deck, flattening his nose and stunning him.

Chance had his hands full, too. His left hand was clamped around the neck of an enemy while his right clenched into a fist and pounded the man's face. But he was taking punishment himself. His opponent was choking him at the same time, and the other man in the fight hammered punches into Chance's ribs from the side.

Knowing that he had only seconds before he would be overwhelmed, Chance twisted his body, drew his legs up, and rammed both boot heels into the chest of the man hitting him. It wasn't quite the same as being kicked by a mule, but not far from it. The man flew backwards and rolled when he landed on the deck. He almost went under the railing and off the side into the river, but he stopped just short of the brink.

With the odds even now, Chance was able to batter his other foe into submission. The man's hand slipped off Chance's throat as he moaned and slumped back onto the smooth planks.

That still left the rich man who didn't like losing.

As Ace and Chance looked up from their vanquished enemies, they saw him pointing a pistol at them.

"If you think I'm going to allow a couple gutter rats like you two to make a fool of me, you're sadly mistaken," the man said as a snarl twisted his beefy face.

"You're not gonna shoot us, mister," Ace said. "That would be murder."

"No, it wouldn't." An ugly smile appeared on the man's lips. "Not if I tell the captain the two of you jumped me and tried to rob me. I had to kill you to protect myself. That's exactly what's about to happen here."

"Over a blasted watch?" Chance exclaimed in surprise.

"I don't like losing . . . especially to my inferiors."

"You'd never get away with it," Ace said.

"Won't I? Why do you think none of the crew has come to see what all the commotion's about? I told the chief steward I'd be dealing with some cheap troublemakers—in my own way—and he promised he'd make sure I wasn't interrupted. You see"—the red-faced man chuckled—"I'm not involved with just the railroad. I own part of this riverboat line as well."

Ace and Chance exchanged a glance. If the man shot them, his hired ruffians could toss their bodies into the midnight-dark Missouri River and no one would know they were gone until morning. It was entirely possible that a man of such wealth and influence wouldn't even be questioned about the disappearance of a couple drifting nobodies.

But things weren't going to get that far.

Ace said in a hard voice that belied his youth, "That only works if you're able to shoot both of us, mister. Problem is, while you're killing one of us, the other one is going to kill *you*."

The man's eyes widened. He blustered, "How dare you threaten me like that?"

"Didn't you just threaten to kill us?" asked Chance. "My brother's right. You're not fast enough . . . and your nerves aren't steady enough . . . for you to get both of us. You'll be dead a heartbeat after you pull the trigger."

The man's lips drew back from his teeth in a grimace. "Maybe I'm willing to take that risk."

Well, that was a problem, all right, thought Ace. Stubborn pride had been the death of many a man, and it looked like that was about to contribute to at least one more.

Then a new voice said, "Krauss, I guarantee that even if you're lucky enough to kill these two young men, you won't be able to stop me from putting a bullet in your head."

The rich man's gaze flicked to a newcomer who'd stepped out of the shadows cloaking the deck in places. Wearing a light-colored suit and hat, he was easy to see. Starlight glinted on the barrel of the revolver he held in a rock-steady fist.

"Drake!" exclaimed Krauss. "Stay out of this. It's none of your business."

"I think it is." Drake's voice was a lazy drawl, but there was no mistaking the steel underneath the casual tone. "Ace and Chance are friends of mine."

Krauss sneered. "You wouldn't dare shoot me."

"Think about some of the things you know about me," said Steve Drake, "then make that statement again."

Krauss licked his lips. He looked around at his men, who were starting to recover from the battle with the Jensen brothers. "Don't just lie there!" he snapped at them. "Get up and deal with this!"

One of the men sat up, shook his head, and winced

from the pain the movement caused him. "Mr. Krauss, we don't want to tangle with Drake. Rumor says he's killed seven men."

"Rumor sometimes underestimates," said Steve Drake with an easy smile.

"You're worthless!" Krauss raged. "You're all fired!"

"I'd rather be fired than dead," one of the other men mumbled.

Steve Drake gestured with the gun in his hand and told Ace and Chance, "Stand up, boys."

The brothers got to their feet. Chance reached inside his coat to a pocket and brought out a gold turnip watch with an attached chain and fob. "I don't want to have to be looking over my shoulder for you the rest of my life, mister. This watch isn't worth that."

"You mean you'll give it back to me?" asked Krauss.

Ace could tell from the man's tone that he was eager to resolve the situation without any more violence, now that it appeared he might well be one of the victims.

"I mean I'll sell it back to you," said Chance.

Krauss started to puff up again like an angry frog. "I'm not going to buy back my own watch!"

"I won it from you fair and square," Chance reminded him. "Unless you think I cheated you . . ." His voice trailed off in an implied threat.

Krauss shook his head. "I never said that. I suppose you won fair and square." That admission was clearly difficult for him to make. "What do you want for the watch?"

"Well, since it came from a famous man, I reckon

it must have quite a bit of sentimental value to you. I was thinking . . . five hundred dollars."

"Five hun—" Krauss stopped short and controlled an angry response with a visible effort. "I don't have that kind of money on me at the moment. That's why I put up the watch as stakes in the game."

Steve Drake said, "We'll be docking at Kansas City in the morning. I'm sure you can send a wire to your bank in St. Louis and get your hands on the cash. That's the only fair thing to do, don't you think? After all, you set your men like a pack of wild dogs on to these boys, and then you threatened to murder them and have their bodies thrown in the river like so much trash. You owe them at least that much."

"Nobody's going to take their word over mine," said Krauss, trying one last bluff.

"Captain Foley will take *my* word," Drake said. "We've known each other for ten years, and I've done a few favors for him in the past. He knows I wouldn't lie to him. You wouldn't want it getting around that you were ready to resort to murder over something as petty as a poker game, would you? Seems to me that would be bad for business."

"All right, all right." Krauss stuck the pistol back under his coat. "It's a deal. Five hundred dollars for the watch."

"Deal," Chance said.

The rich man laughed. "The watch is worth twice that. You should have held out for more."

"I don't care how much it is. I just want you to pay to get it back."

Krauss snorted in contempt, turned, and stalked

off along the deck. His men followed him, even though he had fired them. Evidently that dismissal wouldn't last, and they knew it.

A man with a temper like Krauss's probably fired people right and left and then expected them to come right back to work for him once he cooled off, Ace reflected.

Once Krauss and the others were gone, the Jensen boys joined Steve Drake, who tucked away his gun under his jacket and strolled over to the railing to gaze out at the broad, slow-moving Missouri River.

The gambler put a thin black cheroot in his mouth and snapped a match to life with his thumbnail. As he set fire to the gasper, the glare from the lucifer sent garish red light over the rugged planes of his craggy face under the cream-colored Stetson.

"We're obliged to you, Mr. Drake," Ace said. "You're making a habit out of pulling our fat out of the fire."

"Yeah," Chance added. "If you hadn't come along when you did, we might've had to kill that obnoxious tub of lard."

"Krauss's gun was already in his hand," Steve Drake pointed out, "and yours were in your holsters. He might have gotten one of you, just like you said."

"Yeah, and he might have missed completely," said Chance. "We wouldn't have had any choice but to drill him, though."

"And then we would have been in all kinds of trouble," put in Ace. "The odds of hanging are a lot higher if you kill a rich man instead of a poor one."

"You sound like you have a low opinion of justice," said Steve Drake with a chuckle.

"No, I just know how things work in this world."

The gambler shrugged and blew out a cloud of smoke. "You may be right. We all remember what happened back in St. Louis, don't we?"

CHAPTER 2

St. Louis, three days earlier

Neither Ace nor Chance was in awe of St. Louis. They had seen big cities before. Traveling with Doc Monday when they were younger had taken them to Denver, San Francisco, New Orleans, and San Antonio so the buildings crowded together and the throngs of people in the streets were nothing new to the Jensen brothers.

It had been a while since they'd set foot in such a place. They reacted to it totally differently.

Chance looked around with a smile of anticipation on his face as they rode along the street, moving slowly because of all the people, horses, wagons, and buggies. He was at home in cities, liked the hubbub, enjoyed seeing all the different sorts of people.

Because Doc Monday, their surrogate father, made his living as a gambler, he had spent most of his time in settlements. That was where the saloons were, after all. And although Doc had tried to keep the boys out of such places as much as possible while they were

growing up, it was inevitable that they had spent a
great deal of time in those establishments.

Chance had taken to that life, but Ace had reacted
in just the opposite manner. He didn't like being
hemmed in and preferred the outdoors. He would
rather be out riding the range any day, instead of
being stuck in a saloon breathing smoky air and listening to the slap of cards and the raucous laughter
of the customers. If he had to spend time in a settlement, the smaller ones were better than the big
cities. To Ace's way of thinking, a slower pace and
more peaceful was better.

Ever since Doc had gone off to a sanitarium for a
rest cure, the boys had been on their own, and they
had packed a lot of adventurous living into a relatively short amount of time. Chance was always happy
when they drifted into a town, while Ace was ready to
leave again as soon as they replenished their supplies
and his brother had an opportunity to win enough
money to keep them solvent for a while.

St. Louis was the farthest east they had been in
their travels, with the exception of New Orleans.
There was no particular reason they were there,
other than Chance deciding that he'd wanted to see
St. Louis.

Ace figured Chance might have assumed St. Louis
was like New Orleans, the city he loved, with its moss-
dripping trees, its old, fancy buildings, its music, its
food, its saloons and gambling halls, and especially
its beautiful women. After all, both cities were on the
Mississippi River.

He seemed somewhat disappointed in their present

surroundings, which led him to look around and ask, "Is this it? A bunch of people and businesses?"

"That's generally what a big city is," Ace reminded him.

"Yeah, but it doesn't even smell good! In fact, it smells sort of like . . . dead fish."

"That's the waterfront," Ace said with a smile. "New Orleans smelled like that in a lot of places, too. You just didn't notice it because you liked all the other things that were there."

"Maybe," said Chance, but he didn't sound convinced.

"I guess we'd better find a place to stay. We've still got enough in our poke for that, haven't we?"

Chance grunted. "Yeah."

Something else caught his attention and he pointed to a large saloon with a sign on the awning over the boardwalk out front announcing its name. RED MIKE'S. "I think we should have a look inside that place first."

The place took up most of the block on that side of the street. A balcony ran along the second floor. Ace wouldn't have been surprised to see scantily clad women hanging over the railing of that balcony, enticing customers to come up, but it was empty at the moment.

The hitch rails in front of the saloon were packed. The Jensen brothers found space to squeeze in their horses and dismounted, looping the reins around the rail. Chance bounded eagerly onto the boardwalk with Ace following at a more deliberate pace. He would have preferred finding a place to stay first, maybe even getting something to eat, but once

Chance felt the call of potential excitement, it wasn't easy to stop him from answering.

Considering the number of horses tied up outside, Red Mike's was crowded with customers. Men of all shapes, sizes, and types lined up at the bar and filled the tables. Ace saw buckskin-clad old-timers and burly men in canvas trousers, homespun shirts, and thick-soled shoes who probably worked on the docks or the riverboats. Also in attendance were cowboys in boots, spurs, and high-crowned hats, frock-coated gamblers who reminded him of Doc, and meek, suit-wearing townsmen.

Circulating among the men were women in low-cut, spangled dresses that came down only to their knees. Some of them looked fresh and innocent despite the provocative garb, while others were starting to show lines of age and weariness on their painted faces. All of them sported professional smiles as they delivered drinks, bantered with the customers, and occasionally perched on someone's knee to flirt for a minute before moving on.

In each front corner of the big room was a platform with steps leading up to it. A man holding a Winchester across his knees sat on a ladder-back chair on each platform. They were there to stop any trouble before it got started.

The tactic seemed to be working, While Red Mike's place was loud, even boisterous, it was peaceful enough in the saloon. Everyone seemed to be getting along.

Ace leaned closer to his brother and said over the hubbub, "It's too busy in here. We'd better move along and come back later."

"No, there's a place at the bar," Chance replied, pointing. "Come on."

Ace followed, unwilling to let Chance stay by himself. It wasn't that he didn't trust his brother, but sometimes Chance could be impulsive, even reckless . . . especially in such surroundings.

They weaved through the crowd to the bar. By the time they got there, the space Chance had noticed was smaller than it had been. There was still room for one of the brothers, but not both of them.

That didn't stop Chance from wedging his way into the opening and then using a shoulder to make it wider by pushing one of the flanking men aside. Ace winced a little when he saw that, because he knew what was liable to happen next.

Chance turned his head and beckoned to his brother. "Come on, Ace. There's room now."

No sooner were those words out of his mouth than a big hand clamped down on his shoulder and jerked him around. The man Chance had nudged aside glared down into his face and demanded in a loud voice, "Who do you think you are, boy?"

"My name's Chance Jensen," Chance said coolly. "If this is a formal introduction, you can go ahead and tell me your name."

The man ignored that. "You can't just push a man around like that and expect to get away with it, *boy*. You done left school too early. You ain't been taught all the lessons you need."

"From the sound of it, I have considerably more education than you do."

The big man's face darkened with anger. He was several inches taller than Chance, about the same height as Ace, and probably weighed fifty or sixty pounds more than either brother. His rough clothes and a shapeless hat jammed down on a thatch of dark hair indicated that he probably worked on the docks. Not the sort of hombre to mess with unless it was absolutely necessary, that was for sure.

The man leaned closer and growled. "Listen to me, you little son of a—"

Ace managed to get a shoulder between the two of them and said quickly, "My brother and I aren't looking for any trouble, sir. Maybe we can patch this up by buying you a drink."

Chance began, "We don't have enough money to throw it away buying drinks for—"

Whatever Chance was about to say, it wasn't going to help matters any, Ace knew. He pushed in between them harder, which made Chance take a step back and bump into the man behind him.

Being jostled made the man spill his beer down the front of his shirt. With an angry shout, the fellow twisted around, brandishing the now-empty mug like a weapon. "What in blazes?" he roared. "I'm gonna—"

The place went quiet, but not because of the man's shout.

Ace heard the familiar sound of a rifle's lever being worked and glanced around to see that both men on the elevated platforms in the front corners of the room were on their feet. Their Winchesters were socketed firmly against their shoulders, and the barrels were leveled at the group involved in the confrontation at the bar.

The dockworker who'd been glaring at the Jensen

boys swallowed hard and unclenched his big fists. "Blast it, Mike. Tell those killers o' yours to hold their fire."

A man wearing a gray tweed suit moved along the bar until he was across the hardwood from Ace, Chance, and the other two men. He was short and broad and the color and coarseness of his hair made it resemble rusty nails. "You know the rules, Dave. No fighting in here. My grandfather didn't allow brawling and neither did my father. Neither do I."

Dave glowered at Chance and accused, "This obnoxious little sprout started it, not me."

"Obnoxious," repeated Chance. "That's a longer word than I thought you'd be able to handle."

From the corner of his mouth, Ace told his brother, "Just be quiet, all right?"

Chance looked offended, but Ace ignored him.

"Sorry for causing trouble," Ace went on to the man on the other side of the bar. Judging by the man's attitude and the fact that the dockworker had called him Mike, Ace figured he was the owner of the place, Red Mike himself. "We just wanted to get a quick drink, and then we'll be moving on."

"Speak for yourself," said Chance. "I might like it here. I don't so far, not particularly, but I might."

Mike nodded to the brothers and asked the two offended parties, "If these youngsters were to apologize, would that take care of the problem?"

"Hell, no," replied the man who had spilled his drink when Chance jostled him.

Mike pointed a blunt thumb toward the batwings. "Then there's the door. Get out."

The man stared at him in disbelief. "You're kickin'

me out? I wasn't doin' anything but standin' here enjoyin' a beer when this little piss-ant made me spill it all over myself!"

"Come back tomorrow and your first drink is on me," Mike said. "That's the best offer you're going to get, Wilson."

The man glared and muttered for a moment, then snapped, "All right, fine." He thumped the empty mug on the bar with more force than necessary, then turned and walked out of the saloon, bulling past anybody who was in his way.

"Now, how about you, Dave?" Mike went on. "Will an apology do for you?"

"No," the dockworker said coldly. "It won't. But I don't want those sharpshooters of yours blowin' my brains out, so I'll leave. I reckon that same free drink offer applies to me, too?"

"It does," Mike allowed.

Dave nodded curtly. "You shouldn't take the side of strangers over your faithful customers, Mike. It's these two as should be leavin'."

"You're probably right. Make it two free drinks."

That seemed to mollify Dave somewhat. He frowned at Ace and Chance one more time and said, "Don't let me catch you on the street, boys. You'd be wise to get outta town while you got the chance." With that, he stomped out of the saloon.

The two guards on the platforms sat down again. The noise level in the place swelled back up.

Mike looked at Ace and Chance and asked harshly, "Do you two cause so much trouble everywhere you go or did one of my competitors pay you to come in here and start a ruckus?"

"We're sorry, mister," Ace said. "Things just sort of got out of hand."

Chance looked slightly repentant as he added, "Sometimes my mouth gets away from me."

Mike grunted. "See that it doesn't again, at least not in here." He shook his head. "I don't care what you do elsewhere or what happens to you, either. You said you wanted a drink?"

"A couple beers would be good," Ace said.

Mike signaled to one of his aproned bartenders. "Don't expect 'em to be on the house, though. Not after the way you acted. In fact, I ought to charge you double . . . but I won't."

Ace dug out a coin and slid it across the hardwood. Mike scooped it up with a hand that had more of the rusty hair sprouting from the back of it.

The bartender set the beers in front of them.

Since Mike didn't seem to be in any hurry to move on, Ace started a conversation after picking up a mug and taking a sip from it. "You mentioned your father and grandfather. Did they own this saloon before you?"

"What's it to you, kid?" asked Mike as his eyes narrowed in suspicion.

"Nothing, really," Ace replied honestly. "I'm just interested in history, that's all."

A short, humorless bark of laughter came from the saloonkeeper. "Red Mike's has got some history, all right. The original tavern, back in the days when all the fur trappers and traders came through St. Louis on their way to the Rockies, was over by the docks, almost right on the river. A hell of a place it was, too. Men were men back in those days, especially those